CASTLES
BURNING

A RINEHART SUSPENSE NOVEL

Other Jacob Asch Novels by Arthur Lyons

ALL GOD'S CHILDREN

THE DEAD ARE DISCREET

THE KILLING FLOOR

DEAD RINGER

A RINEHART SUSPENSE NOVEL

CASTLES BURNING

Arthur Lyons

HOLT, RINEHART AND WINSTON

New York

First published in January 1980 by Holt, Rinehart and Winston,
383 Madison Avenue, New York, New York 10017.

Published simultaneously in Canada by Holt, Rinehart and
Winston of Canada, Limited.

Library of Congress Cataloging in Publication Data
Lyons, Arthur.
    Castles burning.
    (A Rinehart suspense novel)
    I. Title.
PZ4.L9898Cas   [PS3562.Y446]   813'.5'4   79-1935
ISBN 0-03-047621-6
First Edition

Designer: Trish Parcell
Printed in the United States of America
1 3 5 7 9 10 8 6 4 2

FOR THE WORLD'S MOST BEAUTIFUL WRECKING CREW

Dee
Susanne
Sylvie
Andy
and Marianna, the All-American
Bicentennial Bitch

CASTLES
BURNING

A RINEHART SUSPENSE NOVEL

The blonde was bent over the chair, precariously balanced on ten-inch platform heels, looking at me through her legs. Her miniskirt was hiked up past the tops of her black nylons, exposing a patch of purple-pantied pudenda, and she wore a faintly surprised expression on her face, as if she had been expecting someone else. She may have been at that, but I had the distinct impression that as long as I had my wallet with me, I could have been the Hunchback of Notre Dame. She looked as if she would be a good sport about little things like that.

The others in the room were cut from the same mold. Some wore elbow-length leather gloves and black leather skirts cut to their hoo-has and leaned against naugahyde bars with cigarettes dangling from their overly lipsticked mouths. Others sat on swaybacked beds in black bras and panties, adjusting garter belts and smoothing down nylons. Others stood on high heels on which only a tightrope walker could keep balanced, their hands on their copious corseted hips and a cold, arrogant light in their eyes that challenged you to name your game. Whatever game you finally named, however, was sure to be cold and quick, for whatever tenderness had once dwelled in any of these girls had died long ago, over-the-counter. They were sex without sympathy, and embracing any of them would be like holding one of those life-sized plastic dolls that came mail order from magazines with names like *Climax* and *Hustler* and *Man's Delight.* Any warmth you got back from them would be your own.

"Well? What do you think?"

Howard Winter stood in the middle of the room, his arms outstretched. He was dressed the way he was always dressed, in a khaki safari jacket with a paisley foulard loosely knotted at the throat, khaki trousers, and chocolate-colored soft leather moccasins. With his bone-white hair and bushy white mustache setting off his big red face, he looked like a caricature of a British big-game hunter, which was just what he wanted to look like.

Besides erotic art, Winter dealt in a lot of primitive art—African and pre-Columbian—and he thought the image good for business. He might have been right. At least none of his clients seemed bothered by the faint trace of a British accent that occasionally crept into his speech, sounding suspiciously like Stewart Granger in *Harry Black and the Tiger,* or the fact that the only big game he had ever gotten close to was at the San Diego Zoo. It gave their dealer a little dash, was all.

"They're pretty strong," I said, trying to make up my mind.

"They're more than that, dear boy," he said. "There is very little being done today that has this kind of raw, cold power."

The canvases were all huge—all over six feet tall—and they were painted with such meticulous, coldly exaggerated realism that they looked like blown-up photographs. Except for the faces. The faces ruined the photo-real effect. They were almost cartoony.

"And the guy who painted these is the one you want me to talk to," I said.

2

"Yes."

"When is the opening?"

"Tomorrow night."

"How much are they going to be selling for?"

"Twenty," he said, sighing ecstatically.

"Thousand?" I asked, stunned.

He turned on me. "Certainly thousand."

I nodded. "And your cut is what? Thirty percent?"

"Thirty-five."

"It must be nice."

"Don't forget," he said, with a tone that sounded slightly offended but probably wasn't, "I'm the one who knows the people who have twenty thousand to spend on a painting. That's why artists sell through dealers and not on the street. It's all in the contacts. Who could Gerry McMurtry call?"

"Good point," I said. "You probably know every rich geek in the city."

He stiffened. "My clients are not geeks."

"Who *is* going to pay twenty grand for one of these?" He started to open his mouth, but I held up a hand. "And don't get all bent out of shape. If I had twenty grand to casually lay down on a painting, I might even buy one. I like them that well. But let's face it, these aren't any Andrew Wyeth landscapes. Who's going to be your typical buyer?"

"You'd be surprised," he said, unblinking.

"I probably would be."

"We live in an erotic age, dear boy. People are no longer ashamed to own a piece of erotic art. They don't have to keep them in the basement for fear of being ostracized. Degas and Toulouse-Lautrec were condemned in their time as pornographers, but what collector wouldn't give his right arm to have an original Toulouse-Lautrec today? Then, too, you must remember—and don't bother to repeat this to any of my clients because I would just deny that I said it—your average collector is usually nothing more than a rich fool who understands only one thing—money. He has absolutely no criteria for judging a work of art except its price and what the dealer tells him. The more he pays, the more he thinks it's worth." He stopped and waved a hand at the canvases that filled the room. "I have eight Gerry McMurtrys in the show, and by the time it closes next month I guarantee I'll have sold all eight. Probably half will be bought by people who don't even *like* them. That's what capitalism has done to art. The only thing those buyers will want to know is whether or not McMurtrys are a good investment."

"Are they?"

"McMurtrys will be selling for thirty in a year or two. Maybe more." He raised a white eyebrow and looked at me speculatively. "You want to buy one?"

"Thanks, but twenty Gs is a little out of my league."

"Maybe we can work something out."

"I just think I'll wait until they come out in paperback."

He shook his head pityingly. "You're going to miss the boat."

"I've missed a lot of them," I said. "One of them was the *Titanic.*"

"Tsk, tsk. Such an attitude. There is absolutely no hope for you, dear boy. Let's go in the office and talk. Susan!"

The blonde must have been hidden by the paintings, because I had not seen her.

She was flawless, with huge green eyes and a deep tan that made her perfect white teeth look even whiter. Her blouse was unbuttoned almost to the navel, and the absence of tan lines across her more-than-ample cleavage made me wonder if the trend continued below.

"Susan Lamb, Jake Asch," Winter said. "I believe you two talked this morning on the phone."

She took my hand and smiled. She may have even said something like "Nice to meet you," but I could not be sure. I was in a trance. I was about to propose, but then held myself back, deciding to spare myself the pain of the divorce. If she was Howard's latest, she was just biding her time, filling in as a receptionist between toothpaste commercials and waiting for Mr. Right to come along. A producer, preferably, but she would probably have settled for a director in a pinch. As soon as she found out I drove a '67 Plymouth and used it to haul my own Jockey shorts to the laundromat, it would be all over between us.

"We're going into the office, Susan," Winter told her. "No calls."

"Yes, sir. Anything else?"

He nodded. "Call Alec and tell him to make our appointment at two."

I watched her walk away. "I'd like to be the lion that laid down with that lamb. Neither of us would get much sleep."

He looked at me warningly. "That's private stock, my friend."

"Come on, Howard. You're too old for the girl. Step aside for a younger man."

He straightened indignantly. "A man is just as old as the woman he feels."

"Yeah," I said. "I remember the last one."

The last one had been named Lori Baskin, age twenty-six, and she was the reason I knew Howard Winter. It seemed that Lori's toothpaste commercials had been a little too few and far between, and when Howard's promised film contacts had failed to come through, Lori had asked him for a little subsidy to her regular receptionist's salary—about ten thousand dollars' worth —just to see her through the year. In exchange for the ten grand, Lori told Winter she would be willing to forget all about the paternity suit her lawyer was set to file on him. Winter and I had mutual friends, and he gave me a buzz and asked me to see what I could come up with.

Lori's gynecologist turned out to be the nervous type, and it didn't take much to get him to admit that he had changed the date of Lori's last period—at her request. On the basis of the corrected dates, I found out that Lori's eggs had been dropping down her Fallopian tubes right around the time she and a girl friend had spent a week in San Diego with two male acquaintances. Exit Lori.

Winter stepped around a painting and signaled me to follow.

The office was small, with brown grass-cloth walls and a scuffed parquet floor. The furniture consisted of a glass-topped drawerless desk, three leather-and-chrome chairs, a glass-and-chrome end table, and a heavy safe that squatted in the corner. There were no paintings in the room, but three large carved African masks adorned the wall behind the desk. On the end table was an eight-inch-high silver statue of a squatting woman, grimacing in childbirth.

Winter saw me looking at the statue. "Tlatzolteotl."

"You do and you clean it up," I told him.

"No, no, no," he said, trying to explain. "Tlatzolteotl is the Aztec Earth Mother. Was, I should say. That statue is four hundred years old."

It could have been four hundred years old or four years old. That was how much I knew about it.

"During the harvest festival," he went on, "they picked a girl to personify the goddess; then they would decapitate her and flay her, and the high priest would dress up in her skin and copulate with the sun. It was a mimic copulation, of course."

"I hope so."

He threw up his hands and rolled his eyes to the ceiling, as if he were giving up on me. He gestured at one of the chairs and sat behind the desk.

6

"Now," I said, picking a piece of lint off my pants, "what does this McMurtry want to see me about?"

Winter steepled his fingers and said: "He wants you to find his wife and son."

"How long have they been missing?"

"Eight years."

It took me a few seconds to recover from that one. "Nice time to start looking for them."

He smoothed down his foulard tie and frowned impatiently. "It's a long story."

"And screwy, too, I'll bet. It already sounds screwy."

"That's only because you don't know anything about it."

"I'm not sure I want to."

"He'll explain it all when you see him."

"I'm not sure I want to do that either. What is this guy like? I'll tell you one thing right now, Howard: if he's one of the Flying Weirdinos, you can forget it. I've had more than one of that troupe lately as clients, and I'm not anxious to have another one."

"No, no," he said, waving his hands in protest. "Believe me, you'll like him. He's really a nice kid. A bit volatile at times, but a good kid. And as you saw, he's loaded with talent."

"So was Van Gogh, but I wouldn't want him to call me up to help him find his ear."

"Don't worry," he said with an edge in his voice. "I'm telling you Gerry's as normal as you or I."

I gave him a dubious look.

"You, then," he said, grinning.

"How long have you known him?"

"Nine years," he said, smoothing down the side of his white head with one hand. "In a modest way, I feel sort of responsible for his career. He brought me some of his slides when he was first starting out. He wanted me to do a one-man show of his work. I recognized his talent immediately, of course, but at the time I was not able to handle his stuff. I gave him the names of a couple of dealers I knew in New York who I thought might be interested, though. It was in one of those galleries he was discovered by Kenneth Merrill."

"The writer?"

He nodded. "Merrill came out with a best-seller, *Sex in America.* You probably remember it. He featured a couple of McMurtry's paintings in the book. From then on the price of his stuff skyrocketed. That was two years ago. I'd lost track of him until then. As a matter of fact, when I first saw the book, I was shook. I recognized the style right away, but the name didn't click. When he'd come to me before, his name had been Ellison."

"Why did he change it?"

He stroked his mustache thoughtfully. "I'll let him explain. You'll talk to him?"

I sighed. "I'll talk to him."

He nodded and called for Susan. She came in smiling. She could have come in scratching and farting, and she still would have had the same effect on me.

"Susan," Winter said, "call up Gerry, will you? He's at his studio. Tell him Jake will be over to see him when he leaves here."

"All right," she said, and left.

I watched her go, then stood up.

"I'll talk to you?" Winter said.

"Probably. If not about McMurtry, about Tlatzolteotl."

He looked confused. "Huh?"

I pointed out the door at Susan Lamb's retreating derrière and smiled. "The next time you scorch your pecker."

TWO

It was too hot for May, but then it had been too rainy for April, too. It was ninety-five with seventy-five percent humidity, and there had been two second-stage smog alerts in the past five days. The Weather Bureau was blaming it on the temperature inversion layer—whatever that was—and promised relief in the next few days when the mass of "moist tropical air" moved in from off the coast. They had been promising that for a week, however, and if it did not come soon, people would be stopping their cars in the middle of the freeway and shooting one another for tailgating.

The address Winter had given me was on Pico near Fairfax, on the edge of the old Jewish section of L.A. Now only the Jews on social security populated the neighborhood. The wealthier ones just drove down occasionally from Beverly Hills or Bel-Air to get some *kishke* at Canter's Deli or pick up a dozen bialys at one of Fairfax's countless Jewish bakeries.

One of the bakeries was downstairs from McMurtry's studio, sharing the bottom floor with an old Rexall drugstore. The building was old, and the architecture was that mishmash of styles that had been dared only in 1930s Hollywood. It had an art deco bas-relief front and a terra-cotta tile roof and arched windows across the second story flanked by Greek columns. Somehow it all went together.

The rich, sweet smells of the bakery followed me halfway up the stairs that led from the street, before deferring to forty years of must. The hallway at the top smelled like a catacomb, and the only light was provided by a dirty skylight in the ceiling. That was a smart move on the landlord's part, but not smart enough. It would have had to be pitch-dark for me not to see the paint curling off the walls and flaying off the ceiling in long strips or the four or five different patterns on the floor, where the dirty linoleum tile had been patched with whatever had been available.

I thought about going back downstairs and buying a half dozen bagels and forgetting about it, but then I remembered that McMurtrys were going to be selling for thirty grand next year, and my feet kept moving.

Most of the doorways in the hall were frosted glass, but McMurtry's was solid and painted black. I knocked on it and waited. When there was no response, I knocked again.

"Okay, okay, hold on," a muffled voice called out, and then the door jerked open.

The man who blinked out at me like a mole coming into sunlight was probably my age—thirty-six—and an inch or two taller than my six feet, but thinner by quite a bit. He had a long, leanly handsome face that ended in a strong chin and was framed by straight, shoulder-length brown hair. He wore a long-sleeved blue denim work shirt, faded blue jeans, and blue sneakers, all of which were liberally smeared with various colors of paint. Perspiration soaked through the front of the shirt in large patches, running some of the colors together.

"Yeah?" he said irritably.

10

"Mr. McMurtry?"

"Yeah?"

"I'm Jacob Asch."

He wiped away the beads of sweat that dotted his forehead and said, "Oh, yeah, sure. Come in, come in."

As soon as I stepped through the door, I knew why he was sweating. The heat in the place was stifling.

The room was completely dark except for the light provided by a projector sitting on a table in the middle of the room. A huge canvas hanging on the wall was being used as a screen.

The picture being projected onto the canvas was of a woman in a low-cut black leather jump suit and knee-high, dagger-heeled boots, complete with spurs. She was sitting on a bed in a sleazy motel room, gesturing at her boots as if she wanted me to lick them. Her hair was a short black wave brushed back from a high-cheekboned face so pale it looked as if it had been dusted with rice powder, and her blood-red lips were parted slightly, giving her a positively vampiric appearance.

McMurtry closed the door. "I guess I forgot what time it was. I get wrapped up in my work."

He hit the lights, and the motel room faded, but the woman in the jump suit remained vivid and strong.

"So that's how it's done," I said, walking over to the unfinished painting.

He came up behind me. "That's how it's done. I project the image onto the canvas, then paint over it. Of course, as you can see, when you blow up a picture that big, all it is is a series of microdots. That gives me a lot of leeway to do what I want to do, especially with color, since all the photographs I use are black-and-whites."

"But it's not photo-realism," I said, leaning close to the painting. "Your faces are almost cartoony—"

"You noticed," he said, pleased. "That's because my work has been greatly influenced by a man named Gene Bilbrew. He was a black artist who used to live here in L.A. before he died. He did a lot of serials for underground comic books in the fifties and sixties. Fetish and SM stuff. Actually, my work is a mixture of illustrative art and photo-realism. Pure photo-realism wouldn't work with images like these. Part of their power lies in the fantasy. In real life, that woman would possess no beauty at all. She would either be a joke or scare you shitless, but those would be the only two ways you could respond to her."

I was held by the cold, vicious beauty of the painting and got a chill wondering what kind of infant that madonna would suckle. "I don't know. She's doing a pretty good job of disturbing me like she is."

A satisfied smile turned up the corners of his mouth. "I'm glad she affects you that way. I don't want people to be tranquil looking at my paintings. They weren't designed to go with wood paneling and hanging plants. This is Hollywood, not Mill Valley. It's a nasty, plastic world out there."

His voice was a soft, steady baritone, almost soothing. He was not what I had expected, but then I didn't really know what I had expected. Certainly nobody this composed. Still, there seemed to be a contained intensity just below the surface that created a strange kind of tension in me.

"I know it must not be a very original question," I said, "but how did you get into painting this sort of stuff?"

He shrugged. "When I was ten years old, I found an old fetish magazine my father had hidden in his room. Black nylon and high-heeled-shoe stuff. It was nothing compared to the stuff that's on the stands today, of course, but then it was considered porn. Anyway, it blew me away. I decided then and there that those were the most powerful images I could paint and that as soon as I could, I was going to blow them up and put them on a wall. I guess you can say all this is a childhood fantasy grown into an adult fantasy."

I remembered my own first exposure to similar material. I had been around the same age, and my reaction had been almost the

12

same. Only with McMurtry, the reaction had stuck a little harder. If he was one of the Flying Weirdinos, at least he was the catcher and not the guy who tries the triple without a net, I decided.

A fan sat on the floor in the corner, making a valiant effort to churn up the air, but it did not seem to be doing much good. The thick, greasy smell of oil paint hung in the room like a fragrant blanket, making it difficult to breathe.

My shirt was sticking to me uncomfortably, and I plucked at it with two fingers. He noticed and said: "For God's sake, take your coat off. I apologize for the heat in here, but I have to keep the windows closed because of the light."

I peeled off my coat and laid it over the back of one of the two rickety wooden chairs nearby.

"You want a beer?" McMurtry asked.

I told him a beer sounded great. He turned off the projector and disappeared through an open archway into another room. While he was gone, I looked over the studio.

It was a large room, and besides being incredibly hot, it was also incredibly shabby. The sick-green plaster walls were cracked and smeared with dirt, the ceiling was watermarked, and the wood floor was so encrusted with drops of paint it looked like a pebble garden. Stretcher bars, some blank canvases, and several gigantic rolls of paper leaned against one wall. Aside from the table that held the projector and another smaller table beside it holding a palette, some brushes, and a half dozen well-squeezed tubes of oil paint, the two rickety chairs were the only furniture in the room.

He came back holding two cans of Ole, handed me one, then pulled the tab off his and tossed it on the floor. I noticed there were a lot of them to keep it company. I ripped the top off mine and looked around.

"Just throw it anywhere," he said. "In this dump it isn't going to make any difference."

He took a couple of deep swallows of beer and looked around.

"You know, this place was my first studio, nine years ago. The first thing I did when I moved back to L.A. was run right over here and find out if it was available. I've done some really good work here." That bit of nostalgia seemed to work on him. His expression softened a little.

I took a sip of beer. It was delicious and ice-cold. "How long have you been back?"

"Four months." He nodded at the two chairs behind me. "Sit down."

I took the chair with my coat on it, and he pulled the other one over to face it.

He lifted the can of beer to his mouth and paused there, peering over it. "Howard gave you a strong recommendation. Four stars."

"Only four?"

"That's Howard's top rating. It's reserved for people who make him a lot of money. Howard likes money."

And blondes, I thought. "I never made him a lot of money."

"You saved him a bundle, I hear. It's all the same thing."

"Paternity cases can get pretty sticky. We lucked out. His turned out to be fairly simple."

"That's what it was? A paternity case?" He smiled. "He never told me. Good old Howard." His tone said clearly that he thought of Winter as something other than "good old Howard."

He rested the can on his knee and leaned forward slightly. "What exactly is your relationship with Howard?"

"There isn't one, really," I said. "I did the one job for him. That's all."

He pursed his lips and nodded, then leaned back. "What did he tell you about me?"

"Exactly? 'A nice kid. Volatile, unpredictable at times, but basically a good kid. And loaded with talent.'"

14

He grunted. "Sounds like something that asshole would say."

"You don't like him too much."

"I don't," he said. "Howard is a first-class, A-one prick. He treats his artists like shit. The only reason he doesn't treat me like shit is that I make him too much money. But good old Howard pulled a few numbers on me a long time ago when I was struggling. He doesn't remember, but I do."

I'd heard a lot of similar stories when I'd worked for Winter, but personally I had nothing against the man. A couple of times he had taken his bwana role a little too seriously and tried to treat me like Kakanga, the gun bearer, but I'd straightened him out, and he'd never tried it again. But McMurtry's dislike for the man was real and obviously went beyond that sort of thing. As a matter of fact, it was the first crack I'd seen in his cool, unruffled front.

I diplomatically decided to skip the story Winter had told me about being responsible for McMurtry's career. He didn't seem to be in the mood for it. "So why do you sell through Winter's gallery?"

"With Howard and me, it's strictly business. He gets me my price and takes his thirty-five percent, and that's it. But I wouldn't trust him as far as I could throw him, and that wouldn't be far, that tub of shit. That's why I asked what your relationship was with him. I don't think I'd want to hire anybody who was a good friend of Howard's. When he recommended you, in fact, I was reluctant to even meet you."

"That's funny."

"What?"

"I told Howard I wasn't particularly anxious to meet you. I had vague visions of some raving, twitching bozo in a rubber overcoat, whacking off in a high-heeled shoe."

He laughed. "I'm sorry to disappoint you."

"It's not a disappointment, believe me."

He took another sip of beer, and the smile left his face. He squinted at me intently and asked, "Did Howard tell you what my problem is?"

"I gather you want to find your wife."

"And son," he added quickly.

"Winter said you hadn't seen either of them in eight years."

"That's right."

My beer was starting to warm up. I drained the can before it got too warm to drink and set the empty down on the floor beside me. "What happened?"

"It's a long story," he said, looking past me.

"That's why I assume you wanted me here. To tell it to me."

"Yes," he said, sighing. "I guess it is." He balked and pointed to the can on the floor. "Before I start, you want another beer?"

I guessed the reason he asked was that he wanted to think about it a little before launching into it, so I said okay and handed him my empty. He left the room and came back with two more beers and sat down splay-legged in the chair.

"Okay," he said. "This is how it went. Ten years ago I was just out of art school, living in Venice and playing the role of the perennial starving artist. That was when I met Lainie. She was going to UCLA and working part time at an art supply store I dealt with at the beach. We'd talk when I came into the store, and then I asked her out, and before I knew it, things got really heavy. We weren't going out a month before she moved in with me."

He tilted the can up to his mouth and took a drink. "I don't know, but I think a lot of the reason I was attracted to her so much in the first place was this aura she gave out of being totally self-sufficient. She seemed like one of the strongest and most together girls I'd ever met, and at the time that was very important because my own head wasn't on straight. Artists are very insecure people, and Lainie seemed at the time to fill a lot of needs in me, kind of plug up the holes. When she got pregnant, there was never any doubt in my mind that marrying her was

16

going to be the solution to all my problems. It was only the start of them."

"What happened?"

He shrugged. "The mask came off. Little by little I found out that all that strength was just a front. Deep down, she was more insecure than I was, and pretty soon things started to come apart. We never argued before we were married, but suddenly we started getting into incredible fights. She would push me and push me, making little taunting remarks, until I would blow up. I didn't realize it at the time—I don't think she did either—but it was all part of the pattern. She was trying to change me into somebody else—the image of the man she carried around with her."

"What man?"

"Her father," he said, then blinked at me as if surprised I was here. "Is it really necessary to go into all of this?"

"I wouldn't know. You're the one who brought it up."

"Yes, and I'm not really sure why I did."

"If you want me to find your wife," I said, "the more I know about her, the better chance I'll have of finding her."

"I suppose." He hesitated, deciding whether to go on, then sighed and said: "Lainie's father owned a chain of shoe stores that went broke right after Lainie was born. He wound up selling shoes in somebody else's store for the rest of his life, and it blew his mind. He was haunted by failure, and not to think about the failure, he drank. Only the drinking just made him think about it more, and it would build up inside him until finally he would explode and take it out on Lainie. That was the only time he would tell her he loved her, when he would beat the shit out of her and feel guilty about it. That stuck with her, and after that all the men she was attracted to were macho, overbearing, sadistic types. I was the first one who didn't fit the mold."

"Why do you think that was?"

"I don't know. Maybe she was unconsciously trying to break the pattern. Whatever the reason, it didn't work. That's why she would goad me into arguments. The only time she would ever get really sexually turned on—after Brian was born, that is— was when I would really lose my temper. That was what got me thinking in the first place; that was when I started to dig to find out what it was all about."

"Did you confront her with it?"

"Sure," he said. "She denied the whole thing. She claimed she hated her father. She said he was just a no-good lush. She wasn't aware of what she was doing because she had ambivalent feelings toward him—even her unconscious ones. She wasn't searching for the *pure* image of her father, but only part of it. She wasn't looking for a sadistic failure; she wanted a sadistic success. That was another reason I had to bail out."

His gestures and facial expressions were electrically animated now, and I guessed his reasons for telling me the story had gone beyond my reasons for hearing it. It was a catharsis. He was explaining the whole thing to himself, not to me.

"Why is that?"

"After Brian was born, I had to do a lot of shit art, just to keep food on the table. I had a connection with a small commercial gallery that would take all the seascapes and wet Paris street scenes I could grind out. I was still developing my own art, too, but then Lainie started finding me more outlets for junk through her connection with the art supply store, until I realized that was all I was doing.

"I don't know if you can understand this, but my art has always been my freedom. Suddenly, one morning I woke up and realized I wasn't free anymore, and I hated Lainie and resented Brian for it. My Vision wasn't seascapes and wet Paris street scenes. It was this." He made a gesture toward the madonna.

"So you split."

He nodded. "I went to the bank and drew out half of what

we had, which wasn't a hell of a lot, and hopped on a bus to New York. That was the last time I saw Lainie. Or Brian."

"Why New York?"

"Any artist who really wants to make it has to go to New York. That's where it's happening. The public doesn't decide who is great and who isn't. It's *told.* And the people who tell it are a small group of collectors and critics and gallery owners in New York. If an artist plays his cards right and is admitted into the circle, he is on his way. But he has to live in New York, and he is allowed to go home only after he's made it."

"You make it sound so conspiratorial."

"That's because it is."

I sipped my beer. "You must have made it into the inner circle. They let you come home."

"Yeah, but it was a long, hard haul, believe me. I've only been getting big prices for my work the past two years. Before that I sold enough to stay alive, but not much more than that. I've paid my dues. I've slept on the floor of my studio with the cockroaches enough nights and eaten enough mayonnaise sandwiches for a lifetime."

"Why did you change your name?"

"One reason was that I didn't want Lainie following me," he said. "I thought she might try. Another reason was that I owed some people some money. Friends. I paid them back later, but at the time I was strapped for cash, and I didn't want them bugging me. I wanted to concentrate on painting without any outside pressure. So I started signing my name McMurtry. I never changed my name legally."

"Have you had any contact with your wife at all since you left for New York?"

He shook his head. His eyes avoided mine. "I thought about writing, to try to explain. But hell, how could I explain? She never would've understood."

"So why do you want to try now?"

"I don't. I just want to make sure she's all right." He hesitated thoughtfully. "Look, given the same circumstances, I would probably make the same decisions I did then. There was no other choice. But that doesn't mean I'm proud of what I did. I didn't have anything to offer her then, nothing except my art, and I was not about to offer that up as a sacrifice. But now I've got something, I'm financially secure, and if she needs anything, I want to make sure she has it.

"And I want to see my son. The last few months, since I got back to California, it's become sort of an obsession with me. After all these years I suddenly want to see my son. Does that sound strange?"

If his motives sounded uncertain, even to himself, at least the sentiment behind them seemed sincere.

"Not necessarily," I said.

"There's also Mona."

"Mona?"

"My old lady," he said, looking down at the beer can in his hands. "We've been thinking about getting married. But we can't do anything until I find out if I'm still married to Lainie. I assume she would've filed for a divorce, but I can't find any record of it in L.A. County."

"Have you looked for her at all yourself?"

"I called everybody I could think of that we knew. Nobody's heard from her in years. It's like she dropped into a hole or something."

"Is her mother still alive?"

"The last I heard."

"Did you try her?"

"I called the number I had for her," he said gravely. "A stranger answered. He said he'd had that number for two years, and he'd never heard of any Mrs. Bowen. Palm Springs information didn't have a listing for her either. But I doubt Lainie would have gone there anyway."

"Lainie's mother was a real strict Catholic, the self-immolating type. Her love was her crucifix, and she pushed everything else in her life away, including Lainie. That was one reason Lainie grew so dependent on her father. All the time we were together, she hardly ever talked to her mother. Maybe at Christmas she'd call her or something like that, but that was about all."

I put my beer down on the floor and took a note pad and pen from my pocket. "What was the mother's first name?"

"Jane."

"B-O-W-E-N?"

"Yes."

"Address?"

His brow furrowed as he tried to remember. "She lived in a trailer park in Palm Springs. Sahara, Arabia, something like that. I remember the name had something to do with Arabs."

I wrote down: "Sahara, Arabia, Arabs?"

"Where were you married?"

"Santa Monica."

"And your name was Gerald Ellison?"

He nodded.

"Where was your wife born?"

"Terre Haute, Indiana."

"She have any relatives there you know about?"

"She never mentioned it if she did. She moved from there when she was little."

"A couple of things up front," I told him. "Everybody's somewhere. I can probably find your wife, but it might take some time. It's been eight years. She might have changed her name, like you. She might be living in L.A.; she might be living in Terre Haute; she might be living two blocks from where you were living in New York. My point is: How much do you want to spend to find her?"

"Whatever it takes," he said without hesitation.

I nodded. "My rate is standard. One-fifty a day plus expenses. Plus fifteen cents a mile. And I'll want a five-hundred-dollar retainer."

"I don't have a checkbook with me," he said. "If you stop by the opening tomorrow night, I can give it to you."

"Tomorrow's fine."

"Then it's settled," he said, smiling.

"Not quite."

The smile dimmed. "Why not? What's the problem?"

"No problem. There are just a few things I think you should be aware of before you decide to go through with this, that's all."

"What kind of things?"

"I had a case similar to yours a couple of years ago, only my client was the other side. The woman's husband cut out on her and her two kids. He just didn't come home from work one day. A couple of years later a friend of the woman called her up and told her that she saw the husband on a plane to Salt Lake City. The woman hired me to find the guy. I found him living in a suburb of Salt Lake, working as a computer engineer. He was remarried and had a kid by the woman. We had a long talk. He said he had run out on his wife, my client, because he'd felt as if he were being smothered, that his life was a total waste. So he left and changed his identity and started over. He begged me not to tell his ex-wife where he was, but I couldn't very well do that. Well, my client had already been granted a divorce, so she couldn't nail the guy for bigamy, but she slapped a nice fat civil suit on him that tied him up for years. In the end his second marriage broke up, and the guy wound up flat on his ass."

"What are you trying to tell me?"

"Like I said, eight years is a long time. The woman is bound to harbor a lot of bitterness toward you. You could find out too late that looking for her was not such a hot idea after all."

"That's a chance I'm going to have to take, I guess," he said.

I sighed. "All right. Just so you know. I'll try to provide you with as much insulation as possible."

His left eyebrow lowered. "How are you going to do that?"

"If I find her, I'll approach her with a cover story. I don't know what right now, but I'll think of something. I'll bring your name up and see what she says. If she reacts like she's going to be the seven-year plague, at least you'll know about it without having to go in cold."

He nodded and rubbed his chin thoughtfully. "Yeah, that sounds good."

"Do you have a picture of her?"

He pulled out his wallet from his back pocket and flipped it open. Carefully he extracted a small, dog-eared color snapshot and handed it to me. The picture was of a pretty brown-haired girl sitting on a couch and holding an infant on her lap. Both the girl and the child were smiling for the camera. McMurtry's face was there in the child's, even at that age.

"The kid looks just like you."

"Yes," he said, as if embarrassed. "I'll want that back. It's the only one I have."

"Sure."

I put it away and stood up.

"Tomorrow night, then," he said, and shoved out his hand.

I shook it, and he showed me to the door. I stepped into the dingy hallway feeling a slight twinge of apprehension. Not about McMurtry. I genuinely liked the guy. That, perhaps, was part of the problem.

Relocating in his old studio, trying to hunt down his wife and son, the man seemed to be trying to forge a tangible link with the part of the past he had fled. After eight years I had wanted to tell him that you can never go home anymore, but I hadn't. I hadn't because it was really none of my business and because I needed the bread. There was always that.

My footsteps made lonely echoes off the walls of the hallway.

I stopped and listened. Not a sound came from behind any of the office doors, not the creaking of a chair, not a cough.

The other tenants in this building know, I thought as I went down the stairs. McMurtry is just going to have to find out for himself.

Sometimes nostalgia just isn't what it used to be.

THREE

It was still hot and smoggy the next morning, and as I drove out of town, I wished I had some of that "moist, tropical air" off the coast in a compressed air bottle so that I could administer a high colonic to that disgustingly ebullient little weatherman on the "Channel Six News."

The air heated up as I drove east through the desert, but ten miles outside Palm Springs the smog miraculously disappeared, as if the movie moguls who lived there had ordered a sky-high invisible wall from Special Effects to protect the sanctity of their winter homes.

The coke-oven wind that blew off the desert carried some sand with it, but I didn't slow down. With my car, a little sand damage might have been an improvement. I did the last stretch of highway at eighty-five, and then the palm trees started, and I took my foot off the gas and coasted into town.

Although its population had swelled in recent years with an influx of blizzard fugitives from back east and general seekers of the "good life," and a vast condominium sprawl had begun on its outskirts, Palm Springs still retained the artificial, well-planned flavor of a movie set.

The palm trees that lined the colored sidewalks were too well manicured and evenly spaced to be real; the streets were too antiseptically clean; the architecture and colors of the posh shops and restaurants and motels that jostled one another for space on the town's main drag were too perfectly coordinated not to have come from Set Design. Even the rugged mountains that served as an immediate backdrop for the city looked like something from a Maxfield Parrish print when the light hit them right. And it seemed as if somebody made the light hit them right a good deal of the time.

The sidewalks were filled with the usual assortment of gawkers and shoppers in various states of dress and undress, all with their heads tilted slightly upward to absorb every available second of sunshine. There were bikinied brunettes in platform shoes and short-shorted sun-bleached blondes with cocoa-butter thighs; middle-aged red-headed dye-jobbed ones in loose-fitting shifts, leading their beast-of-burden tubby-hubbies with their pasty-white hairy legs poking out of their Bermuda shorts and cameras strapped faithfully around their necks. There were even a few gray-haired representatives of the tour group from Vancouver who had already been to see all the stars' homes and were now downtown, intently scouring the faces of passersby, hoping to get a glimpse of just one movie star upcloseandinperson before the group pulled out in the morning for Vegas. And there were the less identifiable ones, the secretaries and insurance salesmen who came down to blow out and bake, who would go back home wearing their tans like merit badges and bask in the envious glances of their friends and co-workers.

I pulled into a gas station and bought a map of the area. The attendant directed me to the public library, and I drove there.

The last listing I could find for Jane Bowen in any Palm Springs directory was 1971, at 22 Mecca Drive, Palm Springs.

26

Mecca Drive was not indexed on my map, so I tried looking in the yellow pages under "Mobile Home Parks." McMurtry had been close; the name of the park was Araby.

It was hidden behind a high wall of oleanders, and I drove by the first time without seeing it. On my second trip I spied the unmarked entrance and turned in.

A plywood camel with a blue blanket painted over its single hump stood in front of the clubhouse, a tired expression on its face. Having to hang around there all day, it could hardly be blamed.

A hundred Mantovani violins drifted peacefully across the pool area where a few octogenarians dozed in the shade. A few others sat in the outdoor hot pool, staring blankly into space. I patted the camel on the hump sympathetically and went into the office.

The manager, Mr. Treekle, was only a youngster—sixty-five or so—and although he was willing, he was not very helpful. He had been running things for only a year and had never heard of Jane Bowen. I showed him the address, and he told me that the current owner of that *mobile home*—having visibly cringed several times from my use of the word *trailer*—was a Mrs. Harriet Poulson and gave me directions how to get there.

In the publicity releases put out by its Chamber of Commerce, Palm Springs boasts the largest per capita ratio of swimming pools of any city in the world, the world's wealthiest Indian tribe, the world's largest aerial tramway, and the world's "most luxurious mobile home park." Araby was not it.

The grounds were nicely landscaped with date palms and cacti and occasional sprays of magenta bougainvillea, but most of the mobile homes in the place were old single-wides to which expandos had been attached to provide more space. Jane Bowen's old place was one of those.

Harriet Poulson was a thin, spry woman of seventy-odd, with the sharp, small eyes and bluish, clawlike hands of a bird. When

I told her who I was, she twittered like a bird, too, and hustled me inside.

The living room was long and narrow, and the fawn-colored paneling on the walls contrasted with the dark furniture that filled it. Most of the pieces were old but looked as if they'd been expensive at one time, with a lot of polished, ornately carved wood that nobody would bother with any more because of the cost of labor.

She put me at a round mahogany table in the dining room, which was nothing more than a space allocated at the end of the living room, and went into the kitchen to get us some lemonade. From where I sat, I could look into the kitchen and, beyond that, down a hallway to a bedroom at the far end of the place. I felt as if I were in the dining car of a train.

Behind me the gossamer curtain liners drawn across the windows turned the morning light a filmy white. On the wall to my right was a desertscape of some smoke trees and purple verbena blooming in front of a mountain range that looked an awful lot like the one behind us. I would have thought that she would have had enough desert outside without importing any. But then, she probably did not get out much.

She came back in with two glasses of lemonade. "I hope it's sweet enough for you," she said in a voice that sounded like a rusty hinge. "I like mine a little tart."

I sipped it. My mouth shriveled up into a prune. I tried to talk normally. "It's very good."

"I squeeze it fresh," she said proudly. "You're sure it's not too tart?"

"It's fine."

"A private detective," she said, sucking in a breath. "That really must be exciting work."

"Not really," I said. "It can get pretty dull. Most of my time is spent sifting through a lot of bureaucratic paperwork and running credit checks, things like that."

She looked disappointed. "I guess they do play things up on television."

I looked around and said: "You have a very nice place here."

She smiled pleasantly. "It's comfortable. The main thing is, it's easy to take care of. At my age, that's important. I used to manage a big house when my husband was alive, but I couldn't do it anymore."

"How long have you lived here?"

"Six years. I bought it in 1972, two years after Kyle passed away. That was my husband, Kyle."

I nodded.

"After Kyle passed on, there was no reason to keep the big house, so I sold it." She paused, then said, as if I would be interested: "We lived in Arcadia."

"Why did you move to Palm Springs?"

"I've always loved the desert. It's nice and quiet. And it's a lot easier for me to get around down here than in the city." She waved one of her claws at me. "But you didn't come all the way from Los Angeles to hear an old lady rattle off this nonsense, for heaven's sake. You wind me up, I'll just sit here and talk your ear off." Her bird eyes narrowed. "Who did you say you were looking for?"

"Jane Bowen."

She thought about it, then shook her gray head. "I don't know anybody by that name. The woman I bought this place from was named Bowen, but it wasn't Jane."

"What was her name?"

She tapped her chin with a bony finger. "Lainie. Lainie Bowen."

"A young girl?"

"Yes. In her late twenties, I'd say."

Bingo. Lainie and my instincts had both been right. After McMurtry had cleared out, she had run home to mother. "Jane was Lainie's mother."

"Ah," she said, "that explains it then. Her mother died the year before she sold me the home. That was why I got it so cheap. She needed the money to pay off the inheritance taxes and things, and she couldn't live here. Not with her baby. Children aren't allowed in the park." She quickly amended that. "To live, that is. They're allowed to *visit,* of course."

"And that's the name she was going by then? Bowen?"

"Yes."

"Lainie is the one I'm really looking for."

Her eyes grew wary. "Why are you looking for Lainie?"

"A distant relative of hers died recently and left her some money. Not a fortune or anything, but a substantial amount. The attorney from the estate hired me to locate her. She seems to have dropped out of sight."

Her eyebrows bunched together in concern. "I wish I could help, but I don't know where she went after she sold me this place. It's too bad, because she deserves good fortune, poor thing. I always felt sorry for her. She was really a nice girl. A little high-strung, but that was understandable after all she'd been through. Her husband ran out on her, you know."

I said I didn't. She nodded. "Left her flat with a baby to take care of and everything. That wasn't too long before her mother died, I guess. All that happening so close together really got her down. We had a couple of long talks about it. She was real attached to her mother. She was still broken up about her passing on, even though it'd been over a year since it had happened."

"Do you know where she was living at the time she sold you the place?"

"She had an apartment, I know that, but I don't know where."

"How about where she worked?"

"She was a salesgirl at one of the department stores downtown. One of the better ones—Robinson's or Bullock's, one of those—but I can't remember which one now."

"In any of the talks you had with her, Mrs. Poulson, did she mention whether she planned to stay in town?"

"Seems she mentioned something about moving, but I'm not sure." She thought for a minute, then remembered something. "She had a boyfriend. Maybe she got married again."

"Who was he?"

"I can't remember his name. I saw him only once. He drove her over here one time when she showed me the place. A real nice-looking boy. She said he was an actor. He looked just like that boy that plays on 'Starsky and Hutch.' I can't remember, though, whether it's Starsky or Hutch. I can never keep those two straight in my mind."

"Don't feel bad," I told her. "I can't either."

"As a matter of fact, when I first saw that series, I thought it was him until I looked real close. From what Lainie said, he was supposed to be going to Hollywood to audition for some show. Maybe she went there." She paused, then said: "To tell you the truth, I hope she didn't."

"Why?"

"Well. . . ." She leaned toward me and lowered her voice. "The day they were over here, I saw him hit her. Right outside by the car. Knocked her down. I talked to her later about it, but she just said that it was her fault, that she'd made him lose his temper."

I thought about McMurtry's tale of Lainie's odyssey. Maybe after all her searching she had finally found her father. "Was he local?"

"I know he was living down here then. He must have had a lot of money, because he drove a real expensive sports car, one of those that cost thirty thousand dollars. Wherever he got his money, though, it wasn't from acting."

"Why do you say that?"

She shrugged. "Because I've never seen him, and I watch television a lot. That's about all I have to do." She looked at her watch. "Matter of fact, I'm missing 'Emergency Hospital' right now."

"I'm sorry."

She waved a claw at me and cackled. "Oh, that's all right. This is much more exciting. I don't get much company anymore. And never anybody as exciting as a private eye." She paused and said distractedly: "John was supposed to get a kidney transplant today."

"John?"

"On 'Emergency Hospital.' "

"Oh." It was a perfect cue to break away. I stood up. "Mrs. Poulson, I want to thank you for all your help—"

"Maybe somebody around the park knows something. About where Lainie went, I mean."

I took a card out of my wallet and handed it to her. "If you do hear something, just call me collect at that number. Anytime."

She winked at me and cackled again. "I'll put the word out. Is that the way they say it?"

"That's the way they say it," I said, winking back, and left.

The pay telephone was by the clubhouse. I tried all the major department stores in town, but none of them had a Lainie Bowen working for them.

The same octogenarians were dozing in their lounge chairs as I walked to my car. These would be Mrs. Poulson's informants, the ones that were still alive anyway. From where I was standing, it was kind of hard to determine just which ones those were.

FOUR

The Riverside County offices were located twenty miles away in Indio, an ugly commercial town surrounded by brooding groves of date palms, which were its main claim to fame.

I found the death certificate for Lainie's mother in the county recorder's office. It said she had died at Desert Hospital on October 9, 1971, of a myocardial infarct. Lainie was listed as the next of kin, with an address of 444 East Ramon Road, Apartment 4, Palm Springs. I took the address down and went down the hall to the clerk of the superior court.

Since I didn't have an exact date, it took a very sugary smile and a lot of silver-tongued charm to induce the girl behind the desk to run Lainie's name through the divorce files, but once she had committed herself it didn't take her long to find it. The divorce papers had been filed on March 16, 1971, and finalized a year later. I had her make copies of the pertinent stuff and went back down to the recorder's office, just to see, on the off chance, if Lainie had gotten remarried, as Mrs. Poulson suggested.

As I stared at the license the clerk handed me, I was filled with that tingly electric excitement that always flowed through me when the pieces came together. To another person it might have looked like just another piece of paper, but to me it was people, and their lives seemed to pulsate in my hands.

On June 20, 1974, Lainie Marie Bowen had married one Simon Alexander Fleischer at 454 Fairmont Road, Rancho Mirage, which was also listed as Fleischer's address. Fleischer's age at the time was fifty-two, which, unless he ate a lot of preserves, let out Mrs. Poulson's Starsky or Hutch. The marriage was the second time around for Fleischer, too; his last wife had died in 1965.

I had the clerk make a copy of the license and went outside to the pay phone. Fleischer's number was listed, at the same address as on the license.

I went to the car and spread the map out on the front seat. The only Fairmont Road in Rancho Mirage was inside Tamarisk Country Club. I hummed to myself as I put the key in the ignition. I was feeling very proud of myself. This bit of business was going to be wrapped up today, nice and neat, with a big red ribbon around it. Asch, you're a hell of a detective.

The series of small, exclusive communities that was strung like rich pearls along the highway to Palm Springs had nice-sounding names—La Quinta, Indian Wells, Palm Desert—and their lush golf courses lay like acres of cash on the white desert sands. Rancho Mirage was the fourth pearl, and just past it, a sign said: FRANK SINATRA DRIVE. It figured.

I turned left, dipped down into a wash, and made a slow pass by the heavy, electronically controlled gate that barred the entrance to the course. There was a phone by the gate, but before I tried that, I wanted to see if there was another way in. I made a U-turn and started back slowly.

A little farther back was a gateless and guardless road. A sign beside it said: TAMARISK COUNTRY CLUB—MEMBERS ONLY. I turned on it. If I liked the place, maybe I'd join.

The road ran between two walls of oleanders for a few hundred yards, then opened into a parking lot that looked like a Lincoln Continental dealership. I circled around the modern stone and glass clubhouse to where the busboys parked, thinking my car would look less conspicuous there, but even their cars were newer than mine. It was enough to give a person a complex.

I left my coat in the car and hoofed it down a cement walk that ran between the back of the clubhouse and several windowless stucco buildings. The metal garage doors of one of the buildings was open, and inside was an old man preparing one of the golf carts that filled the place to be taken out on the course. His eyes took me in disapprovingly as I passed, but I smiled and said hello, and he didn't start shouting for the guards.

The path ran between two hedges out onto the fairway, where it turned into a cart trail. Tall clusters of eucalyptus and oaks and palms shaded the course and gave a green tinge to the hard glare of the desert light. The air had cooled and moistened a bit, but it was still hot, which was probably why the greens were almost deserted. I followed the path, stepping off for an occasional golf cart that whined by, but the hatted golfers driving them didn't pay me any attention.

After a quarter of a mile or so the path crossed a road with an electronic gate across it like the one out front. I stopped and consulted my map. Fairmont Drive was another quarter of a mile down the road. It had its own gate, too. I stepped around it and started looking for house numbers.

From the outside the house did not look like much, just a sand-colored rough plaster wall with a carved oak door set into it. I pressed the button by the door and waited.

The door was opened by a large, thick-shouldered man dressed in black slacks, black shoes, and a black short-sleeved shirt. He was fortyish and had black hair and small pig's eyes and a nose like the hood ornament on an old Pontiac. It was too hot to be dressed the way he was, but I didn't mention it. Maybe he thought he was Lash La Rue. He looked me over, and a faint frown of disapproval tugged at his mouth. "Yes?"

"Is Mrs. Fleischer in?"

"Is she expecting you?" in a tone that said he knew she wasn't.

"No." I showed him my photostat. "I'm a private detective. I'd like to talk to her if she would be kind enough to spare me a couple of minutes."

"What's it about?"

"Are you Mr. Fleischer?"

"No," he said. "I'm an employee of Mr. Fleischer's."

I smiled politely. "It's a personal matter."

The light in his eyes seemed to crystallize. "How did you get in here?"

"Walked," I said, still smiling.

The frown really grew then. He grunted and went over me again with his eyes as if expecting to find something distasteful he had missed before. I never found out if he came up with anything. He closed the door without another word.

I waited some more. Perspiration broke loose from my hairline and made a run for one eyebrow. I intercepted it with two fingers and flicked it onto the ground. Two minutes went by. The man opened the door again and told me to come in.

The plaster wall was a front hiding an open-air courtyard filled with plants. Another carved oak door, this one arched, was recessed into the wall on the other side of the courtyard. He opened it and showed me inside.

A small foyer opened into a white living room, the ceiling of which must have been fifteen feet high. Dark beams sloped across it and through a glass wall, out to a large pool area that had been made to look like a rocky lagoon.

The lagoon was surrounded by tall palms and a lot of semitropical plants, and on the far side of it a waterfall tumbled musically down a dark pumice cliff.

The floor was brown terrazzo tile. In the middle of it was an island of white—a white shag rug on which a white sectioned couch surrounded a chrome-and-glass coffee table. Another cluster of white furniture sat in front of a marble fireplace that was bordered by a band of mirror. By the sliding glass door that led out to the pool was a sunken tile bar backed by mirrors, and beside that sat a five-foot-high white ceramic greyhound calmly staring at me, listening for his master's voice.

Lash La Rue waved a hand casually at the couch on the white island and told me Mrs. Fleischer would be right out. I sat and drummed my fingers on my knees while looking around the room at the paintings on the walls. Most of them were abstracts, and none bore any resemblance to McMurtry's work. I wondered if the woman had kept any of the things he had done in those days before he'd put an egg in his shoe and beat it. I wondered if she knew what they would be worth.

The woman came in assertively, almost striding, and I had the feeling she would come into every room just like that, as if she were ready to take it over. She was tall and still athletically built, with long legs and narrow hips and a well-rounded bust, and she looked solid all over. A lot of tennis probably kept it that way. She wore a blue and gray silk blouse with puffed sleeves and beige slacks and matching leather pumps.

I stood up, and she looked at me without smiling. "Now what is all this about, Mr.—"

"Asch," I said. "Jacob Asch. You're Mrs. Fleischer?"

"Yes."

I put out my hand, and she shook it firmly.

I would not have been able to recognize her from her picture, but that didn't mean much. It was a bad picture. Her face was narrow and well tanned, surrounded by medium-length brown hair that was brushed back in a series of soft waves. She had a wide mouth, with a slightly overlapping upper lip that gave it a touch of pouty wantonness, a classic nose with a long, graceful sweep to it, and ice-blue eyes in which resided a hard intelligence. It was a handsome face—not beautiful by any means—but more interesting than it would have been if it had been beautiful. Even the razor-thin scar that ran alongside her temple to the corner of her right eye I found interesting. The plastic surgeon had done a good job on it, but it was still visible, although barely—shiny and white. I wondered how she had gotten it.

"Shall we sit down?" I suggested.

She shrugged and nodded slightly at the couch. When we were both seated, I smiled and said: "Is your husband home now, Mrs. Fleischer?"

"No. He's in Cleveland. He won't be back until the end of the week."

"Is he there on business?"

"That's where his business is," she said.

"Really? What kind of business is he in?"

"He manufactures conveyor systems," she said, crossing her legs impatiently. "Don't you think you should tell me what this is all about?"

"I'm looking for your ex-husband," I said. "Gerald Ellison."

Her hand moved toward her tanned throat, and confused emotions tugged at her features. She looked as if she wanted to say a lot of things, but all she came out with was: "I don't understand."

"A collection agency back east has been looking for Ellison for six months. He ran up a lot of bills back there, and they were turned over to the agency for collection. A month and a half ago he skipped and went to L.A. The agency called me. I work for them every once in a while, when they need something done on the Coast. I traced Ellison to a place in Santa Monica, where he'd been staying with friends, but I got there two days after he left."

"So what's all this got to do with me? I haven't seen Gerry in eight years."

Her mouth had puckered, as if she found the name distasteful. "No, but you might soon."

Uncertainty moved behind her eyes. "What do you mean?"

"Before he left Santa Monica, he told his friends he was going to look you up."

The assertiveness was completely gone from her gestures now, replaced by a combination of things, fear, anger, anxiety. They were taking their turns working on her. "But how could he find out where I am?"

"People leave a trail of paper behind them all through their lives," I said, shrugging. "All you have to do is know where to look for it."

She looked out at the lagoon. "But *why?* Why would he try to see me now, after all these years?"

I was about to answer that when a lanky, brown-haired teen-age boy padded into the room, chomping noisily on an apple. He wore white duck pants and a short-sleeved pale blue shirt, and his footsteps were muffled by blue jogging shoes. He looked at us questioningly and then started for the door. "I'm going."

Lainie Fleischer's head snapped around as if it were loaded on a spring. "Where?" Her voice was demanding.

The kid stopped and turned. "Elliott's."

The sharpness with which she had responded seemed to embarrass her. She made an effort to smile and softened her voice. "All right, doll, but dinner's at six. Don't forget."

"I won't," he said. He scowled at me, then gave her a concerned look. "Are you okay?"

"I'm fine, dear," she said. "I'll see you later."

"Okay," he said, took another juicy bite out of the apple, and went out.

"Your son?"

"My stepson, actually," she said. "But I look on him as my own son."

"You have another son, don't you?"

"No," she said firmly.

Confusion stuck its finger into my thoughts and stirred. "That's funny. Ellison told the people he was staying with that he was coming here to see you and his son. Brian."

Her face clouded, and she looked at me fearfully. There was no fear in her voice, however. The words came out cold and clear. "He waited about five years too long. Brian is dead."

"I'm sorry," I said, but sorry was not what I was feeling. I was too shocked to feel sorry. "How did it happen?"

"An automobile accident."

"Here?"

"Outside Palm Desert."

"How long ago?"

"Five years." Her eyes drifted out to the lagoon, but she was looking somewhere far more distant than that. After a few seconds she seemed to remember suddenly that I was there and turned back, almost angrily. "In all these years, Gerry has never made any attempt to find out if Brian or I were alive or dead. What right does he have now to come barging into my life?"

Her voice was full of anguish. I couldn't think of anything to say. She did not want me to anyway. "I've finally achieved some measure of happiness, and now he wants to ruin it. It's not fair. I won't let him do it. There has to be some law against it."

I felt sorry for the woman and, at the same time, self-conscious. I was an unwelcome intruder in her life, and I did not want the role. "I didn't mean to alarm you. He may never show up. From what the people in Santa Monica told me, he was having trouble locating you."

"You didn't."

"I'm a professional. He's not."

She seemed to take some solace in that. She stared at me down her eyelids and said: "If you find him, you're not going to tell him where I am, are you?"

"I'm interested in only one thing, Mrs. Fleischer, and that's collecting the money he owes."

"What if he can't pay it?"

"Don't worry," I told her. "The agency will get its pound of flesh, one way or another."

All the emotion had boiled out of her voice now, leaving only a residue of bitterness. She fixed me with an unblinking icy stare. "Well, if you collect it, take two pounds from the son of a bitch," she said in a voice that gave me a chill. "And mail one of them to me."

FIVE

The drive back to Indio seemed to take a lot longer this time. My thoughts kept doubling back to Lainie Fleischer.

I returned to the recorder's office.

According to the death certificate, Brian Ellison had died on February 4, 1973, at approximately 10:00 P.M. The cause of death was skull fracture and cerebral hemorrhage, the result of an automobile accident. The location of the accident had been Washington Street, Palm Desert, and the reporting agency had been the California Highway Patrol. The clerk gave me directions how to get to the local CHP office and I left.

The accident report on file in the highway patrol office ran thirteen pages. At 1040 hours on February 4, 1973, the Indio dispatch was notified of a collision on Washington Street with unknown details. Two units arrived at the scene eight minutes later, to find a blue 1964 Volkswagen, license 456 IJT, at rest off the road, its front end smashed into a tamarisk tree. The driver and registered owner of the car, Lainie Bowen, was found unconscious at the wheel and was rushed by ambulance to the Eisenhower Medical Center. Her son, Brian, age three, was dead in the right front seat. Deputy Coroner Patrick McNeal took charge of the boy's remains, ordering them to be removed to the Fitz-Morris Mortuary in Indio.

Lainie Bowen survived the crash with a concussion, a broken right femur, and multiple facial lacerations. Since there had been no witnesses to the accident, the investigating officers, Bellmore and Ortega, had to piece together details of the accident from the scene and from a subsequent interview with Lainie.

Lainie's recollection of the accident was vague. To the best of her knowledge, it had taken place around ten. She had been driving west on Washington at an estimated speed of 50 mph when she must have dozed off, causing the car to drift across the roadway and into the tree. She told the officers she had been working all day and had been very tired at the time.

None of that was refuted by the accident scene. The speedometer of the car was stuck at 52 mph, and there were no locked skid marks on the roadway, indicating that she had tried to stop. Lainie admitted having a few drinks early in the evening but denied being intoxicated at the time of the accident. The blood alcohol taken at the hospital was .06, tending to bear out that part of her story, too. Since the officers could find no grounds for any legal action against her, they recommended the discontinuance of further investigation.

The sun was tucked safely behind the mountains by the time I got back on the interstate, and by the time I hit Riverside it was dark. The taillights of the cars ahead of me looked like red tracer bullets hurtling down the highway, and my thoughts followed them all the way to their target, L.A. It was after nine when I pulled off the freeway and headed up La Cienega toward Winter's gallery.

I had to park on a side street and walk four blocks to get there, and the minute I hit the front doors I regretted not having gone home to change.

The Beautiful People had turned out en masse for the opening. They stood shoulder to shoulder, sipping white wine and ogling each other with cocaine eyes, their voices hyper and shrill from trying to make their own profound comments heard over the collective cacophony of conversation that filled the gallery like white noise.

Looking over the elegant sea of silk and satin, leather and linen, fur and feathers, I felt uncomfortably conspicuous in my rumpled sports coat. But then I remembered an article I'd just read in a leading men's magazine that the "rumpled look" was in now, and I felt better. I guess the theory was that anyone with enough balls to show up at a formal social function looking as if he had slept in his suit *had* to be important enough to get away with it. I made my way into the crowd with renewed confidence and started looking for McMurtry.

A gaunt model type with black hair frizzed like the Bride of Frankenstein and skin pulled too tightly over her cheekbones floated out of a group of people toward me. I thought she was naked until I saw that she was wearing a dress made of Saran wrap. She paused long enough to give me a penetrating stare from beneath a pair of jet-propelled eyebrows before deciding I was nobody and drifting away. We obviously did not read the same men's magazines.

A bar had been set up just inside the front doors, and Susan Lamb stood behind it, flashing her Close-Up smile and filling glasses with chablis. I asked her if she had seen McMurtry or Winter, and she said ten minutes ago and pointed. I followed the direction of the finger.

I excused my way through the gallery on tiptoe, so as to see above the multitude of turbans and Afros and Egyptian mantles and feathered headdresses, and finally I spotted McMurtry in the back of the room. He was standing with a short, conservatively dressed man with a shaved head. When I saw how McMurtry was dressed, I did not feel so bad about not changing. He wore a badly pressed seersucker jacket with gray slacks, a button-down magenta shirt with no tie, and round-toed Italian sports shoes that could have used a good shine.

" . . . They are an ironic, camp statement about the vulgarity and emptiness of American culture," the man with the shaved head was saying as I came up behind him. "They take the modern process of depersonalization to its logical conclusion. Our whole society is moving in that direction. The recent prurient upsurge is a product of modern advertising, wouldn't you agree? I mean, advertising strips men and women down to their sexual identities to sell their products—"

"Jake!" McMurtry said as soon as he saw me. He excused himself to the bald man and began steering me firmly away. "Jesus Christ, you showed up just in time."

"Why?"

"You saved me from a fate worse than death—listening to a critic."

I glanced back at the man, who was watching us retreat with a rather miffed expression. "Him?"

"The *Times*," he said. "Actually, I'm kind of suprised he showed up tonight."

"Why?"

"Eight years ago I had my first show in L.A., and he blasted the hell out of me in his column. Said my stuff was nothing but porn, and not even good porn at that. So, being a firm believer in the credo of one good turn deserves another, I went out to Bullock's and got a nice gift box and took a shit in it and wrapped it up nice and pretty and sent it to his office with a card that said: 'A token of appreciation for your enlightening contributions to the world of criticism.' "

I laughed. "You signed it?"

"No," he said, taking a sip of wine from the glass he held in his hand. "I'm not totally crazy. Just half. But he knew who it was from."

"From what I heard when I walked up, it doesn't sound like he holds a grudge."

"He can't," he said with a self-satisfied smirk. "A critic can never knock you once you've made it, Jake. He would look like an ass. Once you've made it in the art game, the function of the critic becomes merely to dream up reasons why you have. If you sell for five hundred a painting, you're a pornographer. But if you sell for twenty thousand, you are making—how did it go? —'ironic, camp statements about the vulgarity of American culture.' " He was smiling, but his voice had a serrated edge on it. His eyes were bloodshot, and he looked a little high. He glanced down at my empty hands and said: "You didn't get a glass of wine?"

"Not yet."

"We'll have to fix that right up. I'm never without a full glass of wine at an opening." He leaned toward me conspiratorially. "Actually, it's a prop. Gives me time to think when somebody asks me a question about my art. It also helps to be half in the bag to listen to some of the unadulterated shit some of these idiots come up with. Come on."

I followed him through the maze of paintings and people, stopping occasionally for him to shake hands with a friend or listen to an emphatic "Simply great," or "Maaaarvelous," from a too-enthusiastic admirer. We were almost at the bar when our path was cut off by a dark, diminutive beauty in a white linen peasant dress.

"There you are," she said, slipping her arm through McMurtry's. "I've been looking all over for you."

McMurtry smiled easily now. "Jake Asch, Mona Talbott. My lady."

"Nice to meet you," she said, smiling gently and offering her hand. She had a pretty, high-cheekboned face, the features of which seemed to have been assembled around her large, long-lashed, amber eyes. Her voice was very soft, and there was a gentleness in her manner which relaxed me, yet made me awkwardly aware of why I was here. "Have you ever been to one of these things before?"

"No."

"You're in for an educational experience then," she said, smiling.

"Do the people always dress so—"

"It varies," she said, anticipating what I was going to say. "A lot of the collectors here tonight are Hollywood people. They tend to get a little dramatic."

"There's a girl floating around dressed in Saran wrap."

She waved a hand at me. "That's nothing. There's one wearing a trash-bag dress. One of those black plastic ones."

"She probably paid two hundred bucks for it," McMurtry threw in contemptuously.

"Three," she said. "I asked."

McMurtry grinned sardonically. "I'd like to meet the guy who designed it. He's got to have a great sense of humor. A trash bag designed to hold human refuse—three hundred dollars. Beautiful."

I had the feeling McMurtry would have liked to mail out Bullock's boxes to almost everyone in the room.

We went to the bar, where Susan Lamb poured out three glasses of white wine. McMurtry took a sip from his, then held the glass down on the edge of the bar and brought out his wallet from his inside coat pocket. He took a folded check from the wallet and handed it to me. "Five hundred. I didn't want you to think I'd forgotten."

I hesitated. I did not know how much he had told Mona or how much he wanted her to know. Before I had a chance to find out, a distinguished-looking man with a dark tan and silver hair materialized in front of us. His shirt was open to his navel, exposing a chestful of gray hair and about forty pounds of gold chain. The willowy raven-haired girl on his arm was beautiful but couldn't have been any older than nineteen. The green glitter on her eyelids matched her backless green silk dress, and there were Christmas tree lights in her hair.

The man threw his arms around McMurtry and patted him on the back. "We have to run, Gerry," he said in a thick Italian accent. "You are *bellissimo,* fabulous. We must do a show soon. At my store in New York."

"I'm doing a show in New York in the fall," McMurtry told him. "At Benedick's."

The man made a disappointed face. "Rome, then." He bent slightly and kissed Mona's hand. "Beautiful lady, we will talk again. I have to fly to New York on Monday, but I'll call you when I get back next month. We will set up a show. *Ciao.*" The man whisked his nineteen-year-old out the door and was gone.

"Flore Ricci," McMurtry said.

"He just opened a store in Beverly Hills, didn't he?"

McMurtry nodded. "People were paying two hundred dollars just to get into the opening. He has stores all over. Paris, Rome, New York." He turned to Mona. "Want to go to Rome, honey?"

"I wouldn't mind."

"If anybody told me five years ago I'd be doing shows in Rome, I'd have said they were nuts."

I stared at the check in my hand, handed it back to him. "Two hundred should cover it," I said. "With expenses, it ran a little over that, but we'll call it two even."

His eyebrows bunched above his nose. "Why? What do you mean?"

I glanced over at Mona.

"It's okay," McMurtry said. "Anything you've got to say, you can say in front of Mona. She knows about everything."

I took the business envelope from my inside pocket and handed it to him. He looked at it questioningly. "What's this?"

48

"I found her."

He looked up sharply. "Where?"

"Palm Springs. After you left, she went home to mother. She's remarried now. Husband's name is Simon Fleischer. He's an industrialist from Cleveland. It's all in there."

He shook his head, smiling. "Howard was right about one thing. You sure do get results—fast." The smile faded quickly, and he searched my face eagerly. "Did you talk to her?"

"Yeah, I talked to her."

"What did she say?"

"About what I expected. I gave her a scam story about being a bill collector looking for you. When I mentioned your name, she looked at me like I was one of the Hounds of Hell."

He frowned. "What about Brian? Did you see Brian?"

All the way back from Palm Springs, I had been trying to think of a way to amputate painlessly that part of the past he was seeking. I had not been able to come up with any. "There was an accident in 1973. She was driving. Brian was killed."

His mouth dropped open slightly, and he stared at me glassy-eyed, as if he didn't understand what I was saying. Then, suddenly, he did understand, and his features went slack, and he began breathing heavily. "Jesus Christ."

His weight leaned against the bar, and he bowed his head. Mona laid a hand gently on his arm and watched him with concerned eyes. "God, honey, I'm so sorry."

They stood that way for a while, not saying anything; then McMurtry looked up at me. His eyes were watery. "Is her address in here?"

I nodded. "Yeah. But I wouldn't recommend you trying to see her."

"Why not?"

"For the reasons we went over already. When I talked to her, she made it clear she didn't want to see you again. In fact, she told me in so many words that if I found you and cut out your heart with a dull Exacto, she wouldn't get all broken up about it. If you dropped in on her now, there would be no telling what she'd do. Her husband has a lot of money, and money can buy a lot of juice. She could make life miserable for you if she put her mind to it."

"I don't care. I have to know what happened to Brian."

I pointed at the envelope on the bar. "The accident report is in there. It'll tell you what happened."

He shook his head. His lips formed a tight dark line. "I want to hear it from her. I have that right."

I was experiencing mixed emotions. I liked him, and I felt sorry for him, but I also felt sorry for Lainie Fleischer.

"I'm not sure you do," I said. "I talked to the woman. She has obviously been through enough the past eight years without having it all dredged up again. You wanted to make sure she was all right. She is. So let it lie. No matter how trite it may sound, you can't bring your son back. No meeting between you will do that. All it can possibly do is create more problems, not solve any."

The muscles in his jaw tightened visibly, and there was a hunched violence in his shoulders that made me nervous. Mona seemed to see it, too.

"Maybe Jake's right," she said weakly. She put her hand on top of his, but he withdrew his own with a jerk. He stared at a fixed spot behind the bar, then finally said softly: "Yeah, maybe he is. Fuck it. Maybe I don't have any right. No right at all."

He downed his wine in one gulp, then slammed the glass back down on the bar. Too hard. The sound of the exploding glass put an abrupt end to the conversations around us. Heads turned.

"You're bleeding," Mona said, grabbing McMurtry's hand. The broken stem of the glass had opened a gash in the webbing between McMurtry's thumb and forefinger, and it was bleeding freely. I didn't know whether McMurtry had broken the glass intentionally or whether he had merely misjudged the force he had used putting it down, but the anger seemed to have drained from his neck and shoulders, as if someone had pulled a plug. He was staring at his bleeding hand with detached curiosity.

"Do you have a handkerchief?" Mona asked me urgently.

I shook my head.

Susan Lamb came up with a linen napkin, and Mona used it to wrap McMurtry's hand deftly.

A group of concerned onlookers had begun to coagulate around us, trying to see what had happened, and McMurtry waved them back, smiling. "It's all right. Just a little scratch."

They disbanded slowly, buzzing with excitement about the event.

"We'd better make sure there isn't any glass left in the cut," Mona said.

"Goddammit, it's *all right.*"

A tension grew between them, then was snapped by a loud voice shouting: "Gerry! Gerry!"

Howard Winter's head bobbed like a big red balloon over the crowd. He was beaming as he bulled his way through to the bar. "Things are going splendidly, splendidly," he said breathlessly, then as an afterthought: "Hello, Mona, dear. Jake, good to see you. Gerry, Mrs. Fowler had just bought *Exotique Photo Album #3.*" He stopped when he saw McMurtry's hand. The blood was already soaking through the napkin. "What happened to your hand?"

"Just a little accident."

"Mmmmm," Winter said. "Anyway, she wants to meet the artist. I told her I'd bring you over."

"Who is she?"

"The wife of Harold Fowler, the president of Fowler Associates. The biggest advertising agency on the Coast. He's here with her."

"What do they want to talk to me for? They're not buying me."

They're buying a goddamn work of art. Either they want it or they don't want it."

"Look," Winter said. "That woman is paying twenty grand for that painting. For twenty grand, you can talk to her."

"Thirteen grand," McMurtry corrected him. "We can't forget about your seven, can we, Howard?"

"Thirteen, then," Winter said testily.

McMurtry turned to Mona. "I think you're right. I think we'd better see if there's any glass left in this cut."

"You can do that in a minute," Winter said. "These people are good customers."

"Yeah, well then, go back there and turn on your phony English accent and charm the socks off them, Howard. I'm just not in the mood to stand around and listen to a lot of horseshit from some asshole advertising executive and his wife. Not tonight. Not now. That's it. If they want the painting, fine. If they don't want it, that's fine, too. Frankly, I don't give a shit."

Winter's eye was caught by a movement in the crowd. "It's too late. Here they come now."

Mrs. Fowler was a tall redhead in a bright-green dress who looked as if she could have been a show girl in a Vegas line ten or fifteen years ago. She was running interference for her husband, who was flabby and pale and at least a foot shorter than she. He was wearing a very bad hairpiece and an expression that said he wanted nothing more than to get the hell out of here and go home.

McMurtry took one look at the approaching couple and said: "Fuck 'em. Come on, Mona. Let's get out of here. Asch, I'll mail you a check for the two hundred in the morning."

Winter grabbed his arm. "You can't leave like this—"

"Watch me," McMurtry growled, twisting his arm free.

"The son of a bitch," Winter muttered as he watched McMurtry's back disappear through the door.

He did not even seem to be aware of my presence. His face broke into a placating smile, and he started toward the obviously puzzled Mrs. Fowler. "Gerry extends his deepest apologies, Sarita, but he had to rush over to the emergency room. He cut his hand very badly on a broken glass. . . ."

I drifted toward the door, and Winter's voice faded into the happy chatter of the crowd.

SIX

I don't believe in ESP. Maybe that is a natural outgrowth of my personality. I am a born skeptic, and things that make other people go wow usually just make me shrug or get me down on my hands and knees to look under the table for wires. Still, it was odd that I should have been thinking about Erica when the phone rang.

I had been thinking about her quite a bit lately, ever since I met Lainie. Her ghost had come to float more and more through my mind, and she was one ghost that scared the hell out of me, probably because if she knocked on my door tomorrow, even knowing what I know, I could not honestly tell myself I wouldn't welcome her right back into my life again. I had even been entertaining thoughts of calling her up to see if she was still married, which was like considering playing Russian roulette with five bullets in the gun.

Erica was a CPA. At least she had been a year ago, when I'd met her. She was intelligent and fiercely independent, and although at first I had been intimidated by her strength, I was also incredibly attracted to it. During the six months we spent together, I reached some kind of high. Every free moment we were together, and we shared everything, from our bodies to our innermost feelings. Or so I thought.

I had walked through the whole thing eyes straight ahead, with a euphoric smile of love plastered inanely across my face, until I fell right into the pit. The one with the spikes and the live tiger at the bottom. Even if I had been looking down, I don't know if I would have seen it. She had covered it over too well with palm leaves.

One night it was "I love you, I love you"; the next, she was staring at me coldly and telling me she was marrying someone else, next week. "I don't love him," she had told me, "but he asked me, and I don't think you ever will. I want to be married, and I don't want to wait."

My mind could not absorb the shock. I'd tried to argue with her, but my arguments were tentative, fumbling. Hers were insane. The self-confident, controlled exterior peeled away, layer by layer, until she was screaming at me to get out. I felt like Ronald Colman in *Lost Horizon,* watching the woman he loved wither up into something ugly and scary that he did not know at all.

For two months after that I'd walked around like a zombie in a jute mill. Gradually, however, I worked myself back to the point where I was functioning normally. I had even managed to bury Erica. Until Lainie came along and dug her up.

When I'd first met Lainie, I had not made the link between her and Erica; that had come a few days later. Just what it was in Lainie that had triggered it, I was not sure. Aside from the fact that they both were handsome women and had the same cold blue eyes, the physical resemblance was slight. The connection in my mind was rooted in something else, something felt more than seen.

Maybe it had been the way her assertive, composed front had

crumbled when I had mentioned McMurtry's name, or maybe my imagination was just coloring it all in from what McMurtry had told me about her. But I could not shake the feeling that there were two Lainies, just as there had been two Ericas, and that Lainie's face was just a mask, a cuticle that had formed by exposure to the air.

So now Lainie and Erica had become somehow inextricably intertwined in my mind. McMurtry's old obsession had resurrected my old obsession, and I was thinking that it would be better for both of us if we tried to rebury them and walk away. The ringing of the phone killed any possibility of that.

A woman's voice said urgently: "Jake, this is Mona Talbott."

"Oh," I said, a little suprised. "Hi, Mona."

"I have to see you. Gerry is missing."

"What do you mean, missing?"

"He hasn't been home for two days. He hasn't called, nothing. I'm really worried. The police just called a few minutes ago, and the questions they were asking were really strange. I don't know what to think—"

"What police?" I asked, trying to catch up with her.

"The Palm Springs police. Some detective there. Gerry went there two days ago. He hasn't been back since."

Palm Springs. He couldn't leave it alone. "Where are you?"

She gave me an address in Malibu. I told her I would be there as soon as I could.

It took me a good forty minutes to get through the snarl of traffic on the Coast Highway to the turnoff to McMurtry's place. A strong offshore breeze cooled the beach, but a few hundred yards into the foothills the air began to heat up again.

The house was half a mile up the hill, a trapezoidal wood-and-glass structure with a shake roof. Mona opened the front door as I pulled up and parked. She had on a pair of jeans and a red V-necked cashmere sweater.

I said hello, and she said hello back and tried to smile. Her face was pale and drawn. Even the amber light in her eyes seemed diluted, drained of color, like watered-down scotch.

The living room was small, with a rust-colored carpet and art deco furniture. The beamed ceiling slanted up to a skylight, and two and a half of the walls were rough dark wood. These were covered with paintings, all of them good, but none of them McMurtrys. Of the other walls, one half was a red-brick fireplace, and the other was glass that looked out onto a redwood porch. She suggested we go out there.

We settled in two deck chairs. The hot breeze blew up the hill, carrying with it the faint steady hiss of the ocean. In spite of the heat, she sat holding her arms, as if she were cold.

"Okay," I said. "What happened?"

She took a breath. "On Thursday Gerry came home all excited. He said he'd gotten a call at the studio from some man in Palm Springs who said he had information about Brian's death—"

She was speaking rapidly, but the cadence of her voice was uncertain, almost panicky, like a singer who had lost the rhythm of the band. I interrupted her to get her back on cue. "What kind of information?"

"It was about the accident, that's all I know. Gerry didn't even know. All the man would say was that if Gerry was interested, he should be in Palm Springs at eleven the next morning, that he would explain then."

"Did he give his name?"

She shook her head. "He said his name wouldn't mean anything to Gerry, so it didn't make any difference."

"Where were they supposed to meet?"

"Some place on Palm Canyon Drive. A street corner. There's a bench, and Gerry was supposed to wait there."

"Why all the cloak-and-dagger stuff?"

She shrugged. Her movements were electric, jerky. "I don't know. Gerry didn't like it either, but he felt like he had to go.

Ever since he found out about Brian, that's all he's been thinking about. He hasn't been able to work at all."

She looked down at the hands in her lap and began rubbing her thumbs together.

"He was supposed to be back that afternoon. I waited until nine that night, and when he still didn't call, I called the police station in Palm Springs. I was worried he might have gotten into an accident or something. I talked to some sergeant, I don't remember his name, and he said Gerry hadn't been in any accidents, and then he asked me how long he'd been missing and I said since morning, and he said he couldn't do anything until I filed a missing persons report and that I couldn't do that until the person had been gone for twenty-four hours. So I waited until morning and went down to Santa Monica and filed a report."

"Why didn't you call me then?"

She touched her head. "I should have. I just—I don't know —I guess I just wasn't thinking straight."

"Okay. Go on."

"Then this morning that detective called and started asking all sorts of weird questions—"

"The Palm Springs detective."

"Right."

"But you filed the report in Santa Monica."

"Yes. I called Palm Springs back before I went down there, but they told me to report it to my local police station. They told me it didn't matter where the report was filed, that the information would go out the same way. They were even kind of rude. I had the feeling they didn't want to be bothered with it."

"They changed their minds fast."

"That's what I thought."

"What kind of weird questions did he ask?"

"Like, has Gerry been talking about Fleischer or his son a lot lately, or did I know if he's made any long-distance calls to the

Fleischer house or if Gerry had made any remarks about getting even with Lainie—"

"Getting even? Getting even for what?"

She bit her lip. "For Brian's death. He kept trying to imply that Gerry blamed Lainie for it."

"Did he?"

She jumped at that. "No. I think he blamed himself more than her. I told the detective that, but he didn't seem to believe me. He kept asking questions about Gerry's state of mind, as if he were crazy or something. Then, when I asked him what he was trying to get at with these questions, he turned real nice and said it was just routine. That was when he started asking questions about you."

That gave me a little jolt. "How did he know about me?"

She leaned forward anxiously. "Lainie told him."

"Lainie?"

She nodded. "Gerry saw her."

"When?"

"A few days after you gave him those reports."

"What happened?"

"Just what you said would happen." She sighed and looked out at the ocean. "I told him you were right, but he had to talk to her. He wanted to see if she had any pictures, anything he could have as a memento, but I guess the scene got really nasty. He said she came apart when she saw him. She screamed at him and told him he hadn't cared about Brian when he was alive, why should he now that he was dead? I guess Gerry became upset. He has a tendency to react. He said some things he didn't mean, and one thing led to another, and I guess he pushed her or something because she had the houseman throw him out, physically."

"I saw a taste of his temper at the opening."

"You have to understand the strain he was under, getting the show ready, then finding out about Brian like that. And he'd been drinking. Gerry should never drink. He's a different person when he drinks. Normally he's the gentlest man I've ever known."

Far out beyond the breaker line, a sailboat leaned hard into the wind, trying to keep its balance. Her face softened as she watched it, as if she sympathized with its struggle. She had one of her own going. "Gerry is a very sensitive man. He's a success, but deep down he doesn't really know how to deal with that. People don't understand that. He harbors a lot of resentment about the way the whole art game is set up, and he feels guilty about having played the game and won, about a lot of the things he had to do to make it. When he drinks, sometimes those feelings boil up to the surface, and he turns bitter and cynical. He's hard to take when he's like that, even for me. It's gotten him into trouble sometimes."

"What kind of trouble?"

She hesitated and squinted into the sun. "He's gotten into some fights in bars, but it's not his fault most of the time. People just take the things he says wrong."

"Lately?"

"He got into a bad one last week. At a place down the highway called the Blue Whale. Some other artists and movie people hang out there, and Gerry likes to go there. He says he can usually find some good conversation."

"What happened?"

She shrugged. "I guess somebody was talking about some new movie that just came out, and Gerry made a remark about it being a piece of garbage. An 'artsy-craftsy, jacksy-offsy movie,' he called it. Anyway, words went back and forth, and the thing snowballed, and the guy and Gerry came to blows. Gerry got the worst of it, I think."

"Has he ever hurt you?"

"Oh, no. Never."

"Has he been drinking a lot during the past two weeks?"

She nodded, her eyes dropping to her lap. "That was one reason I was worried about him getting into an accident."

"Did you tell any of this to the detective when he called?"

"No."

"Was he drinking because of what I'd found out? About Brian?"

"Yes. But he was coming out of it. Thursday—the day he got the call—was the first day he'd gone to the studio since you gave him those reports. He said he felt like working."

"I'd like to take a look around his studio."

She leaned forward hopefully. "I'll get the keys."

I followed her inside and waited while she went into the other room and came back out with a set of keys. I took them and asked: "What kind of car is Gerry driving?"

"A black seventy-eight Cutlass."

"License?"

"WRT nine-ninety-one."

I jotted that down. "I'll get back to you as soon as I find out something."

At the door she touched my arm and smiled gently. "Thank you. I was going out of my mind. I didn't know who else to turn to."

"Don't worry," I told her. "Everything will be okay."

I went down the walk and paused at my car to stare out at the ocean. It stretched endlessly toward the horizon and beyond, violet blue except where the sun played white upon its surface. It was beautiful, but it had always filled me with a cold, unreasoning fear. I could never swim in it without having nebulous, protean visions of monsters with huge, waiting jaws lurking unseen in the darkness below.

I didn't know why, but I had some of those same feelings now, with both feet on solid ground.

SEVEN

I went to my place and threw some things into a flight bag — two shirts, a pair of slacks, toothbrush, razor, the usual overnight garbage—and told the answering service I would be out of town for a day or so. Then I drove over to McMurtry's studio.

The stairway was still permeated with sweet bakery smells; the hall was still deathly quiet. The entire building seemed to be tensely silent, waiting with tired resignation for the wrecking crews.

Nothing seemed to have changed in the studio either. The heat and greasy smell of paint still hung heavily in the air. From her position of ascendancy on the wall, *Madonna #4* was still inviting me to lick her boots. On a closer inspection I saw that venetian blinds had been partially painted in behind her, but that was all that had been added in two weeks.

A palette was caked with dried oil paint on the table by the painting, and an opened beer can sat beside it. Some liquid sloshed in the bottom of the can when I picked it up. I put it down and went into the other room.

A dirty tile drainboard that held a double sink ran the length of the room, anchored on the far end by a small refrigerator. The porcelain in the sink was brown with dirt and age. Another doorway beside the fridge led back into the studio, and by the doorjamb was a wall phone.

The phone had a switch on it to cut off its ring. He would use that when the work was going well, I supposed. Phone numbers were scribbled in pencil around the phone. None of them was the right area code for Palm Springs, but I took them down anyway. There didn't seem to be a message pad anywhere. The wall was handier, I guessed. When it got filled with numbers, you could always paint it.

The refrigerator was well stocked with beer and bottles of Poland mineral water. Other than that, there was just some greenish cheese wrapped in cellophane and half a loaf of dark bread.

The cupboards above the sink were empty except for a well-depleted fifth of Jack Daniel's and an unopened fifth of Finlandia vodka. He had good taste in booze, and from the looks of things he drank it straight from the bottle; there were no glasses.

The set of cupboards on the opposite wall were stacked deep with magazines. I pulled them down and started browsing through them.

They would have probably been worth quite a bit, but only to a collector. There were a few of the modern, slick-papered girlie mags in the bunch—*Penthouse, Club, Chic*—but most of the collection was pure fetishism, and at least twenty years old. The titles were *Exotique* and *Bizarre,* like the photographs in them, especially the bondage stuff. The models were very restrained in every conceivable position—spread-eagled to chairs and on crosses, hoisted up on pulleys, chained to walls, hog-tied, gagged, their faces encased in leather masks. Others were having their bottoms spanked by jackbooted Amazons in black leather panties.

Another stack in the cupboard was old comic books, with the

same SM themes. In all of them, trussed-up half-nude females waited for a fate worse than death, expressions of terror burned into their faces, while the villains leered ecstatically at their respective plights. The victim was invariably the "good girl"—wholesome, innocent—and I thought of the Marquis de Sade's comments about the boredom of virture.

The images disturbed me, not out of any offended sense of moralism but because of what they represented. If they were part of McMurtry's Vision he was right. They were not sensual; they were the opposite. Apathy, not sensuality, removes conscience. Without apathy, the acts depicted in the pictures would never be possible. Apathy, when it runs deep, can be hard to detect. It can kill the roots of the soul without killing the plant on the surface.

All the way to Palm Springs, my thoughts were tied up like the girls in McMurtry's magazines. They kept wanting to tell me something, but the gags in their mouths prevented them. I drove through the town, which seemed to be filled with the same tourists as two weeks ago, and into Cathedral City.

Cathedral City was a sort of slum suburb of Palm Springs, a small, junky town of clapboard houses and auto supply stores and thrift shops and gay bars, with an occasional massage parlor thrown in, just to spice up the stew. It was where all the illegal aliens and Mexican dishwashers who worked in Palm Springs' posh eateries lived. The rents were cheap, and the landlords didn't ask too many questions.

I pulled into a gas station there and called the Fleischers' number. Simon Fleischer answered. I didn't try to get tricky this time. I told him who I was and asked if he could spare me a few minutes. He sounded less than pleased about the prospect but relented.

Lash La Rue was waiting inside the steel gates when I drove up. He was wearing yellow today and the same look of disapproval, only not so faint this time. He inserted a plastic card in the slot in the control box, and the gate slid open. He walked back to the black Lincoln without saying anything and took off. I followed him to the house.

He parked the car in the driveway, and I left mine on the street. We went through the courtyard, and after opening the front door with a key, he led me through the living room, down one leg of the glassed-in U that flanked the lagoon.

The U ended in a room that had been lifted from an old Sydney Greenstreet movie. It had a white tile floor and white plaster walls and was filled with fan-backed rattan furniture and arica palms. Several ceiling fans rotated slowly overhead. They were not doing much to churn up the air, but they did add to the effect.

The man sitting in the high-backed rattan chair was no Sydney Greenstreet, in age or stature. He was slightly paunchy but held his fifty-odd years fairly well. He had a tanned, heavy-chinned face, short gray hair about the texture of steel wool, and gray-green eyes that were small and quick and crinkled at the corners. His nose was slightly bulbous and had a bluish tinge from the burst capillaries under the skin. That could have been from heavy drinking, although I doubted it. If he did do any drinking, I would have been willing to bet it was all after five. There was a disciplined firmness in his face that said everything he did would be carefully regulated.

He watched me without saying anything. Lainie Fleischer didn't say anything either. She was standing behind him, her hands resting on the back of the chair, trying to disintegrate me with a death-ray stare.

"You want me to stay, Mr. Fleischer?" the houseman asked from behind me.

Fleischer waved him off. "I'll call you if I need you."

He watched the man go, then sat very still for a few seconds, sizing me up like a weight guesser at a carnival. "Okay. You're here. What do you want?"

His tone was peremptory, unfriendly, but then I hadn't really expected anything else. "May I sit down?"

He shrugged and gestured at a chair.

I sat down, and we stared at each other for a few seconds; then I said: "As I told you on the phone, I'm a private detective—"

"I know all about you and what you are," he said distastefully. "The only thing I don't know is what you want. So why don't you get down to it so I don't have to tolerate your presence in my house any longer than necessary?"

"I'll try not to dirty your carpets while I'm here."

"Just get on with it."

I was not sure just how much he knew about the situation, so I hesitated to plunge right in. "Do you know who Gerry McMurtry is?"

"I told you, I know all about you. That means I know all about McMurtry."

"McMurtry is missing. He hasn't been home since Friday morning."

"So?"

"So his girl friend is worried about him. She asked me to see if I can find him. I thought he might have tried to get in touch with your wife."

His eyes narrowed. "Why would you think that?"

I could almost hear the wheels turning inside his head. "For one thing, he told the girl he was going to Palm Springs. For another, I understand he came here about two weeks ago to talk to your wife. I thought he might have tried again."

Lainie could not contain herself any longer. She stabbed a finger at me accusingly and said: "You lied to me. You told me you were a bill collector. If I had known you were working for Gerry, I never would have talked to you."

"I'm sorry about that, Mrs. Fleischer, but it seemed like the best course at the time. I was merely trying to protect my client—"

66

"Protect?" she said shrilly, stepping around the chair. "Protect? That's cute. But tell me just who's going to protect people from him?"

"I'm sorry if there was trouble—"

Her eyes widened in disbelief. "Trouble? No, there wasn't any trouble. I just thought the man was going to kill me, that's all. He was totally out of his mind. If Norm hadn't been here, I don't know what would have happened. And now this. If he—"

"I'll handle this," Simon Fleischer said sharply.

She turned away angrily and crossed her arms, then dropped into a nearby chair. She stared out the window, her lower lip trembling with emotion. I could hear her breathing from across the room.

"Have you seen or heard from McMurtry since he came here?" I asked. All I wanted to do now was learn that one answer and get the hell out of there.

Simon Fleischer locked stares with me challengingly. "That's what I'm waiting for, to hear from him. Isn't that what you're here for?"

I shook my head in confusion. "Pardon me?"

"Don't you have a message from him?"

"Message? What kind of message?"

"About my son."

Now I was really confused. "What about your son?"

"McMurtry has him."

I tried to absorb that, but somehow my mind wouldn't. "Wait a minute. Your son is missing?"

"You know goddamn well he's missing," he snarled.

"What makes you think McMurtry has him?"

"Friday night Donnie went out on a date. At nine o'clock he left the girl at Sambo's and told her he would be back in twenty minutes. He said he had to meet a man named Gerry. He never came back."

"And you assume this 'Gerry' was McMurtry?"

"Who else would it be?"

"What about this girl? Are you sure she has her story straight?"

Lainie gestured impatiently. "What are you implying? That she's a liar? Pam is a nice girl. What reason would she have to lie?"

"Okay, so assuming she's telling the truth, it could all be a coincidence. There are a lot of people named Gerry."

Fleischer leaned forward and put his hands on his knees, causing the rattan chair to creak dryly. "But there is only one who dropped out of sight the same day as my son. The same day he told his girl friend he was going to Palm Springs. And there is only one who forced his way into my house and assaulted my wife and called up here repeatedly, threatening the welfare of my family."

My mind was like a three-hundred-horsepower motor attached to two-inch wheels. It raced and roared, and the tires smoked, but it wouldn't go anywhere. "He called here?" I asked, trying to give my thoughts some traction.

"Four or five times in the past ten days."

"What did he say?"

He hesitated. " 'Tell Lainie I'll get even.' "

"That's all?"

"That's enough," he said. "The meaning is clear enough."

"Who did he talk to when he called?"

"Norm, my houseman."

"Did he identify himself?"

"He didn't have to. Norm recognized his voice."

I shook my head. "I think it would be rash to jump to any kind of conclusion from that, Mr. Fleischer. I mean, what he said could mean almost anything—"

"I know what it means," Fleischer said belligerently. "The man is sick. He should be locked up. In his twisted mind he blames Lainie for the death of his son. When he was here, he actually accused her of having perpetrated the accident, on purpose."

"Maybe in the heat of the moment he said some things he didn't mean, but I can't believe he would harm a child."

He looked at me contemptuously. "My wife has a different opinion."

"But it doesn't make any sense," I argued. "Why would he go after your son, even if he blamed your wife for the death of his own? That would be getting even with you, not her. You had nothing to do with the accident."

Lainie's head jerked around. There were white lines around her mouth. "Because he knows how much I love Donnie," she said. "When he came here two weeks ago, he started talking about 'our' son. I told him I had only one son—Donnie. That was when he came unglued. He kept asking how could I say something like that, and I said because it's the truth, and then he started accusing me of all sorts of terrible things. He grabbed me and started shaking me and then threw me down. That's when I screamed and Norm came in." She shivered and grasped her arms as if feeling for the bruises from the scene. "He's doing this to hurt me. He wants to take away my son because he thinks I took away his."

She looked at her husband apologetically, and her eyes grew moist. "I'm sorry, darling. It's my fault. You never should have married me. . . ."

Fleischer went to her and tried to quell her protestations with comforting pats on the shoulder.

"Have you received any kind of note? A ransom demand, anything like that?"

Fleischer looked up at me red-faced. His small gray eyes pinned me accusingly. "Not yet. That's what I'm waiting for."

It finally dawned on me why I had been granted as long an audience as I had. Fleischer's mood had been precariously balanced between outright hostility and a grudging curiosity ever since I had arrived. "Wait a minute, you think I—?"

He stared at me silently.

"Let's get one thing straight, Mr. Fleischer," I said. "I'm sorry if there was any trouble when McMurtry came here. I had a feeling there might be; that's why I advised him against it. I told him your wife had a new life and that he had no right to upset it and that he couldn't change the past. You can check all that out if you want. I have not seen or talked to McMurtry in two weeks, since the day I gave him my report. The first I even heard that he'd been out here was this morning when Mona Talbott called me. You may not like me or what I do for a living —I don't like it sometimes—but I'm straight, and my business is straight. I'm not into snatching kids, and I don't like people who do. If you have any doubts about that—any doubts at all —I can give you the names of half a dozen people in law enforcement in L.A. who would be happy to relieve you of them."

He caught the angry tone in my voice and backed up a little. But not much. He was not the type to back up much, no matter if he was wrong or not. "What you say may be true, Asch, but that doesn't change things. My son is still missing, and I'm still holding you personally responsible. You have the responsibility of checking on your clients before you take on a job. McMurtry is a madman, and you turned him loose, and I'm telling you right now that if anything happens to my son, you'll think the world had fallen on your back."

I gave him my best Atlas shrug. "I thought that a long time ago," I said. "You've talked to the police about this, obviously. What do they think?"

He gestured abruptly and grunted. "Nothing. They're idiots. That one moron—McDonald or whatever his name is—thinks Donnie took off on some joyride. He won't come right out and say it, but I know that's what he thinks. I can tell by his attitude."

"What about the FBI? You could try them."

He stood up from the arm of Lainie's chair where he had been sitting and turned his back on me. "I've talked to the local agent. He won't do a damned thing. He says they can't come into it unless there's proof there has been a kidnapping—a note or something."

He turned and indicted me with a gray stare as if I had something to do with that.

"Has Donnie ever taken off before without telling anybody?"

He squinted at me, his body tense. "What are you trying to say? That the police are right and Donnie has just gone off on a joyride? Or that he's run away from home?"

"It has happened—"

"Not with Donnie. He's a happy boy. He would never do anything like that. Why should he? He's always had anything he's ever wanted."

"Kids don't always run away because they're unhappy, Mr. Fleischer. Sometimes they just do funny things. Especially when they get around their friends. One kid gets an urge to take off and go somewhere, and the group follows."

"None of Donnie's friends would do that," he said, dismissing the suggestion. "They all come from good families. I pay $5,600 a year to make sure of that."

His voice assumed a heavy confidence at the end, as if by reciting the amount he were cementing a contract from which none of the parties could escape.

"You send him to a private school?" I asked.

"Piedmont. We started it up last year. The kids at the high school down here are into dope and God knows what. We didn't want our children exposed to that."

"Who is 'we'?"

He lifted his chin slightly and struck an aristocratic pose. "Myself, Danny Klein, Walter March. Some of the better people in the desert."

I looked over at Lainie, but she refused to meet my gaze, as

71

if I were an unpleasant reminder of her rather unaristocratic origins. "Have you checked with his friends at school?"

"Of course we've checked," Fleischer said. "Do you think we're idiots?" He made a gesture to the door. "I don't really think we have anything more to say to each other, Asch."

I stood up. "Okay."

"Norm!" Fleischer yelled.

I held up a hand. "It's all right. I can find my way out."

As I walked past Lainie, she looked up at me hatefully. "How much did my ex-husband pay you, Mr. Asch?"

"Two hundred dollars."

"Two hundred dollars." Her mouth turned up sardonically at the corners. Her eyes were pale, cold. "That's all? That's all you get for ruining lives? Your morality comes cheap."

I didn't say anything. I just went to the door.

EIGHT

The khaki-uniformed policewoman at the front counter told me I could find McDonald in the Detectives' Room and pointed to a door to her right.

Beyond the door were a hallway and another counter manned by another policewoman, who shunted me through yet another door, which said on it DETECTIVE DIVISION.

The room was large and gray and somber, and the coffinlike desks that filled it gave it the atmosphere of an undertaker's parlor. Only two of the desks were occupied, and neither of the occupants was dressed like a cop, but then, hell, this was Palm Springs. One of them had on a white short-sleeved shirt with green flowers all over it—orchids or hibiscus or one of that crowd. Tropical flowers have never been my strong suit. The other had on an open-necked navy sports shirt with white stitch-work on the collar and epaulets on the shoulders. Like a bee, I went straight for the flowers.

I did not make a bad bee. The name plaque on the desk in front of him said: DETECTIVE RON MCDONALD.

Ron McDonald. Jesus. I could have done a lot with that one. Ronald McDonald and His Hamburger Helpers. Instead, I just said: "Detective McDonald?"

He looked up from the arrest report he had been going over and leaned back. "Can I help you?"

"My name is Asch," I said, putting out my hand.

He raised his eyebrows and took it. "Ah."

He had a dark mustache and thinning brown hair and a jowly, good-natured face that I discounted right away. I've never trusted good-natured faces on cops.

"I just got a call about you." There was a brown folder with a case number on it in front of him, and he fingered it while he talked.

"From Simon Fleischer."

"Uh-huh. He wanted me to hunt you down and find out just what you're doing down here."

"I told him what I was doing down here."

"Yeah, but I somehow don't quite think he believed you. Sit down."

I slipped into the chair in front of the desk, and he picked up a package of Salems and shook one out. He offered it to me.

"No, thanks. I don't smoke."

He nodded, lighted the cigarette with a gold lighter he materialized from his pocket, and leaned back, exhaling casually. "You saved me a phone call. I was going to give you a buzz anyway."

"I figured you might."

"You're working for the Talbott broad?"

"More or less."

"What does that mean?"

"There hasn't been any official arrangement made. I told her I would take a look around for McMurtry. I guess you could say I'm working for her." I took out my notebook, scribbled down three names, then ripped out the page and handed it to him.

He read the names aloud: "Sergeant Al Herrera, LASO; Jim Gordon, DA—Organized Crime; Ray Mayfield, Robbery-Homicide—LAPD. Yeah, so?"

"I just thought you might want to check with somebody. People usually like to know who they're talking to. Especially cops."

He put the list down on the desk. "You left off Frank Capek."

"You talked to Frank?"

"After I talked to the Talbott broad this morning." He pulled a glass ashtray across the desk and tapped the ash from his cigarette into it. I noticed that the bottom of the ashtray said: "Ocotillo Lodge." I wondered what the towels in the detectives' rest room would say on them. He twirled the ashtray with his fingers and said: "McMurtry was your client, right?"

"That's right."

"Exactly what did he hire you to do?"

"Find his ex-wife and kid."

"And you found her."

"You know I found her."

He nodded and took another drag from his cigarette, letting the smoke dribble slowly from his lips. He stared at me for a while, then asked: "Why did you lie to Mrs. Fleischer when you went to see her?"

"For the simple reason that considering the circumstances, there was bound to be a lot of animosity on her part toward McMurtry. My first duty was to my client. I thought the bill collector story would give him a little insulation in case she wanted to get nasty."

"From what she says, he's the one who got nasty."

"I didn't know about that until Mona told me this morning. I advised McMurtry not to try to see the woman. I didn't see anything but trouble coming from it."

"I guess your advice didn't stick."

"I guess not."

"Have you heard from McMurtry lately?"

"The last time I talked to McMurtry was two weeks ago, when I got back from Palm Springs and told him what I'd found out."

"How did he react to that?"

"You mean about his wife and son?"

He nodded.

"He was upset, but hell, anybody would have been upset."

He paused, as if trying to determine exactly how to word the next question. "Would you consider him emotionally unbalanced?"

"Not at all."

He rested his palm on top of the brown folder and said: "Then you wouldn't put too much credence in Fleischer's theory that McMurtry has gone bonkers and snatched his kid."

"I don't know anything about it except what he told me. It *is* kind of a coincidence that McMurtry went to Palm Springs and disappeared the same day as the kid—"

"Too much of one for me," he said flatly.

I crossed my legs and shifted in my chair. "What do you mean?"

He stubbed out his cigarette and smiled without putting too much effort behind it. "If you were planning to kidnap the kid, would you tell your girl friend you were coming down here and that you'd be back the same night, knowing that when you didn't come home, she'd probably call the cops and report you missing?"

"Probably not," I admitted.

"I wouldn't either."

"What about the phone calls?"

"Mona Talbott says McMurtry has been home every night and that he hasn't been making any phone calls."

"The houseman recognized his voice."

"*Now* he recognizes his voice. Before, he didn't know whose voice it was. Lainie Fleischer is filling in all the blank spots for everybody. She knows it's him because she wants it to be him."

"What about Donnie telling his date he was going to meet a man named Gerry?"

"Yeah, there's that," he said significantly.

I waited for him to amplify on that, but he just began rubbing inside his ear with a finger. He took the finger out and inspected the end of it for wax, and I said: "Fleischer doesn't think you're taking this thing seriously enough."

"Yeah, I know," he said in a tired voice. "He calls me up every half-hour to tell me. Every agency in the state has the kid's license number and his description. I don't know what else he wants me to do. Hell, he asked the feds to come in on it, and they turned him down cold. You know why they turned him down cold? Because it doesn't add up to kidnapping, that's why." He leaned over the desk and began counting on his fingers. "A, there's no ransom demand, no note, nothing. B, the kid was driving a car, and the car is still missing. C—and here's one that Fleischer doesn't admit to—the kid has problems at home, and he'd talked about splitting before. D, he runs around with a flaky crowd. Add those up, and you don't get kidnapping, you get runaway."

"What flaky crowd?"

He shrugged, and his voice grew irascible. "Some of the kids he goes to school with."

"Flaky, like police-business flaky?"

He nodded. "None of it has ever gotten to court, of course. Their parents made sure of that."

"Fleischer gave me a big spiel about how his kid's friends only came from the best families—"

"Oh, they do," he said. "They're all juice people. And most of them need all the juice they can get because they've usually got all the problems to go with it. They've all got nice big homes surrounded by nice high walls so that nobody can see what's going on inside, and they all get their pictures in *Palm Springs Life*, sipping cocktails at the opening of the Racquet Club or wherever it's chic to be seen. Only the caption underneath the picture doesn't say that the old lady's glass is filled with Perrier water because she just got through drying out in a sanitarium in Arizona or that after the photographer snapped the picture, they had to rush over to the hospital, where their daughter is having her stomach pumped from ODing on Tuinals, or hop over to the PD to pick up their son, who got all fucked up on Quaaludes and got pinched driving the wrong way on a one-way street."

As he spoke, his voice picked up acidity.

"You sound bitter," I said.

"Bitter? Me? Naw, I'm not bitter. I've just been through all this before, and I'm not going to start foaming at the mouth and get all worked up because Simon Fleischer calls me up every twenty-five minutes and tells me I couldn't find my ass with two hands and radar. Because when the kid does turn up, I know Simon Fleischer will be back on the phone to the chief trying to get the arrest report filed under T for Trash. Me? Bitter? Naw. I just understand that when you get the kind of money concentrated in one place that we have here in Palm Springs, a lot of people start to see the main function of the police department as to protect that money."

"You could always move."

The suggestion seemed to surprise him. "Move? Hell, I wouldn't want to work anywhere else. I love this town. It's the big city without the tall buildings and the traffic and the smog. Hell, you name me another town this size where you can stand out on the main drag and eventually meet everybody in the world—from crown princes to movie stars to Mafia shooters. I wouldn't think of moving."

I wondered why he was telling me all this. He seemed to be working off steam. Perhaps he saw us as kindred spirits under a common siege by the Simon Fleischers of the world. I hoped so. That might make it easier to get what I wanted. "You said Donnie has problems at home. What kind of problems?"

His face suddenly lost its good-natured expression. He gave

me a coplike stare. "What does it matter to you, Asch? You're just looking for McMurtry."

I thought about that. I did not really believe that McMurtry's disappearance was causally related to Donnie Fleischer's, but I had to be sure. I didn't like to admit to myself that Lainie's parting remarks had gotten to me, but they had. "Simon Fleischer just about accused me of being in on the kidnapping plot—"

"I wouldn't lose any sleep over that," he said.

"I'm not. But if McMurtry has gone off the deep end and done something to his son, I'm partly responsible. Morally, if not legally. I'm the one who turned him loose on them."

He shrugged. "You were hired to do a job. You did it."

Maybe he was right. Maybe it was just my Jewishness coming out. After a thousand years of being hated by everybody, you begin to feel there must be something hateable about you. A black man comes into his house and finds his wife in bed with another man, he shoots the man. A Mexican shoots his wife. A Jew says, "It must be my fault," and shoots himself.

"Maybe you're right, I don't know," I told him. "Still, it's nice to think you're helping. When the time comes that you start screwing up lives instead of helping, maybe it's time to get out of the business."

He tapped the top of the desk thoughtfully, then grabbed his cigarettes and lit up another one. Without looking at me he said: "From what some of his friends say, the kid and his old man fight like cats and dogs. He's talked about running away, but the only thing is that Fleischer is kind of tight with a buck, I guess, and the kid never had enough money in his pocket to make it very far. He's bounced the idea off a couple of pals at the school who are apparently better financed, but nobody has ever taken him up on it. From what I gather, the kid's a smart-mouthed punk, and nobody could stomach the idea of taking a long trip with him."

"They say anything else interesting?"

He smiled and put his hands on his chest. "Hell, I'm a cop and over thirty. What are they going to tell me? My own kids won't even talk to me. They're at that age now where they're starting to see all cops as the Enemy. Of course, my ex helps that right along, may she rest in pieces." He paused, then asked: "You have any kids, Asch?" He seemed to be working himself into a friendly mood.

"No."

"Married?"

"Used to be."

"Hear from her much?"

"The last time, I think, was three years ago."

He nodded and pursed his lips. "You're lucky, brother. My ex is like Godzilla. Built along the same lines and has the same temperament. All it takes is for me to be two days late with a support check and she comes out of the bay breathing fire."

I tried to move him from Tokyo Harbor back to Palm Springs. "What about the girl Donnie was out with Friday night? Pam . . ." I snapped my fingers twice. "Pam, jeez, what's-her-name. . . ."

"Conner."

"Right," I said. "Conner."

"What about her?"

"I'd like to talk to her."

"You're over thirty, too."

"Yeah, but I have a way with kids. It's in the karma."

He shrugged. "You want to talk to her, I can't stop you."

"Where does she live?"

He put out the second cigarette and shook his head. "Sorry. Her parents have juice, too. They find out I've given out their address. . . . You know how it goes."

The uniformed policewoman from out front poked her head through the door. "Ron, Captain Galbraith wants to see you."

McDonald stood up. "I'll be back in a minute," he said, and went through the door.

I sat for a minute or so, drumming the top of the desk with my fingers. I could have called every Conner in the phone book and asked for Pam, but maybe there was an easier way. I looked over at the detective four desks away in the navy blue shirt. He was absorbed in some reports and was not paying any attention to me.

I put my hand down casually on the top of the brown folder and began easing it across the desk. When it was in front of me, I flipped it open, all the time keeping my eyes on the other cop. He still was not looking. The top report was an interview with the Fleischers. Three pages down was Pam Conner's interview. I took down the address, then shut the folder and pushed it back across the desk, five seconds before McDonald came back in.

"I've got to go," he said, clearing the papers from the desk top and locking them in the center drawer. He shook his head. "Just got a rape call from the Riviera. The Swinging Singles convention is up there. Five thousand of them. They come in three times a year. I don't know what gets into them, but when they come here, they turn into animals. They get stoned and walk around nude and jump one another's bones. I swear to God, they fuck in the hallways, on the diving boards, anywhere. Then they go home to their secretarial jobs and their paper filing and build up steam for the next trip down."

I stood up, and we shook hands. "Well, thanks for your time."

"Don't mention it. And I meant what I said: I wouldn't lose any sleep over this thing. The kid will turn up, and under his own power."

I nodded. "One more thing you might be able to help me with. Can you recommend a good place to stay? One that won't cost an arm and a leg?"

"Try the Royal Western on South Palm Canyon. It's new, and pretty nice, from what I hear."

I said I would, and he looked over my shoulder and shouted: "Jimbo! Come on. We're going to the Riviera."

The detective with the navy shirt looked up from his work and grinned widely. He stood up and clapped his hands together. "All *right*."

McDonald looked at me and winked. "See? How could I ever move? What other city would pay its employees to go to a stag show?"

From its vantage point overlooking the entire valley and set into the stark rock face of the mountain, the Conner house resembled some Near Eastern white-walled fortress guarding the entrance to the Khyber Pass. The only thing that spoiled the effect was the fenced-in tennis court that flanked the front of the house.

Nobody answered when I rang the bell. I consulted my watch: 3:35. I went back to the car and listened to the radio. After ten minutes of the same old disco shit I turned it off and sat sweating in silence.

Below, the city was strewn across the sand like wreckage from some treasure ship that had been washed up on a white and waterless shore. Beyond the sand the slanting afternoon light threw shadowy wrinkles on the mountains that ringed the valley, reminding me of old men. The air was clear, except for a dirty smudge of smog that hovered tentatively at the entrance to the pass. Maybe it was waiting for night, thinking it could sneak in under the cover of darkness.

A blue Corvette came roaring up the hill and pulled into the Conners' driveway. The driver kept the motor running while a slightly pudgy teenage girl got out on the passenger's side, her arms laden with books. She slammed the door and waved goodbye, and the car backed out and started back down the hill. I got a glimpse of the driver as he passed, but not a good one. A thin-faced boy with long brown hair.

I got out of the car and started across the street. "Pam?"

She had a key out and was almost at the front door when she heard her name and turned around. As she did, she dropped one of her books.

"Allow me," I said, and stooped to pick it up.

"Thanks," she said. "Who are you?"

Her dishwater-blond hair was long and straight, and her round face was cute in a baby-fat kind of way and liberally daubed with freckles.

"My name is Asch," I told her. "I'm a detective. I'd like to talk to you about Donnie Fleischer."

"He still hasn't come home?"

"No."

"That's really weird. I mean, people just don't disappear."

"Fifty thousand do in this country every year."

She blinked disbelievingly. "That many?"

"That many. May I come in?"

"Yeah, sure. I guess."

She inserted the key in the lock and pushed open the front door. As she stepped in, a miniature gray poodle came clacking into the tile foyer, wagging its tail furiously. Pam put her books down on a mirrored table and bent down to scratch behind the dog's ear.

"Hello, Fritz. Aren't you a pretty boy today?"

The dog licked her hand with his pink tongue and then sniffed around my feet. "That's Fritz," she said, straightening up.

"Hello, Fritz," I said, bending down to pet the dog. He accepted my hand appreciatively and trotted off into the living room.

"Anybody home?" Pam yelled, moving out of the foyer. When no answer came back, she looked over her shoulder and said: "Mom must have gone shopping. Come on into the living room."

The room was a long rectangle of white—white walls, white carpeting, white furniture, white drapes. I felt as if I were in the middle of a blizzard. I wondered why desert dwellers were so enamored of white. On the exterior it was functional, but inside it seemed to serve no purpose except perhaps to remind the inhabitants of the winters most of them had fled to come out here. The only break in the whitescape was outside the sliding glass doors. The brown rocks of the mountain came down to the edge of the white decking, and the ubiquitous swimming pool sparkled blue in the afternoon sun.

"Sit down, Mr.—" She put her hand to her mouth in an embarrassed gesture. "I'm really sorry, I forgot your name."

"Asch," I said, sitting on a snowy sofa. "You can call me Jake. Or you can call me J. Or you can call me JA. But you doesn't have to call me Mr. Asch."

She snickered. "Okay. I'll call you J."

She plopped down in a chair and curled her legs up underneath her, and the dog came over and jumped on her lap.

"You just getting home from school?" I asked.

"Um-hmm," she said, stroking the poodle's head. His tongue rolled out of his mouth contentedly.

"Piedmont?"

"I don't go to Piedmont anymore. I go to the high school." She gave me a quizzical look and said: "You weren't with the other detective before, were you?"

"I'm not with the police," I said. "I'm a private investigator."

She seemed to pull back. "You working for Donnie's father?"

"No. A relative." It wasn't a lie, not technically. Mona Talbott had to be somebody's relative.

The girl nodded and said: "It's really weird. You know, I was so mad at Donnie Friday night I could've killed him. I waited at Sambo's for an hour and a half for him to come back, and I finally wound up calling my mother to come and pick me up. She was really pissed. Then when the police came by and told me Donnie hadn't been home yet, it really blew me away. I didn't know what to think."

"Do you and Donnie date a lot?"

"We do things together. I don't know if you'd call it dating, really. We're good friends. I understand Donnie. A lot of people don't."

"How is that?"

She shrugged. "He's just different around me than he is around other people, that's all."

"Different how?"

"He's more natural. More himself. He doesn't put on an act."

"He puts on an act for other people?"

She raised an eyebrow. "Sometimes. It depends on who he's around. Donnie's really an insecure person in a lot of ways, and a lot of times he tries to impress people."

"Tell me about Friday night."

She shifted in her chair and said: "Donnie picked me up a little before seven, and we went to the show. Then we drove around a little and talked, and then we went to Sambo's to get something to eat. That was around nine-thirty, I guess."

"What did you talk about while you were driving around?"

"Buddy Holly."

I looked at her strangely.

"That was the show we saw. *The Buddy Holly Story.* It's really good. Neither of us knew who Buddy Holly was before we saw the show. I mean, he died before we were born. But we were wondering what it would've been like to grow up back in the fifties."

When I talked to girls like this, I was overwhelmed by a feeling of being out of sync, of belonging to another cycle of things. Buddy Holly's death had been a major trauma for me. I owned a whole other set of heroes and villains, and it was unreal to me to think there was an entire generation out there that had no recollection at all of the assassination of John F. Kennedy.

"What was his state of mind?"

"What do you mean?"

"Did he seem happy, upset, depressed?"

She looked away. "He was a little uptight."

"What about?"

"I guess he'd had an argument with his father about something earlier. I don't know what it was about."

"Then what happened?"

"We went to Sambo's, like I said, and Donnie ordered a hamburger, and then said he had to meet a man named Gerry and that he'd be back in a few minutes."

"Did he say who this Gerry was?"

She shook her head, and a long strand of blond hair fell across her eyes. She brushed it back with a flick of her hand and said: "No. But I know he was an older man."

"How?"

"The way Donnie talked about him," she said, as if that made it final.

"Did he say why he was going to meet this Gerry?"

"No," she said, and looked down at the dog in her lap. She was avoiding my gaze, and I was sure it was because she knew more than she was telling.

"Pam, I'm not out to bust anybody. My only interest is finding Donnie. He may be in trouble, and he may need help. If he does, now is not the time to be holding anything back."

She searched my face earnestly. "You really think he could be in trouble?"

"I don't know."

She took a deep breath and began to fidget with the seam of

her jeans. "Donnie was supposed to buy some dope from this Gerry."

"What kind of dope?"

"Grass."

"Did you tell the police that?"

"I didn't want to get Donnie in trouble," she whined. "I didn't think he'd be missing this long. I just thought he'd taken off somewhere and would be back."

"Is Donnie into drugs?"

"Not really. He'll smoke a joint at a party or drop a 'lude once in a while, but it's more to go along with the other kids than anything else. Donnie is really insecure in a lot of ways, like I said. He can't stand to feel left out of things."

"You're talking about the kids from Piedmont?"

She nodded and looked outside.

"Do they do a lot of dope?"

"A *lot,*" she said. "Even the teachers at Piedmont are fried out of their skulls half the time."

I had to smile at the irony of it. To prevent their innocent children from being exposed to the big bad dope users at the high school, the desert's "better people" had bunched them for $5,600 a year.

"Is that why you left there?"

"That was one of the reasons. All my friends have always been at the high school anyway. I never hung around with the Piedmont kids. I could never stand them."

"Why not?"

She made a face. "They're such snobs. I mean, my parents have money, okay? But I don't look down on people that don't. Those kids do, though, and it always used to bug me. Like when I was going there, my friends at the high school always used to come by and pick me up after school, and the Piedmont kids would sit out on the lawn and wait to see what kind of an 'old' car they'd be driving. That was their big entertainment for the day. I mean, they'd really get off on it. They'd point and laugh and say, 'You're not really going to ride in *that*?' because it wasn't a new Porsche or Mercedes or something. It was sick. I could never understand why Donnie ran around with that crowd. They never liked him. All they did was use him."

"How?"

She looked at me. The light from the sliding glass door leading out to the pool hit her eyes obliquely, turning them from brown to green. "Like the dope thing. Donnie will buy some grass or some coke, and half the time he won't even do any of it. He'll just take it to school and give it away to play the big shot. He always tries to play the big role around those kids. That's one thing that always bugged me about him; he always has to talk big and try to impress everybody. It's only because he's lonely. He wants people to like him, but he goes about it the wrong way." She hesitated, then went on. "It used to make me sick last year when he'd come to school with some dope, and all the kids would buddy up to him and tell him how great he was and pat him on the back and everything, and then, when he'd leave, they'd all laugh and tell each other what an asshole he was. I've tried to tell Donnie how they are, but he won't listen. He thinks all those kids are his friends."

"Do you have a yearbook from last year?"

"Yeah."

"Can I see it?"

She shot out of the chair, launching the dog onto the carpet, and bounced out of the room. Fritz walked in circles for a while, and then, presumably operating on the theory that any warm body was better than none, he jumped up on the couch and lay down beside me.

Pam came back a minute or so later holding a thin blue book. Engraved on the cover were her name and "Piedmont '78." The entire book was no more than thirty-five pages.

"Looks like a pretty small school."

"I think there are twenty-eight students."

"In the whole school?"

"Yes."

"How many teachers?"

"Six."

The photographs in the book were all incredibly self-indulgent. Each student had his own page of pictures, and in all of them the kids seemed to be everywhere but on campus. They sat in deck chairs, lay on beds, sprayed each other playfully with hoses, strolled downtown with their arms around each other, but there were no shots of anybody studying. Interspersed with the pictures were poetical quotes by e. e. cummings, Lord Byron, W. H. Auden and quotes from recent songs by David Crosby, Joni Mitchell, Mose Allison, and Cat Stevens. Compared to the more traditional poets, the quotes from the songs had an alienated, painful, sometimes bitter flavor to them.

On Donnie's page were two pictures. In one he was swinging a golf club. In the other he had his arm around the shoulders of a horse-faced blonde. "Who's that?"

Pam looked at the picture. "Ms. Curtis. She's the Spanish teacher at the school."

The quote on the page next to the picture was from a Neil Young song:

> *Don't let it bring you down*
> *It's only castles burning*
> *Just find someone who's turning*
> *And you will come around.*

"Who does Donnie hang out with?"

She came over and sat next to me and started flipping the pages. She stopped when she got to a picture of two lithe, long-haired clones, standing in front of a gorilla cage at the zoo. "The Donovan twins. Marv and Steve." She turned the page and tapped it with her finger. "Jim Fedders." Two pages later she stopped again. "Andy Bowles."

She pointed out three or four more, and when she had finished, I closed the book. "Are all those kids heavy dopers?"

"Not all of them. Andy Bowles isn't. The Donovan twins are the worst. They're always messed up on reds. I don't know how they even function half the time."

She went back to her chair, and Fritz followed on her heels.

"You think Donnie might have taken off with any of them? Just to be going?"

"I doubt it. Not now."

"Why not now?"

"Finals are coming up next week. Donnie wants to finish up with good grades so he can get into SC. They have a good golf team there. That's what he really wants to do more than anything, be a pro golfer."

"How are his grades?"

"Good, in spite of himself. Donnie doesn't really apply himself. But then he doesn't have to. Grades come easy for him. He's really smart."

"Has he ever talked to you about running away?"

"He's looking forward to getting away from—to leaving town. He's looking forward to college. But I've never heard him talk about running away. Not in the sense you mean."

"You started to say 'getting away from.' Getting away from what?"

"I don't know," she said sulkily. "Things."

"I heard he has problems at home," I pressed her. "That he and his father don't get along too well."

She looked at me warily again.

"He never mentioned that to you?" I asked skeptically.

"What does it matter? I don't see what it has to do with anything."

"If what you've told me is true, Pam, Donnie has been hanging around with a pretty fast crowd. The kind of peole who hang around the edges of that kind of crowd can get pretty nasty. I know. I've known a lot of them. They're like hyenas waiting around a herd of antelope for a sick one to wander away from the group. If Donnie is in trouble, knowing what he's running away from might help me determine what he's running to."

She sat there, raking her lower lip with her teeth, then tilted her head down and said: "You're not going to repeat this to Mr. Fleischer—"

"I promise."

"That's the main source of Donnie's problems," she said. "His father."

"How so?"

"Donnie feels like his father doesn't really care about him. He's never had a family life to speak of. His mother died when he was really young, and Donnie was raised by nurses and maids. Even when they lived in Cleveland and he wasn't flying back and forth, I guess Mr. Fleischer was never home. He was always at their plant or out somewhere. Donnie talks all the time about how all his father cares about is his business. That's one reason he identifies with the other kids at Piedmont."

"Why?"

"Because that's the main pastime over there, to sit around and talk about how much you hate your parents."

"How about you, Pam?"

"Hey, I love my parents. They're fairly strict with me, but I'm glad they are. At least I know they care about me." She bit her lip and looked around guiltily as if the empty house were evidence of perjury against her. "Those kids get anything they want, but deep down they all feel like they're being bought off."

Here, kid. Take this money and go play somewhere; just don't bother me. So they went somewhere, and they spent it. They spent it on fast cars and booze and uppers and downers, anything to take the pain out of the American Dream.

Pam went on to tell me a story about one of her old girl friends at Piedmont. The girl hated her socialite model mother, who spent a great deal of her time checking in and out of rest resorts with nervous breakdowns, and resented her jet-set building contractor father, who was always flying off somewhere and leaving her with the mother. Because the mother was thin, the girl would stuff herself with chocolates, trying to get fat, and the more the mother would try to get her to reduce, the more she would eat. Because the mother always dressed chicly, the daughter would wear nothing but sweat shirts and jeans. In an attempt to get the girl to improve her appearance (her own *social* appearance, for after all, what would her friends think if they saw her daughter dressed like that?), the mother would periodically take her out shopping and make her buy the most expensive latest styles. And as soon as the girl would get home, she would throw her four-hundred-dollar outfits on the floor and stomp on them with dirty shoes before putting them on. *That* was showing her.

She finished the story, and I said: "I hear part of the trouble between Donnie and his father is not that he's too loose with his money, but that he's too tight with it."

"That's true," she said. "They have gotten into some fights about that. Like about the car."

"What car?"

"Donnie's car. When Donnie turned sixteen last year, his father bought him a Pinto. He really wanted a sports car—he begged his father for one—but his father said kids today don't know the meaning of money, and a Pinto was good enough for a sixteen-year-old. He was probably right, but Donnie felt self-conscious driving to school in that car. The kids would all rib him about it and make him feel inferior. That made him resent his father even more." She paused and leaned toward me. "You've got to understand: Donnie wants to feel like he belongs —to anybody. That's why it's so important to him to impress the kids at Piedmont. Only it's hard to impress that crowd if you haven't got a lot of money to burn. That's why Donnie tries so hard to play the big role by making up stories."

"What kind of stories?"

"Oh, you know. He tries to come off real worldly when he's not. He's always talking about how many dope connections he has and how his family are big-time Mafia people in Cleveland. It's funny, because a couple of girls at Piedmont have parents who really are big-time Mafia people from Chicago. They just laugh at him. And then like the first day Donnie came to school. His father had just moved him out from Cleveland, and he rode up to school in this big black limo with two men. Everybody in school wanted to know who the new kid was. Well, Donnie went around telling everybody that his father was in the Mafia and that the two men with him were his bodyguards. He said his father always made sure they were with him because he had been kidnapped once in Cleveland. It was just a story, of course. The two men were Norm and Mr. Fleischer. But Donnie got a few wows out of that one, until all the kids caught on."

"Norm," I said. "You mean the houseman."

"Yes." She nodded. "He's worked for the family I don't know how long. Actually, he's been sort of a father figure to Donnie. Donnie feels closer to Norm and his stepmother than to his own father."

"He gets along with his stepmother, then?"

"Oh, yes," she said emphatically. "They're very close."

"Getting back to this dope thing, would you know where Donnie buys his stuff?"

She shook her head.

"You know who would?"

She squinted at me nervously. "You're not going to tell this to the police?"

"I can't promise you that. If it's important, the police should know."

She nodded and after a hesitation said: "Tommy Walsh might."

"Who is Tommy Walsh?"

"A record producer from L.A. At least, that's who he says he is. I know he's loaded with money. A lot of the Piedmont kids hang out at his house. Donnie took me to a party there a few weeks ago."

"Where?"

"Farrell and Alejo. He rents the house. I don't know the address, but you can't miss it. The music is on all the time, and it's so loud the house shakes. I hear he pays the neighbors a hundred dollars apiece not to complain to the police about the noise. He's got an incredible stereo system hooked up in there. He's got a huge mixing board in the back, just like disc jockeys have, huge JBL speakers hanging from the ceiling, everything."

"What happened at the party?"

"Nothing much. Everybody was too stoned for much to happen. All the Piedmont kids were there, and a couple of the teachers, and everybody was passing around dope. There were so many drugs there I couldn't even believe it. Everybody was just lying around, totally wasted. I spent about ten minutes there and asked Donnie to take me home."

"You think Donnie could have bought his dope from Walsh?"

"I doubt it," she said. "Tommy gives it away like candy."

"How old is Walsh?"

"I don't know," she said, shrugging. "Thirty maybe."

"He lives by himself?"

"He lives with a roommate. A man. I think they're queers, but I'm not sure. They act pretty straight. They were really very nice the time I met them. They were probably the only ones at the party that weren't stoned at all."

"Do the cops know about Walsh?"

She shook her head. "I thought about telling them, but I

didn't. I didn't want to get anybody in trouble. I didn't want Donnie's parents to find out he'd been hanging out there."

I picked up the yearbook. "May I borrow this for a day or two? I promise I'll return it to you."

"Yeah, I guess so."

I stood up and smiled. "Donnie is lucky to have a friend like you, Pam. Thanks for your help."

She sighed as if relieved it was all over and walked me to the door. Fritz tagged along. At the door I said: "I'll be staying at the Royal Western Motel. If you think of anything else that might help me, I'd really appreciate it if you'd give me a buzz there."

She said she would. I went down the walk, the yearbook tucked underneath my arm, feeling like anything but a valedictorian. I felt old and jaded, and holding that yearbook only made me feel more old and more jaded. Buddy Holly was dead. Long live Buddy Holly.

I tossed the book onto the front seat of the car and got in. The smell of charcoal drifted by on the breeze. Someone was having an afternoon barbecue. Or maybe it was just the smell of castles burning.

I started the car, thinking I'd be goddamned if I was going to let it bring me down.

TEN

The Royal Western was a modern, characterless three-story motel in the south end of town. My room turned out to be on the second floor in the back. It was small but clean and had a tiny balcony overlooking the pool, so that I could catch all the noise from the kids splashing below.

I unpacked what little I had brought, then undressed and stood under a hot shower for a long time, loosening some of the knots that had bunched at the back of my neck. By the time I'd shaved and changed clothes the knots had tightened up again, as I thought about the people I still had to talk to tonight.

On the advice of the desk clerk I walked across the street to a place called Lyons English Grille. After devouring a thick cut of rare prime rib and a large baked potato and downing two vodka-rocks, I felt better, almost good enough to go visiting.

It was getting dark when I left the restaurant and walked back to the motel. There were no messages for me at the desk. I picked up my key and was halfway out the office door when two men came in. I excused myself as I brushed shoulders with one of them and started for my room. I was almost at the stairs when someone shouted my name. The two men from the office were striding briskly toward me.

They were both a little under six feet and looked in shape for being in their forties, and both had dark hair that was neatly combed and parted, but there the similarities ended. One of them had a squared-off granite jaw and neat, precise features and had never quite lost that rah-rah college look he had had when he'd played running back or wide receiver for Pitt or Notre Dame or whatever school he'd attended back east. The other one, on the other hand, looked as if his face had been assembled from spare parts that had not been designed to go together. His eyes were not the same size or quite in line, and his ears stuck out from his narrow head, and his mouth was too fleshy for his bony face.

When they reached me, the square-jawed one asked: "Are you Jacob Asch?"

"I don't know," I said. "What does he look like?"

He pulled out his ID. "We're with the FBI. I'm Special Agent Garth. This is Special Agent Haber."

I looked at their open-necked sports shirts and knit slacks and soft-leather loafers. "I thought you guys were alway supposed to wear dark suits."

"That was the *old* FBI," Haber said. "We're the new FBI."

I nodded.

"We *used* to be with the old FBI," he went on.

"But now you're with the new FBI."

"That's right," he said, proud he'd made his point.

"We'd like to ask you a few questions," Garth said.

"About what?"

"Your relationship with Gerry McMurtry."

Fleischer's phone calls must have finally paid off. "What twenty million dollars won't buy."

Garth's eyes narrowed. "Huh?"

"Nothing," I said. "We can talk upstairs."

We went up to my room, and I turned on the light and sat on the edge of the bed. Garth took a chair, but Haber was the restless type. He roamed about the room, peeking in the closet and the bathroom, trying to look casual as he took everything in. By the time Garth started the questioning he had finished his tour and come to rest against the bureau.

Garth ran me through my initial contact with McMurtry, my visit with Mrs. Fleischer, McMurtry's subsequent disappearance and what I knew about it, and my thoughts on the disappearance of Donnie Fleischer, of which I had few. Garth sat through it all trying to look like the Lincoln Memorial, while Haber leaned forward intently, searching my face for telltale signs that I was lying—tics, twitches, nervous gestures. He seemed disappointed when I did not display any.

"Would you be willing to submit to a lie detector test about what you've just told us?" Garth asked.

"A lie detector test? What for?"

He gave me a friendly smile. "It would help us out. Kind of get Mr. Fleischer off our backs. Off yours, too."

I sighed. "When?"

"How about now?" he asked. "It won't take long."

I thought about it. I didn't relish the idea, but I didn't relish the idea of Fleischer calling all over the state about me either. If it was going to be the easiest way to get rid of him. . . . "Okay," I said.

They had a gray Ford sedan out front. Haber drove, and I sat up front with him. As we drove through town, I noticed that the unreality of the place was even more striking at night. Everything was floodlit, including the palm trees, and the entire town was suffused with a soft pastel glow. Even the more seedy honky-tonk motels took on an almost ethereal luminescence, their stucco harshness washed out in a bath of blue and amber and green light.

At the other end of town Haber pulled into the parking lot

of a sprawling two-story motel called the Sands. He parked the car and got out. "This way."

I followed them down to a door four rooms down, and Garth stopped and knocked on it. It struck me as a strange place to be administering a lie detector test, but I didn't say anything. The government often worked in ways too mysterious for us mere mortals to understand.

The door was opened by a fat gray-haired man with a great round face and more chins than a Chinese phone book. His eyes were weak and watery, but that might have been because of the constant dribble of smoke from the cigarette dangling from the corner of his mouth. He was coatless, and his white shirt was slightly dirty and covered with burn holes from where his ashes had dropped. He nodded at us and walked away from the door without saying anything.

The room was typical motel fare: cheap cloth furniture; a sagging double bed; plaster walls covered with abstract prints from Sears; a flimsy chest of drawers. The one item that was different was the metal briefcase-size box on the table in front of the curtained window. The lid was open, and the attachments were all laid out next to it, wired up and ready to go.

The fat man took the cigarette out of his mouth and offered his hand, smiling. "Pete Mercante," he said.

"Jake Asch," I said.

"Nice to meet you, Jake," he assured me. "Ever take a lie detector test before?"

"Yeah."

He smiled happily, then mashed out his cigarette in an ashtray beside the box. "Then I don't have to go into any long dissertation about how it works. If you'd like to sit down, we can get started."

Mercante put me in a chair on the side of the table away from the controls, and Garth and Haber leaned against the walls with their arms folded as the polygraph man attached a cuff to my upper arm to measure my blood pressure and then put an accordion tube around my chest to monitor my respiration. Mercante's teeth and fingernails were brown with nicotine stains, and he smelled strongly of tobacco. He also fidgeted quite a bit as he attached the equipment. A nervous polygraph operator. That was all I needed.

After he attached the last piece of apparatus, a set of finger rings that were actually electrodes to detect changes in perspiration, he sat down on the other side of the table and began fiddling with the controls. I felt like Frankenstein's monster. All I needed was a couple of electrodes in my neck and I would be ready to take on the Wolfman.

He began by running a couple of test charts to get a level of my reactions. The questions were all basically harmless—my name, my father's name, my occupation—spiced up with an occasional zinger, like "Have you ever smoked marijuana?" just to see how I would respond to stress.

The principle behind it was very simple, known by primitive man for thousands of years. When the mind is trapped, the body reacts. It sweats; breathing becomes more rapid; the heart beats faster. There are ways to beat the machine, of course, but it is a lot harder to beat it when a good operator is working the controls. By the time he had run the third test chart, chain-smoking the whole time, I knew Mercante was good, nervous or no.

"Okay," he said, stretching. "We can start now."

Wanting every edge I could get, I asked: "Can you put out your cigarette? The smoke bothers me."

He looked down at the burning stick between his fingers, as if surprised it was there. "Oh, sure."

He put out the cigarette and began running me through the same innocuous list of questions, only this time the zingers were not about marijuana; they were about McMurtry: how had I met him; how long had I known him; when was the last time

I spoke to him. Everything was going along just peachy until he asked: "Do you have any knowledge of the disappearance of Donnie Fleischer?"

"No," I told him, but I thought of Pam Conner, and I felt my pulse quicken. I had not told the FBI about her.

I watched Mercante's face, but it remained as expressionless as a bowl of creamed corn. He asked a few more irrelevant questions, just to get my reaction level down, then paused and studied the chart intently. "Are you involved in any way in the kidnapping of Donnie Fleischer?"

The needle must have gone off the paper. I looked over at Garth and Haber. "Donnie Fleischer has been kidnapped?"

The two men stared at me poker-faced.

"When was Fleischer contacted?"

"This afternoon," Garth said finally.

I felt betrayed. I wanted to rip all the wires off. "I don't care much for your approach."

"That really hurts my feelings," Garth said.

"Why the hell didn't you tell me that back at the motel?"

He stared at me coldly. "You still want to take the test?"

I rankled inside at the insinuation but took a couple of deep breaths, trying to hold down my anger. "Why the hell wouldn't I?"

"I don't know," he said, smiling slightly. "But if there's a reason, he'll find out."

I turned to Mercante. "Ask me that question again."

After two more tests Mercante leaned his great hulk back in his chair and lit up another cigarette. He glanced at Garth and said: "He's clear on everything but Question Eight. I'm still getting a reaction on it."

Garth leaned over his shoulder. "What question is that?"

"'Do you know anything about the disappearance of Donnie Fleischer?'"

There was no way around it, so I told them what Pam had laid on me, about Gerry-the-dope-dealer and Tommy Walsh. Mercante ran two more charts on that story, brushed an ash off his shirt, and said: "It checks out."

"Okay?" I asked. "Satisfied? Now take this shit off me so I can get the hell out of here."

Garth watched impassively as Mercante removed the accordion tube from my chest. "I don't know," he said. "I don't know if I'm satisfied or not. Why didn't you tell us that in the first place?"

"If you'd leveled with me instead of trying to play Junior G-man, I might have," I said, meeting his eye.

"You know, you'd think you'd have wised up by now, Asch. You've already gone to jail once for withholding evidence in a criminal investigation—"

"Correction," I said, holding up a finger. "There wasn't any investigation. The investigation was over, and nobody wanted any information pertinent to it. What they wanted was the name of the source I used for the story I wrote about the trial, and I was never formally charged for withholding evidence or anything else. I was cited for contempt by a judge who had a castration complex and who didn't think the First Amendment had anything to do with freedom of the press.

"But hell, you already know all that, Garth, and I want you to know there are no hard feelings on my part for bringing it up. I know you didn't mean anything personal by it, that it was just a way of lashing back at all those reporters that say all those nasty things about the FBI bugging bedrooms and burglarizing doctors' offices—"

"Don't push it, Asch," Garth said, sticking his jaw out. "You don't have any big newspaper to protect you now."

"It didn't do such a hot job the first time," I said. "Anyway, what are you going to do, Garth? Just what the fuck are you going to do? Threaten to have my license yanked? That's straight out of every cheap private detective novel I've ever read."

"It could be done," he said, his face reddening.

"'Tain't that easy, my friend," I told him. "Anyway, I'm not all that crazy about the business. The work isn't that steady, and the pension plan sucks."

"I guarantee it'll happen, Asch," he said, pushing his face at me. "That and a whole lot more if word about any of this gets out to any of your media buddies or anyone else. We're putting a lid on it. Tight. That means you don't poke around anymore looking for McMurtry; you don't ask anybody any questions; you don't talk to anybody. In fact, the best thing you could probably do would be go back to your apartment in L.A. and lock your door and take your phone off the hook and don't come out until this is all over. Because I'm telling you right now, if there's a leak, I'm coming right at you."

Mercante removed the cuff from my arm, and I rotated my shoulder, just to feel the freedom of motion. "There's just one thing you're forgetting. I have a client—"

"Not now you don't," Garth said. "Right now you've got shit."

"What am I supposed to tell Mona Talbott?"

"That's your problem, buddy." His voice was as tender as a barbed-wire fence. "You just forget about McMurtry. Forget about Donnie Fleischer. Just put it all out of your mind."

If it were that simple, I thought, there would be no problem. No problem at all. Only it wasn't.

They drove me back to the Royal Western and dropped me off. I watched them leave, then walked down the street to a liquor store and bought a pint of Old Granddad. I had a feeling I was going to need grandpappy's worldly-wise solace tonight.

It was a nice night for a walk. The air was warm, and a huge, flattened-out yellow moon hovered over the horizon, rivaling the town's chromatic glow. A gentle breeze blew off the desert, setting up a musical rustling in the fronds of the palm trees.

I could see how people could get swept up by it all. It was a perfect Valentino night for sheikhs and sand dunes. Come to Palm Springs. Romantic fantasies fulfilled for a weekend.

I went up to my room wishing I had a romantic fantasy to fulfill. At the moment all my romantic fantasies were Tap City.

ELEVEN

I woke up at 7:40, for no reason I could think of, except that I was being punished for past sins. I say I woke up. I should have said most of me woke up. My tongue was still asleep, and my mouth felt like the inside of a cotton picker's tote bag. Courtesy of Old Granddad.

I showered and dressed and drove to a coffee shop down the street, where I read the paper over coffee, scrambled eggs, and more coffee. There was nothing in it about the Fleischer kidnapping or anything else of much importance either.

After breakfast I drove around aimlessly for a while, thinking about my options, then went back to the motel. There was a message at the desk that Simon Fleischer had called and wanted me to call him back as soon as I got in. I was not particularly in the mood to listen to him tell me how he was going to have me ground into a fine powder and blown away, but I went up to my room and called him anyway.

He answered the phone himself. "I want to talk to you, Asch. It's important. Can you come out here right away?"

I told him I could, and he said: "There's a liquor store on Frank Sinatra Drive, just off Highway One-eleven. My house-man, Norm, will meet you there in fifteen minutes. He'll be driving a white Mark Five."

"Why don't I just drive out to the house?"

"No. The house may be being watched. Just look for the car. He'll go into the liquor store and buy something. While he's in there, go to the car and get in. Keep down so nobody will see you, in case he's being followed."

I told him I would be there in twenty minutes.

Norm was right on time. The Mark pulled into the driveway of the liquor store and parked in back, and while Norm was inside the store, I got into the car and scrunched down in the seat. A few minutes later Norm opened the door and put a large shopping bag on the seat between us. "Anybody see you?" he asked.

"I don't think so."

He grunted and started the car. His eyes were glued to the rearview mirror all the way to the house.

Garth and Haber were in the living room as I walked through, with two other men who had FBI indelibly stamped on their faces.

"Good morning, gentlemen," I said cheerfully.

Garth was the only one who did not return the greeting.

Fleischer was in the den, sitting behind a semioval polished mahogany desk. His tan seemed to have faded, and his face looked gray and drawn. He asked me to sit down and told Norm to close the door on the way out.

I sat down in a gray chair in front of the desk. It was pigskin, as was all the furniture in the room. The walls were tan suede, except for one, which was floor-to-ceiling bookshelves. The books were all bound in leather, and their titles were engraved in gold. They looked very old.

He caught me glancing at them and said: "That collection is

worth a fortune. They're all originals. I have a copy of Hobbes's *Leviathan* there from 1651 that is priceless."

I nodded, and he cleared his throat self-consciously, as if realizing how ridiculous that had sounded under the circumstances.

"I'm sorry about your son," I said. "You may not believe that, but I really am. I'm sure they'll get him back."

"They'd better. If that man harms a hair of Donnie's head, he'll wish he'd never been born." He turned his gaze away from me as if being careful not to direct the threat at me.

"What man?"

"What do you mean, what man? McMurtry."

"There's no proof it's McMurtry—"

"The FBI lab lifted a thumbprint off the note," he said slowly. "McMurtry's thumbprint. They also found some of his prints in Donnie's car. It's McMurtry, all right."

There it was. I had not believed it, even last night, because I had not wanted to believe it. Even now, confronted with the physical evidence, I somehow still could not accept it.

"They found Donnie's car?"

"Just where the note said it would be."

"When did the note arrive?"

"Yesterday afternoon. According to the postmark on the envelope, it should have arrived yesterday. Somehow it got screwed up in the crush of weekend mail."

"Do you have a copy of it?"

He picked up a photostated sheet from the desk and handed it to me.

Fleischer:

> We have your son. To prove it, his car is
> parked in a driveway at 444 West Patencio Road.
> He is all right, but he won't be unless you do
> exactly what we say.

The ransom is $400,000. It must be in circulated, unmarked bills of new issue—twenties and some fifties. You will put the money in a cream-colored suitcase, which is how you will deliver it. When the money is ready, place an ad in the classified section of the *Desert Sun*: "Son, we want you back. No questions asked. Love, Dad." When we see the ad, we will call you at ten that same night and tell you where to deliver the money.

Do not try to get cute. If the police are notified, it's bye-bye, Donnie. Do not bother to try and trace the calls. We will not repeat instructions, so you will not have time.

Everything has been meticulously planned, so do not try to outguess us. The time it takes to get from your house to the drop site has been carefully calculated. If you fail to show up in the time allotted, or if police are spotted in the area, it's bye-bye, Donnie.

I put the note down and looked up. "But *why*? It still doesn't make any sense to me."

"Of course it doesn't. The man is insane."

"But what motive could he have for something like this?"

"I told you, he's trying to punish Lainie. He's trying to get at her through Donnie. He wants to take Donnie from her like he thinks she took his son from him."

I shook my head. "That's hard for me to swallow, Mr. Fleischer. McMurtry would have to be totally out of control to make that kind of connection, and I can't believe he came completely unglued in a week. Besides, this letter doesn't sound like the product of a revenge-crazed mind. The person who wrote this is in control of himself. He's been thinking about it carefully, and for a long time."

"A lot of schizophrenics may appear normal at times," he said. "Even downright brilliant."

"Okay. Let's grant he's schizophrenic—which I don't—why the ransom? If he's doing it for revenge, why bother with the money at all?"

His face was tensely grim, but there was something else there below the surface, a physical sickness like the faint smell of tainted meat. "The FBI thinks maybe he got into it and got scared. The man has never killed before. They think perhaps he got into the situation impulsively and has now found himself incapable of going through with it. And now he needs the cash to get away. At least that's what they're hoping."

"McMurtry's a successful artist," I argued. "He's got money. Why would he need yours?"

"Because he knows he can't get to his own. The minute he were to try, he would be grabbed." He hesitated and stared at me searchingly. "Let me ask you something, Asch. You know the man. Tell me honestly, do you think him capable of murder?"

"Not from what I've seen, no."

That seemed to reassure him a little. He leaned back. "That note says 'we.' Do you think he would be in this with anybody? What about his girl friend?"

"You can count her out. As far as anyone else being involved, from what I've seen of the man he's a loner."

"*That's* why I wanted to talk to you," he said emphatically. "You're the only person who's had any prolonged contact with the man recently. You might be able to tell us which way he's likely to jump when things start happening."

I was not sure what he was getting at, so I didn't say anything. That seemed to make him uncomfortable. He shifted in his chair and said: "Do you know anything about me, Asch?"

"Not much."

He put his elbows on the desk and leaned forward. "You know I'm a rich man. Let me tell you how rich. I have a

110

company in Cleveland—Fleischer-Chalmers Power Systems—that grosses twenty million a year. I own part of a bank and controlling interest in an auto-parts business that grosses another five million a year. My companies employ hundreds of people who make products that are sold all over the world." He recited it like a litany, almost religiously, and as he went on, his voice began to swell as if deriving strength from the incantation. "The point I'm trying to make is that I'm used to making decisions. Important decisions. That comes with any position of power. But in the next few days I'm going to have to make some decisions I find myself totally unprepared for. Ever since the FBI got here last night, I feel like I'm being swept away on one of my own conveyor systems and I can't stop. I don't like the feeling."

"The FBI is experienced in these things," I said, still not sure where he was going.

He stood up and faced his bookshelf with his hands locked behind his back. "That's not the point. The point is my son's life is at stake here, and I can't let myself be carried away by arguments that may endanger him, no matter how good those arguments sound. The purpose of the FBI, its reason for existence, is to apprehend criminals. I don't give a goddamn about criminals. I want my son back." His head dropped, and his voice grew quiet. "It's a funny thing. You devote your entire life to building up something, and you never realize how little it all means until something like this happens. My whole life has been my business, but I'd give it all up—everything I own—if it meant getting Donnie back safe and sound."

"I'm sure the safety of your son is their primary consideration, Mr. Fleischer."

He turned to face me. "Maybe. But if you get chest pains and go to a doctor and he tells you you have to have a bypass, you'd want a second opinion, wouldn't you? No matter how good the doctor is?"

I found the analogy strange, but I conceded I probably would.

He nodded as if that settled it. "Well, I don't have anybody I can go to for a second opinion. At least nobody who's had any experience in a situation like this."

He kept looking at me, and I said: "I'm not sure what you're asking, Mr. Fleischer. Are you asking me to be your second opinion?"

He moved his head as if it caused him pain. "Yes."

My head was swimming from the man's personality changes. "But why me? Yesterday you were ready to have me drawn and quartered—"

"Things have changed since yesterday."

"How?"

"The FBI cleared you, for one thing. We know for sure it's McMurtry, for another. You know the man. You have a rapport with him. If he contacts us directly, you might be able to reason with him. God knows, Lainie and I can't."

"Is that all?"

"No," he said slowly. "I did some checking on you last night. I talked to a man in Los Angeles whom I trust like I trust few men. He told me I was all wrong about you. He said you were tough, competent, and as straight as they come, and coming from him, that's as good a recommendation as you can get."

"Who is he?"

"His name is Myron Greenbaum."

"Never heard of him."

"He's a friend of Allen Beck's."

Now I understood. Allen Beck was a big television producer whose son had been reported missing from his private school a year or so back by Beck's ex-wife. Because the Becks had been involved in a bitter custody suit, the FBI suspected some hanky-panky and refused to move on the case until a ransom note was delivered. It took me three days to find the kid. He was in a roach-infested shack in Topanga Canyon with one of the ex-wife's boyfriends—a burned-out acid-freak drummer. The ran-

112

som note was there, too. The drummer had dropped too much acid and Jack Daniel's and had forgotten to mail it. Beck naturally did not have too many nice things to say about the FBI after that.

"I'm not sure the feds are going to be particularly thrilled about having me around. Especially Garth."

"Don't worry about Garth," Fleischer said. "He isn't going to be in charge of the investigation. He's just running things until Inspector Norton gets here this morning."

"This Norton might not be tickled pink about it either."

"I don't care who's tickled pink and who isn't. They have to do what I say. It's my money and my son. If I say you're working on the case, you're working on the case."

The order in which he had put the two struck me as a significant slip, but then maybe I was being unfair. "What about the money?"

"My brother is in L.A., arranging for it right now. He flew in from Cleveland last night."

"Speaking of Cleveland," I said, "did this happen there before?"

"What are you talking about?"

I told him what Donnie had fed the kids at Piedmont, about having been kidnapped. He made a gruff gesture. "I don't know why he would make up a story like that. It never happened."

"Can you think of any enemies you might have, anyone besides McMurtry who might want to strike back at you this way?"

"Every man in a position like mine has made some enemies along the line," he said. "It's unavoidable. But I can't think of anyone who would perpetrate anything as horrible as this."

I thought about what I was being offered. If I didn't owe it to him, I owed it to Donnie. "All right, Mr. Fleischer. I'll be your second opinion."

"Good." He smiled and sat back down, and as he did, his

whole demeanor changed. His back was erect; the self-confidence was back in his gestures. He pulled out a checkbook and said: "Now, how much do you want?"

I had not even thought about money. "We can take care of that some other time—"

"I'd rather take care of it now," he said. "It's a quirk of mine. When I pay a man, I know he's my man. I've found that's the only way I can be sure of anyone."

Except your son, I thought. "Make it out for five hundred," I said, wondering what he thought he was buying for that. A handshake would have probably bought more, but the man had never made the motion. He tried to solve everything, all his problems, with an exchange of paper.

He made out the check and handed it to me, and I put it in my pocket and turned to go.

"Where are you going?" he asked.

"To Indio. I want to look through the coroner's files. Something set McMurtry off, and I want to find out what. If we do make contact with him, the more information we have to work with, the better off we'll be."

"Good thinking," he said, as if talking to one of his junior executives.

"When I'm ready to come back, I'll call the house, and Norm can pick me up at the liquor store again. I doubt the house is being watched—if McMurtry's alone, he couldn't be watching both Donnie and the house at the same time. But there's no sense taking any chances."

He nodded, then turned away. The silent agreement stretched out between us, that neither would mention the other possibility, that maybe Donnie didn't need watching anymore.

I left before the agreement could be broken.

TWELVE

The coroner's report was a packet of material that included a copy of Brian's death certificate, autopsy and toxicology reports, and various other reports spelling out the time of death and the circumstances under which the body of the victim had been found. There was also a receipt of personal property, listing what was found on the deceased and the name and address of the person who claimed the articles. Brian Ellison had died wearing his clothes, but there had been nothing in them, so consequently Lainie had not bothered to claim them.

I went over the accident reports again, but there was nothing there I had missed the first time. The toxicology report was negative. No toxic substances had been found in Brian's urine, blood, intestines, or liver.

Likewise, there was nothing very shocking in the autopsy reports. The external examination of the body showed evidence of trauma—hematoma and contusion—on the forehead just above the left eye. There was a triangular-shaped burn scar on the right forearm and a slight physical deformity of the left wrist, but both of those appeared to be the result of old injuries and not from the accident.

Brian's cardiovascular, respiratory, endocrine, biliary, and digestive systems were all normal. The skeletomuscular system was free from fractures, except for that left wrist, which, according to the pathologist, had been fractured at least a year before and had healed abnormally.

The only serious injury evidenced from the accident had been to Brian's head, apparently when he had hit the dashboard. The medical examiner had found the brain displaced on the left temporal region directly below the hematoma, and blood was found in the subdural spaces above the left eye. There was no evidence of skull fracture. Cause of death: cerebral hemorrhage due to automobile accident.

There was a Marie Callender's right next to the liquor store, and I grabbed a bite to eat there before phoning Norman. He picked me up fifteen minutes later.

In the garage a man in overalls was working in the front seat of the Seville, installing a tiny microphone on the visor above the windshield. He glanced up briefly as I walked by, then turned his attention back to his work.

The Fleischers, Garth, and Haber were in the Sydney Greenstreet room, along with two men I had never seen before.

Fleischer was sitting in his regular chair: he gestured at the two men. "Asch, this is Inspector Norton of the FBI. And my brother, Zach."

Both men rose to shake hands. Norton must have been a leftover from the old FBI. He was wearing a dark suit. A tall and gristly forty-five, he looked as if he probably jogged or played a lot of racquetball to keep in shape. He had brown hair with a distinguished touch of gray at the temples and an unlined, ascetic face. His dark eyes were unreadable except for the faint trace of suspicion in them.

Fleischer's brother was short and squat, with more hair on

the backs of his hands than on his head, and a potato nose like Fleischer's, but without the bluish color. He could have been younger or older than his brother; I couldn't tell. His eyes were old and baggy from lack of sleep, and gray lines of worry creased his face, making him look older than he probably was.

We sat down. A tape recorder with a headset was set up next to the phone by Fleischer's chair. Another red phone had been installed nearby to leave the main line free for the Call.

"Inspector Norton was just going over the plan," Simon Fleischer said. "Go on, Inspector."

Norton crossed his legs. "The plan is basically No Interference. Our first priority, of course, is to get Donnie back safely. When the kidnapper calls, we can't let on we have any clue to his identity. That may spook him. We've got to lull him into a feeling that everything is running smoothly. We've got to assure him his instructions will be followed to the letter, but at the same time I think we should make it a prerequisite for delivery of the money that we get some proof that Donnie is alive and well."

"What about the phone?" I asked.

"What about it?"

"Have you put a trap on it?"

Norton frowned unpleasantly, then cleared his throat. "I've put a request in to the Justice Department to get taps put on both this phone and McMurtry's home phone. I'm expecting an answer sometime this afternoon."

"This afternoon will be too late."

"Not necessarily."

"You might be able to get pin registers installed in one exchange," I said, "but what if the guy calls from outside Palm Springs? You can't possibly get all the exchanges in the area covered before tonight—"

Simon Fleischer listened with growing irritation before breaking in. "Traps? What the hell are you people talking about?"

Norton glowered at me as if I were an understudy who had

just upstaged him. To steal back the scene, he turned quickly to Fleischer and said: "Phone calls are normally controlled by the caller, Mr. Fleischer, as you know. If the caller hangs up, the connection is broken. But with a device called a pin register, a phone line can be held open even after the caller hangs up. The call is trapped, in effect, and the phone company can trace it."

"What's he talking about 'exchanges' and all that?" Fleischer said, waving a hand at me.

Norton sighed. "Every telephone number within a certain exchange is fed through a central office. That's where the pin register is installed—at the central office of the exchange."

"I see," Fleischer said. "So if the caller calls from another exchange, this pin register or whatever will be useless."

"That's correct."

"Can't you put these things in all the telephone offices in the area?"

"We could, but it would take time—"

"Well, what's the goddamn holdup?"

"The people in Justice are very leery of granting court orders for phone taps these days," Norton said apologetically. "Ever since Watergate, the mention of the word *wiretapping* sends them into a panic."

"Did you tell them at Justice that the kid doesn't belong to any political party?" I broke in.

A flush creeped up the back of the FBI man's neck. I was beginning to enjoy my role as devil's advocate, striking back at my interrogators. Fleischer seemed to approve of it, too. He glanced over at Lainie and nodded, as if to say, "See, I told you," but could not catch her eye. She sat staring at the lagoon, her blue eyes unfocused and slightly glassy, like the recently fired glaze on a ceramic flower pot. Tranquilizers could have caused that.

"Justice is aware of the urgency of the problem," Norton snapped.

"I'm glad to hear it." There was no advantage in pressing that further, so I asked: "How is the drop going to be covered?"

"Our agents will be out cruising, waiting for the call. They are right now, in fact. And they're all well disguised. As soon as we learn where the drop is to be made, agents in that area will be dispatched to establish a perimeter of surveillance. The license numbers of any cars entering or leaving the area will be recorded. We've installed a transmitter inside Mr. Fleischer's car, so that we will be able to hear everything that goes on from the time he leaves the house."

"What if your agents pick up McMurtry's car?"

"It will be tailed, but from a distance, and discreetly. I've made it clear to all my men, the drop is not to be interfered with in any way unless I give an emergency order."

"How many agents do you have working on it?"

"There are a hundred and fifty in town now. By tonight there will be two hundred. We've taken over the Sands as a command post. Everything will be monitored from there."

"What about other law enforcement?"

"I've been assured the complete cooperation of the county sheriffs, the highway patrol, and the Palm Springs police. They've all been instructed to keep their black-and-whites out of the drop area, and they've been told not to attempt to intercept McMurtry if they happen to spot him somewhere."

"Do you plan to have somebody go along on the drop?"

"Our engineers are installing air-conditioning units in the trunks so that one of our men can ride with Mr. Fleischer as an extra security measure—"

Fleischer's smile turned into a scowl. "The note said I was to be alone—"

"It also said you weren't to call the police. Don't worry, everything will be all right. It's just an extra security precaution."

"That's fine," Fleischer said, "but what if I get stopped? What if McMurtry or whoever shows up wants to look in the trunk?"

"He won't," Norton said with complete self-assurance. "You

probably won't even have any direct contact with the kidnappers at all. The last thing a kidnapper wants is to be identified."

"You say 'probably,' but you can't be sure. McMurtry isn't your normal kidnapper. He's mentally unbalanced."

"All the more reason to have someone along with you," Norton argued. "If there's trouble, you're going to need help. We won't be far away at any time, but if someone tries to harm you, you'll need assistance immediately—"

"If someone intends to hurt me," Fleischer argued, "your man won't be able to get out of the goddamn trunk fast enough to stop him." He looked at me. "How about it, Asch?"

"It might be a good idea to have someone there," I said. "If McMurtry is out for revenge on your wife—" I paused and looked around. Lainie was watching me now. "I guess that's the theory we're working on—he might make you a target, too."

Norton nodded, but Fleischer shook his head stubbornly. He passed me a petulant look, as if annoyed that I would challenge the wisdom of his decision. "No," he said. "I can't take the chance. If something happened and your man got excited and shot McMurtry or whoever, we'd never know where Donnie is."

"I don't think you should go," Lainie spoke up.

Everyone looked at her.

"I think one of these people should go. It's their business. They know about these things. You're not well enough to go through an ordeal like this."

Fleischer's face grew firm. "The note said I was to go. I'm going. And I'm going alone."

"Simon," Fleischer's brother said, leaning forward, "Lainie has a point. You have to think about your heart. Something like this could be too much of a strain—"

Fleischer waved away the suggestion. "I didn't develop a heart condition yesterday. I've had it for years. It would be just as much of a strain sitting here, waiting to hear something. More. It's the waiting that's killing me now. It's like dying."

Norton watched the scene with a look of sorrowful concern. He stood up and said: "I want to talk to Asch, fill him in on some details of the operation. Mr. Fleischer, I suggest you try to get some rest before tonight. You're going to need it."

Norton motioned to me, and I followed him. We went down the hall and stopped in front of a door. He knocked, and the door was pulled open by a young man wearing a shoulder holster and a haircut I had not seen in twenty years—a "flattop with fenders," I think they used to call it. The man greeted the inspector and stepped back to let us in.

The room was a bedroom, and the queen-sized bed in the middle of it was covered by a crazy quilt of money—twenties and fifties, all neatly wrapped in paper-banded bundles. Like Pavlov's dog, I felt my mouth immediately begin to water at the sight of all that green. It dried up quickly when I looked at the agents standing around the room with twelve-gauge pumps cradled in their arms.

A prissy-looking photographer moved around the bed, taking pictures of the money.

"People's Exhibit A," Norton said. "All the serial numbers have already been recorded."

The photographer popped off two more flashbulbs, then said: "I'm done."

"Get those developed as fast as you can," Norton told him. "I want them ready before tonight."

We went out of the room, and he closed the door behind us. In the hallway he stopped and turned around. He paused reflectively and said: "I had a long talk with Garth about you. He's not at all happy you're here."

"That grieves me deeply."

His jaw hardened like quick-setting cement.

"We might as well get one thing straight right now, Asch. I'm not interested in your opinions of Garth or me or the bureau. The only reason you're here is that Simon Fleischer wants you here. Why that is, I'm not sure, but it doesn't matter. He's made that abundantly clear. It's his money and his son, and he can do what the goddamn hell he pleases. But I'm telling you up front. I don't want to be tripping over you, and I don't want you second-guessing us. We have a job to do here, and contrary to what you may think, we know how to do it, so don't get in our way."

"Okay," I said. "While we're at it, I might as well get a few things said. I don't know what Garth told you about me, I'm not even sure why he's got such a hard-on for me, but contrary to what you or he may think, I'm not a hot-dogger and I'm not an ambulance chaser. I'm not in this for the money, and I'm not in it for any headlines I can grab to promote business. I'm in it precisely for the reason you said—Fleischer wants me in it—and because I feel a measure of responsibility for what's happened. If I can help, fine. The minute I feel like I'm hindering instead of helping, I'll bow out gladly. But while I'm here, you can rest assured I have no intentions of telling you your job or undermining your decisions with Simon Fleischer, if that's what you're afraid of. As far as I'm concerned, you're running the show."

His eyes searched mine, and the tension in his jaw slackened. "Okay," he said, nodding curtly. "Now, tell me about McMurtry."

"What do you want to know?"

"Who could be in this with him?"

"I've told Fleischer that from what I know of the man, he's a loner. He has a typical artistic temperament. Egocentric, cynical, alienated. Because of his Vision—that's what he calls it— he sees himself as standing apart from the mass. He's also impulsive. All that would make it unlikely he'd be able to form any partnership with anybody on something like this. But that's just a layman's opinion."

"It's the best one we have to work with right now," he said. "You say he's impulsive. Violent-impulsive?"

I told him about McMurtry's scene at the opening and his occasional beer brawls. He listened tight-lipped. "I'm no psychologist either, but add that to the pictures he paints, and I come out with a squirrel. I don't like it."

"What about the phone call he allegedly received at his studio?" he asked.

I told him what I knew about that. He listened thoughtfully, tugging all the while on his upper lip with a thumb and forefinger. When I was done, he said: "It's always possible there was no phone call at all, that he just made it up."

"So then why tell his girl friend he was going to Palm Springs? That made a pretty obvious trail for the police to follow."

He folded his arms and began pacing in front of me. "Assuming there was a call—and I'm not convinced there was—what if the caller had been making plans for a long time? What if he somehow found out about McMurtry, and his argument with Lainie Fleischer, and exploited his emotional state to recruit him?"

I shook my head. "If somebody was planning something like this, he'd get somebody in it he could trust, not somebody emotional like McMurtry. It's more likely that whoever it was who made the call met McMurtry and told him something that blew his mind. Something about the death of his son that set him off."

"What?"

"That's the $64,000 question," I said. "Have you checked out this Walsh character?"

He nodded. "So far he seems to be pretty much who he says he is. He's originally from New Orleans. Family's got a lot of money there, I guess. He came to L.A. two years ago and set up a record company."

"What about the possibility of an inside job?"

"Who have you got in mind?"

"How about Norm?"

He shook his head. "He's been with Fleischer for ten years. And he really likes the kid. He also checks out on the lie box."

"What about Donnie?" I offered. "He's talked about getting out from under the old man's thumb. One of his obstacles has been money. Maybe he saw himself a way to get it."

"That has crossed my mind," he admitted.

I told him about Donnie's kidnapping tale and about his bragging about his family's big-time Mafia connections.

"If that's true about Fleischer having mob ties, I want to know about it. I'll check it out."

We started down the hall, and he seemed to hesitate. "Asch, I want you to do me a favor."

"If I can."

"Fleischer shouldn't go on the drop alone. Too many things can happen. I want you to talk to him, try to reason with him. Maybe he'll listen to you."

"I'll try, but I doubt it'll do much good. He's a hard man to get through to. He listens when he wants to and shuts down his mind when he doesn't."

"For his sake, as well as the kid's, I just hope we get this over with quick." He turned to me and said: "You don't have a family, do you, Asch?"

"No."

"I do. A son and a daughter. That's why I feel sorry for Fleischer. I can put myself in his position. I know what I'd feel like if it was one of mine out there. It would be the not knowing that would get to me, the uncertainty of it. I've been in charge of a lot of kidnapping cases, and I've never gotten used to it, the waiting. The waiting is like dying, but it's a constant, slow dying."

I didn't look at him. "I just hope the waiting is the only dying that comes out of this."

THIRTEEN

Norm was in the kitchen, making coffee. I poured myself a cup and sipped it, leaning against the sink. I tried questioning him about his relationship with the Fleischers and about the family troubles, but I didn't get much worthwhile, maybe because he was afraid of losing his job or maybe because he didn't think it was any of my business.

He did confirm that there had never been any kidnapping in Cleveland, that Donnie sometimes told stories like that "to get attention." I wondered just how far Donnie would go to "get attention." Norm also gave me his version of McMurtry's visit: He had been out back when he heard Mrs. Fleischer yelling, and upon running into the room, he found her on the floor and McMurtry standing nearby with his fists clenched. Lainie had been practically hysterical; she said McMurtry had pushed her over the coffee table. She told Norm to throw him out, but before he could, McMurtry stalked out, saying that he "would be seeing her again."

After five more minutes of listening to Norm's taciturn monosyllabic grunts, I gave up and asked him the way to Donnie's bedroom. He reluctantly pointed to the hallway across the pool and told me it was the third door down.

The door was open, and I went in. The room was blue, the walls pale, the drapes and the spreads on the twin beds a darker royal blue. Expensive-looking stereo components and a color TV lined the wall facing the beds, and above them was a bookshelf filled with paperbacks and school textbooks. A rolltop desk stood in the corner, and on top of it were several golf trophies, along with a color photograph of Donnie standing on a golf course with Arnold Palmer. The pictures on the wall were all pen-and-inks, some abstract originals that looked like Rorschach blots and a copy of a Ralph Steadman drawing of a group of reptilian corporate executives standing at a bar, drinking glasses of blood.

I turned on the light in the walk-in closet. It was packed with sweaters, shirts, slacks, and jeans, all with expensive labels. The rack on the floor must have held twenty pairs of shoes, from Adidas tennies to hundred-dollar Ballys. His golf clubs leaned against the wall in the corner, along with a pair of skis and a tennis racket. I came out and turned off the light, and a voice said: "What are you doing in here?"

Lainie stood in the middle of the room with her arms folded.

"Just looking around."

"What for?"

I was still the Enemy. "Look, Mrs. Fleischer, I know you don't like me, but we're all on the same side. We're all trying to get Donnie back."

She didn't say anything but continued watching me. I stepped over to the desk and indicated the trophies. "He must be good."

She looked at them, and her expression softened. "He is. He won that one in the Junior Nationals this year. He came in third. We were all very proud of him."

"You feel close to him, don't you?"

"He—we fill needs in each other. His mother died when he was very young."

"Your husband being away so much must have brought you closer together."

"Simon is a busy man," she said regretfully. "He doesn't get to spend as much time with Donnie as he would like."

I stared at the trophies. "I hear they quarrel a lot."

"They quarrel sometimes, but no more than other fathers and sons." Her tone was defensive now. "They're both stubborn and hotheaded."

"What did they quarrel about Friday night?"

She shot a hard glance at me and made an offhanded gesture. "Donnie wanted to drive across country with some friends after graduation. Simon said no. Why did you ask that?"

"No special reason." I fingered the driver held by the little man on top of the Junior Nationals trophy. "Can you think of anything McMurtry might have told Donnie that would have made him mad enough at you that he would have wanted to leave home?"

Her back stiffened. "What, for instance?"

"I don't know. You were the one who was married to him."

"I don't have the faintest idea of what you're talking about."

"What did McMurtry and you argue about the day he came here?"

"I told you," she said, thrusting out her jaw. "Brian. The accident."

"Something must have set him off, though. Something you said—"

"Nothing set him off," she said. Her voice was like ground glass. "He didn't need anything to set him off. He was set off before he got here. I told you, the man is insane."

"He wasn't a few days before, when I saw him," I said. "That's my point."

She put her hands on her hips and widened her stance. "What? Just what *is* your point?"

"You really hate him, don't you?"

"Of course I hate him. He's trying to destroy me. He tried it before and failed, and now he's trying it again."

"You mean before, when he left you?"

Her cheeks flushed. "Yes. He was to blame for Brian's death, not me: he was the one who deserted his own son. I told him that. I told him he was the one."

"Is that why he pushed you?"

She squinted at me and said: "What are you trying to imply?"

"I'm not trying to imply anything—"

"But you are," she said, her voice rising shrilly. "You're trying to imply that somehow I'm responsible for what's happened to Donnie, just like he said I was responsible for what happened to Brian. You're trying to shift the blame from yourself, just like he tried to shift the blame from himself."

"Mrs. Fleischer, I'm not—"

"Get out," she said quietly. She stepped forward, breathing hard. The white scar on her forehead throbbed angrily. "Get out of my son's room."

I got out.

Norton was right. The waiting was like dying.

The minutes died hard, each of them going out like a mortally wounded hero in a 1930s movie, making speeches and sending messages to his lover, until you wanted to say, "Enough already," and drop a rock on his head just to shut him up.

The court order for the taps on Fleischer's and McMurtry's phones finally came in, and Inspector Norton spent a lot of the afternoon on the red phone, trying to make arrangements with the phone company to have as many pin registers as possible installed before ten. I spent most of my time in the garage, watching the mechanics work on the cars, in an effort to stay out of Lainie's way.

At six Norm served sandwiches and coffee. Although my appetite had long ago become a casualty to anxiety, I managed to force down a tuna sandwich to keep up my strength. I was sitting at the kitchen table with the two agents who had been guarding the money, sipping a cup of coffee, when Simon Fleischer came in, his face distorted by rage.

He came over to the table and shook a finger at me. "Asch, stay away from my wife."

"Believe me, I'm trying."

The agents went on eating as if they were deaf and dumb.

"She says you've been badgering her."

"I wasn't. She just took it wrong. I was just trying to determine—"

He tapped me on the chest. "You don't try to determine anything. Just stay away from my wife and stay out of my personal affairs."

The remark struck me as strange, considering the circumstances. "It would seem I'm already involved in your personal affairs. I thought that was why you hired me."

"I hired you as a logistical adviser and as a liaison man to keep me informed about what the FBI was doing. That's all."

The FBI men looked at each other uncomfortably.

"All right, Mr. Fleischer," I said. "I'll give you some logistical advice. Let them send an agent with you tonight."

"No," he said sharply. "I've already made my position clear on that."

"You could always change it."

He stuck his chin out. "I'm not paying you to argue with me, Asch. You're not working for the FBI, and it might do you well to remember that. You're working for me, and I expect you to back up my decisions."

It was finally out in the open. The man approached everything like a corporate board meeting, and he had hired me to pack the board in his favor. The funding for my department would continue as long as I voted correctly, with the prez. I wanted to tell him to shove it, but I couldn't. Things were too far along to get out now.

We stared at each other, and he said: "Have I made myself clear?"

"Perfectly."

He rolled his shoulders back and nodded. He was in control of the situation again. He turned on his heel and stalked out, and I said: "Yassah, boss. Yo sho nuff made yosself clear."

The FBI men snickered as I Stepin-Fetchit-shuffled out the door.

The hours dragged by unbearably. Tension tightened inside the house like the mainspring in a watch, and I went outside to find a release. I lay out by the lagoon for a long time, listening to the ghostly whisper of the rainbirds out on the golf course watering down the greens for tomorrow's golfers, wishing it was all over and that this was a real lagoon, far away. My mind drifted, and I was lying on the sand, baking in the sun, and Erica's brown, hard body was next to me. I cursed to myself. There she was again. . . .

My thoughts were broken up by the feeling of a presence behind me. I turned to see Lainie standing inside the sliding glass door, watching me. Her figure was dark, backlit by the living-room lights. She stayed like that watching me for a long time, totally motionless, then let the curtain go and disappeared. The night air seemed suddenly chilly, but I didn't want to go back into the house. Not yet. I waited about ten minutes before I finally did.

At 9:30 everyone was gathered in the Sydney Greenstreet room. Nobody talked much, and as 10:00 approached nobody talked at all.

Ten came and went, then 10:05. Fleischer's eyes were glued to the phone. At 10:10 he jumped up and smacked a fist into his palm. "The note said ten. Why the hell doesn't he call?"

"He'll call," Norton said certainly.

"Maybe he's changed his mind—"

"He hasn't changed his mind. He'll call. Take it easy."

Fleischer turned on him angrily. "Sure, take it easy. That's easy for you to say. It's not your son."

Norton's face darkened momentarily, but then the calm mask of confidence slid back over it, and he said: "He'll call, Mr. Fleischer. Just try to keep calm. Donnie is going to need you to stay as cool as you can tonight. So for his sake, quit conjuring up horror movie scenes for yourself."

"The inspector is right, dear," Lainie said.

Fleischer scowled resentfully at Norton but grudgingly sat down. At 10:27 the phone rang, launching him out of his chair.

Garth moved swiftly to the tape recorder and slipped on the headset, and Norton went with Fleischer to the phone. Garth pressed the "Record" button and nodded, and Fleischer lifted the receiver. His hand was trembling. "Hello? Yes, this is he."

He looked at Norton and nodded. "Yes. Yes, I've got the money.... Yes, it's just like you wanted it.... Okay, just a second. I've got to get something to write with." He picked up a pen and begain scribbling furiously on the pad beside him. "Yes.... Right. The black Seville. Got it.... Cathedral Canyon to Terrace. Right on Terrace to Valley Vista. Right again."

Garth caught Fleischer's eye and made a hand motion for him to slow down.

"Yes. Wait. You're going too fast.... There, I've got Valley Vista.... To the fence, make a left.... A gate. NO TRESPASS-ING. Sections of sewer pipe.... Right, I've got it. Let me repeat it back to you, just to make sure."

As he recited the instructions, Norton waved a hand and formed the word *Donnie* with his lips. Fleischer caught it and said: "Look, I've done everything you wanted. What about Donnie? ... That's what you say, but how do I know you're telling me the truth? I want some proof he's alive and well."

Fleischer nodded at us. A self-satisfied smile spread across his lips, as if he were proud of his firmness under fire, but then the smile died, and his eyes widened in horror. "No, no, don't do that! Please! No, no, I'll do it your way."

Fleischer took the phone away from his ear and looked at us

blankly. "The bastard. The dirty bastard. He said if I wanted proof, he'd send one of Donnie's fingers. The one with the ring I gave him for his birthday."

He started to put the receiver down, but Norton seized his wrist before he could hang up. "Sorry," Fleischer said. "I forgot."

Norton handed the phone to a young agent named Matthews and told him to see if the phone company had trapped the call, then said: "I don't like it, but we don't have any options."

He went across the room to the table on which a large map of the area was spread. He ran his finger down the index. "Terrace, Terrace, here it is. It's in Cathedral City." He traced his finger over the map. "The only dead end off Valley Vista is Channel. The gates must be there."

"He said I'd see some big concrete sewer pipes in front of them," Fleischer said. "I'm supposed to throw the money over the gates. He said it should take me ten minutes to get there, but that he'd give me an extra ten, in case something happened."

Fleischer's brother stood up abruptly. "Let me go, Simon."

"No. He said *me*. By myself."

"He won't be able to tell us apart in the dark—"

"That's right," Lainie said, nodding frantically. "Zach can do it. You're not well enough, darling. It's too much of a strain—"

Fleischer took her hand off his arm. "We're wasting time."

Norton said to Garth: "Take the suitcase to the car."

Garth shuffled out with the suitcase, and we all followed. Norton put the money on the front seat of the Seville and went to the gray Ford. He opened the trunk and pulled out a twelve-gauge pump-action shotgun. Fleischer pointed at the gun. "What's that for? I told you nobody goes with me."

"But—"

"We've already gone through this. No."

Norton shook his head at Garth, then sighed in resignation.

He removed a .38 Police Special from the holster at the small of his back and said: "Okay. But at least take this."

Fleischer looked at the gun blankly, then reached for it. He tucked it into his waistband and got into the car.

Norton bent down to the window. "We'll be monitoring you all the way. If you need help, just say so. Somebody will get to you right away."

Fleischer nodded stiffly and started the car. He slammed the Seville into reverse and peeled out of the driveway. Norton watched him go, then said: "Garth, you drive. Let's move."

I got into the back seat of the Ford, and Norton and Garth sat up front. There was a map there, and Norton spread it out on his lap. As Garth started the car, Matthews came through the garage door. "No go," he told Norton. "The call must have come from one of the exchanges that aren't covered yet."

Norton nodded, his face registering nothing, and pointed a finger at Garth. "Okay. Let's get this show on the road."

The electronic gates all seemed to be moving in slow motion, and it took us two days to get out of Tamarisk. The taillights of the Seville were nowhere in sight when we turned onto Frank Sinatra Drive.

Norton turned on the interior light and picked up the microphone from the dash. "All units. This is Abel-One. The drop site is Channel Road, Cathedral City. A gate with a NO TRESPASSING sign, concrete sewer pipe in front of it. Pickup will be on the other side of the gate. The money is on its way. All units get into position."

The road dipped, and as we approached the highway, we picked up Fleischer's first transmission. "I'm at Van Fleet in Cathedral City. Traffic is bad."

We turned onto the highway and drove into town, and the traffic immediately turned to molasses. The night crawlers were out in force, and the gay bars and shit-kicker watering holes were doing a land-office business.

We hit a red light in the middle of town, and Garth banged his palm angrily on the steering wheel. "Come on, change. Change."

"I'm turning left on Cathedral Canyon Drive," Fleischer said.

Norton looked at Garth. "We're falling too far behind him."

"What do you want me to do?" Garth snapped back, waving a hand at the light.

The light finally changed, and we took off, but we did not get far. The two lanes ahead were clogged by a camper and a lowered metal-flake-blue Chevy filled with six Mexicans. The two cars crept along side by side at twelve miles an hour, oblivious to the fact that the world was behind them, waiting to pass. The back of the camper was plastered with stickers from various national parks, and one on the back said: DON'T TAILGATE.

Garth hit his horn and rode up the camper's exhaust pipe, but the driver was obviously not the type to take a hint. We went on like that for a while, and then the Chevy accelerated, and Garth swung into the lane behind it. As soon as he did, the driver slowed down again. A toy dog sat in the back window of the Chevy, bobbing its head up and down at us mockingly.

"Fucking beaners," Garth muttered.

"I'm on Terrace now," Fleischer said.

I looked at my watch. Fleischer had been gone eight minutes. Garth kept banging his hands on the steering wheel. Inspector Norton's face looked like a plaster mask in the rearview mirror.

At the next intersection the Chevy signaled and turned right, and Garth punched it, barely missing the bumper of the car ahead of us, and cut in front of the camper. The driver of the camper hit his horn and turned on his brights. "Fuck you, buddy," Garth said, flipping him off.

"I've reached the fence"—Fleischer's voice broke in—"and the road is curving around to the left. . . . Wait."

Norton leaned forward, his body tense.

"There's a dirt road that runs along the fence and bears to the left."

Norton consulted the map quickly. "I don't see any other road."

"I'm staying on the regular road," Fleischer said.

"Good," Norton said softly.

We sailed through a yellow light, and Garth said: "Cathedral Canyon is just up ahead."

Fleischer's voice crackled over the speaker. "I'm crossing a street called Grandview. Wait a minute. I'm not on Terrace anymore. This street is called Charlesworth." His voice was swelling with intensity. "He didn't say anything about any Charlesworth. He said take Terrace to Valley Vista. He said the road that goes along the fence, but I can't see the fence. It's to my right somewhere, but I can't see it. There are only houses here. I'm going back to the dirt road."

Norton looked up from the map. "He didn't go far enough. Valley Vista is up farther."

"I'm turning around."

Norton slapped the map violently. "Don't turn around! Shit!"

The light at Cathedral Canyon was red for us, of course. Garth put on his signal and got into the turning lane.

"I'm at the dirt road," Fleischer was saying. "This must be it. It follows the fence. There are some houses. No, wait. There's a sign. . . . This is a private road."

I leaned forward over the front seat to hear better.

"It's a dead end. It's a goddamn dead end, and there are no gates. I must not have gone far enough on the other road. I'm turning around. . . ."

I looked at my watch. "Twelve minutes."

"I'm—I'm not moving. My back tires are stuck in the sand. I'm putting it in reverse. Jesus Christ! The car—oh, no. The car is stuck! It's stuck!"

"Shit," Norton said, slugging his leg with a fist. "He's goddamn coming apart. I had a feeling something like this was going to happen. I never should've let him go alone."

Cathedral Canyon ran up the hill and dead-ended in a cinder-block wall. Garth turned right onto a dark street lined with shake-roofed tract homes. There was no traffic at all, and Garth must have been doing sixty by the time the road steepened and climbed into the foothills. From our vantage point, Cathedral City did not look so bad. It spread out below us like phosphorescent foam.

There was a tense, silent lapse, and then Fleischer's voice filled the inside of the car: "The car is stalled! It won't start! It won't start!"

We could hear him turning over the ignition again and again.

"He's freaking out," Norton said through clenched teeth. "He's going to have a goddamn heart attack if we don't get to him. Step on this piece of shit!"

Our headlights caught the steel of a cyclone fence up ahead, and Garth kept his foot to the floor as the road curved away from it. I leaned forward, my eyes straining to pierce the darkness.

"There it is!" I shouted, pointing to the dirt road. It veered off to our right about fifty yards ahead, and Garth did not bother to slow down as we left the concrete. All three of our heads slammed into the headliner of the car as we hit a deep rut in the road, and Norton screamed for Garth to take it easy.

The red of the Cadillac's taillights glowed just ahead, and Garth slammed on the brakes. We skidded to a stop, and the three of us hit the doors at the same time and ran though the thick cloud of dust made by our sudden stop to the Seville.

Fleischer was still trying to start the car, like a man in a trance. "You've flooded it," I said. "Let it sit. You'll kill the battery."

"The gates," he said, hitting the key again. "We have to find the gates."

He was fixated on turning the ignition key like an aberrant

laboratory animal. He paid no attention to me. I grabbed his arm to stop him, then said as gently as I could: "We have to get the car out first. Let me try."

He looked up at me with glazed eyes. They seemed to be trying to recognize who was talking to him. He was in shock.

I tugged his arm gently, and he came out of the car. "The gates. . . ."

"Get him back to your car," I told Garth quietly.

As Garth and Norton helped Fleischer, I walked back and inspected the rear wheels. They were sunk almost to the hubcaps in soft sand. He had obviously panicked trying to get himself out and managed only to dig himself in deeper.

I took off my coat and jammed it down in front of one of the tires, then ran over to where Garth and Norton were easing Fleischer into the Ford. "Give me your coats."

Norton looked up. "What for?"

"I need some traction to get that car out of there."

"We don't have time for that now," he snapped. "It's already been twenty minutes."

"He said the black Seville," I said. "If he sees a gray Ford, he might panic."

"All right, but if it doesn't work, we're going to have to use the Ford. There won't be any choice."

They peeled off their coats, and I ran back and stuffed them in front of the tires. I jumped in the car and hit the ignition. The engine turned over but wouldn't fire up. I tried it again. Norton came trotting over. "What's wrong?"

"He's flooded it," I said. "We're going to have to wait a couple of minutes."

"We don't have a couple of minutes."

The car was a few feet away from a backyard fence, and behind it a dog was barking furiously. "Shut the fuck up," I said.

Norton's head jerked around, as if it had been slapped. "The dog," I said.

I hit the ignition again. The engine sputtered and coughed, then caught. I pumped the accelerator twice to make sure it stayed alive, then put it in gear and gave it just a little gas. The car rocked forward, then rolled backward, and the tires began to find traction as the coats were pulled underneath them. Garth and Norton ran behind and began pushing and the car rolled free.

I leaned out of the door and shouted: "Okay, now where do I go?"

"Up to Valley Vista, hang a right," Norton said. "Go to Channel, make a left. That should put you back along the fence. The gates should be there. Look for the concrete sewer pipes stacked up in front of them."

I nodded and lead-footed the accelerator. All the way down the dirt road I cursed the car's spongy suspension; then I hit the concrete and spun the wheel sharply to the right and nearly lost control of the beast. The car fishtailed, but I cut the wheel into the drift, and it righted itself just before I hit somebody's mailbox.

The ascent of the road sharpened, and I crossed two more streets. I was at Valley Vista. "Turning on Valley Vista," I said to the microphone on the visor.

The fence was ahead of me now, fifty yards and closing. A street sign just in front of it said CHANNEL. So far so good. I turned left, and the road steepened. I slowed down, looking for the gates.

A dirt embankment rose behind the fence and dropped into a sandy wash. The moon hung over the landscape like a yellowed skull.

About a quarter mile up the hill I spotted a padlocked gate and stopped. There were no concrete pipes in front of it. There was nothing in front of it. Son of a bitch.

"There's a gate here," I said, "but no pipes. Maybe there's another gate farther up. I'm going to see."

A half mile up, the road ended in a half-finished housing project. I stopped and stared at the wooden frames. They looked like skeletons in the moonlight. Tonight everything reminded me of death. "This can't be it," I told whoever was listening. "I'm going back to the gate."

I hung a U and went back to the gate and stopped in front of it. I started to get out of the car, and then my hand touched something cold and hard on the seat next to me. The gun. I picked it up and tucked it into my belt and turned off the headlights. I got out of the car.

Down the hill the dog was still barking. The breeze that blew against my face felt cold, but I knew it was really warm. My whole body was clammy with sweat. I wondered what eyes were watching me from the darkness, if any eyes were watching me at all.

I bent down and inspected the ground in front of the gate. The dirt was marked by large circular indentations, as if something heavy had been standing there recently. Something like sections of concrete pipe. That could have been it, I reasoned. The pipes might have been there when the kidnapper had checked—probably for the building project up the street—then removed some time since. I had to assume that that was what had happened. I didn't have any choice. There wasn't any time left. There hadn't been any time left ten minutes ago.

I opened the door of the car and lugged the suitcase over to the gate, grunting. I never realized how heavy $400,000 could be. I swung it with both hands from the knees, once, twice, then let it go.

It sailed over the fence, and I watched as it hit on the other side with a dull thud. It must not have been one of those suitcases they dropped from airplanes on television because when it hit the ground, the latch broke open, spilling money out all over the sand. Several of the paper bands holding the money together broke on impact, and the breeze picked up the loose bills and scattered them across the desert floor.

Leave it to the government, I thought, to put $400,000 in a cheap suitcase.

I stood there, my mind torn about what to do, but then I said to hell with it, I couldn't hang around any longer, we were already way overtime. I got back in the car and drove back to the dirt road.

As I pulled up behind the Ford, Norton trotted up to the car. He had a walkie-talkie in his hand. "You found it okay?"

"I sure as hell hope so."

"Garth is going to take Fleischer back. He doesn't look so hot. He'll take the Seville, just in case somebody is watching to make sure it comes back down the hill."

I nodded and got out, and Garth eased Fleischer out of the front seat of the Ford and helped him to the Cadillac.

"Come on," Norton said to me, and moved off. We hurried, crouched down along the fence. About three hundred yards up, there was a hole in it, and I followed him through it, and we flattened down against the ground.

We were on the dirt embankment that ran along the edge of the wash, another three hundred yards or so from the money. From there we had a good view of the whole wash. It was a wide flash-flood channel, dotted with boulders and creosote bushes, flanked by mountains on the other side.

Norton picked up the walkie-talkie and said quietly: "This is Inspector Norton. All units in position, report."

Five responses came back. I looked out at the night, wondering where they were. No cars had come up or down the road since we had arrived. Maybe Norton was commanding an army of invisible men.

We waited.

A thin wisp of cloud moved across the lower part of the moon. The dog was barking again. We waited some more.

"Inspector," a voice said over the walkie-talkie.

Norton jerked the instrument up. "This is Inspector Norton."

"This is Garroway, Inspector. I'm about half a mile down from the drop site. I've picked up some movement in the wash. It looks like a man on foot. He's about a hundred yards away from me, and he's moving up the wash toward the money."

"Can you get an ID?"

"Negative. He's too far away. Male Caucasian, young, fairly tall; that's all I can determine. He's got a stocking cap on. Wait. He's stopped. Now he's moving again."

"Looks like this is it," Norton said, his voice tense.

Then something broke the silence, a distant buzzing, like a swarm of angry bees, and the inspector's body stiffened.

"The man has stopped again," Garroway said. "He's gone behind a rock. I can't see him anymore. There are . . . wait . . . I can see headlights coming up the wash. It looks like . . . Jeeps or dune buggies. . . . It *is* dune buggies. Three of them."

"Can you see the man?" Norton asked him urgently. "What about the man?"

"Negative. He hasn't come out from behind the rock."

I could see the headlights now, moving in erratic arcs up the wash. The buzzing got louder and louder until it turned into a throaty growl as the motors labored in the soft sand.

They passed by us, and I got a good look at them. They were Bandidos, one of the two-passenger type of buggies used in off-road racing, built low to the ground and protected by a full roll cage. As well as their normal headlights, they each had a pair of high-intensity Lucas lamps mounted on top, and the entire desert seemed to be crystallized in their calcinated glare. Human voices drifted up the sides of the wash, whooping and hollering as the buggies spun doughnuts in the sand.

Norton watched them go by and said through clenched teeth: "What the hell else could go wrong? That's all we need now, a bunch of fucking dune buggiers. Go, go on, just keep going. . . ."

I held my breath as the headlights of one of the vehicles struck the suitcase and then veered off. I let it out with a sigh of relief, but then sucked it up again when the lights made a wide circle and doubled back. The driver of the buggy stopped in front of the money and hit his horn to attract the others.

Norton struck the ground with his fist. "Shit, shit, shit!" That seemed to get it all out of him. He picked up the walkie-talkie and said: "Garroway, what about the man?"

"Negative. No movement now."

Norton turned to me, his eyes filled with a helpless rage. "We have to move. If those people take off through the desert with that money, we may never get it back. Those goddamn machines don't even have license plates. We'd never be able to trace them."

He said into the walkie-talkie: "Garroway, you keep your infrared scope trained on that rock. Those buggiers have found the money. I'm going down to lift it off them. All units, I want both ends of the wash sealed off, in case they get by us. All four-wheel-drive vehicles stand by to intercept. No sirens and no lights. Okay, let's move."

He set the walkie-talkie down on the ground and said to me: "You ready?"

"I've always wanted to be an Israeli commando."

"Now's your chance," he said. "Just remember one thing, we don't know who those people are down there, so don't get loose. We'll come up behind them: that way we'll be out of their lights. Above all, it's got to be done quietly. No noise."

"Right," I said, and took the .38 from my waistband.

We scrambled down the bank and ran bent over toward the lights. The soft sand was like mush, and it did not take long before my breathing was labored. We ran a zigzag pattern from creosote bush to creosote bush until we were about fifty feet from the buggies, and then Norton stopped me and indicated he was going to circle around and come in from the other side. I gave him a few minutes to get into position and ran in a crouch to the back of the closest buggy.

The drivers had parked to form a semicircle of light around the money, and all of the riders were inside it, talking excitedly. There were three men and two women and a young boy who could not have been more than thirteen. They all wore jeans and windbreakers, and several of them had on billed caps. In the glare of the spotlights they looked like some motley assemblage.

I crawled alongside the buggy and looked inside. The interior was stripped down to essentials: a dashboard, two seats, and a gearbox. There were no weapons and no compartments one could be hidden in.

"Who do you think left it here?" one of the females asked in a shrill voice.

"How the shit should I know?" answered a tall, sandy-haired man. He was one of the men with a cap. "Who cares anyway? Let's just take it and get the hell out of here."

"Les can carry it in his lap," another said. "We'll all meet back at my house and figure it out there. Who knows who might come back for it? It might be some kind of Mafia payoff or a dope buy or something."

"Maybe we'd better leave it," the woman suggested.

"Leave it my ass," the man shot back. "Let's just get it in the car and get the hell out of here."

I peeked around the tire. The sandy-haired man closed up the suitcase and, while the others chattered their agreement with the decision, picked it up and started toward me. When he got up alongside the buggy, I leaned out from behind the tire and leveled the .38 at his chest. "Just stay like that, mister. I don't want to see you fucking blink."

I did not have to worry about that. His eyes were like saucers. Up close, I saw that his cap had a patch on it that said "CAT." The man stared at the gun and whined: "We weren't gonna keep it, mister, honest. We just found it. We won't tell anybody, I swear. Just don't hurt us."

"Shut up," I told him. "Just walk on over here, out of the light." When he got behind the buggy, I said: "Now put the suitcase down, and put your hands on top of the car."

The man did as he was told, and I came up behind him and frisked him quickly. I stepped back from him just as the thirteen-year-old came up, kicking sand. "Hey, Dad, what are you—"

He saw me, and the sentence died in his mouth, but the mouth stayed open. "Over here," I told him.

"Please, mister," CAT-hat started again. "Please don't hurt us. I swear we won't tell anybody."

"Nobody is going to hurt you," I said, feeling guilty now for frightening them. Some Israeli commando. Able to strike fear in the heart of any thirteen-year-old boy.

Norton scrambled up behind me, a .38 in his hand. "Everything under control?"

I nodded. "He's clean."

CAT-hat still had his hands on top of the car. He said over his shoulder: "Look, man, we can't identify you. I swear none of us got a good look—"

"Turn around," Norton said, cutting him off.

The man turned around slowly, and Norton flashed his ID in the light. "We're with the FBI. I want to see some identification."

"Yes, sir," the man said, letting out a sigh of relief. "Thank God. I thought you guys were dope dealers or something."

He dug into his back pocket and came up with a wallet, and Norton opened it. "All right, Mr. Ferguson," he said. "I want you to get back in your car and drive down the wash just the way you came up. You will be met by FBI agents on the way down. We have this entire wash sealed off, so don't get any bright ideas about taking off. It wouldn't do you any good, even if you made it out, which you wouldn't. We know who you are and where you live."

"But we haven't done nothing," the man protested.

"I know that," Norton said. "Just do what I tell you to do."

"Yes, sir, yes, sir," CAT-hat said. He pointed at his wallet. "What about my wallet?"

"You'll get it back."

The man licked his lips. He obviously did not like it, but he was not about to argue about it. "Come on, Les, get in the car."

The two of them climbed quickly into the car and started the engine with a roar. CAT-hat pulled his buggy around in a circle and started back down the wash, and the other two followed. We stood watching their taillights get smaller as they bounced across the desert floor. "They'll be in custody by the time we get below," Norton said. "I didn't know how else to handle it."

"What about the money?" I asked.

"All we can do is leave it and hope the guy is still around and hope that he's even crazier than we think he is."

"Why is that?"

"Because," he said, picking up the case, "only a crazy man would touch it now."

FIFTEEN

Norton put the phone down and looked over the room. "He didn't take it. They're picking it up now."

Fleischer stared at the FBI man and blinked. His eyes were sunken and bloodshot, and his face looked jaundiced in the weak yellow light that seeped through the living-room curtains. "My boy is dead."

"We don't know that," Norton said. "That's a lot of money to walk away from. Personally I don't think he's going to do it."

Fleischer shook his head weakly, then buried his face in his hands. "He's dead."

Zach reached over and touched his brother's back. "You can't think that way, Simon—"

Lainie moved from her chair and put her arm around her husband's shoulders. "We have to keep hoping. We can't give up hope. He's still alive. I *know* he's still alive."

"We have to go on that assumption," Norton said firmly.

Fleischer's head snapped up suddenly, and he glared hotly at Norton. His eyes were like two smoldering bits of coal that had burned their way into his face. "You blew it, Norton. You were in charge, and you blew it. You're responsible for my boy's death."

"Look, Mr. Fleischer," the inspector said in a patient tone, "I know how you must feel, but we can't give way to panic now. What happened out there couldn't be helped—"

"Like *hell* it couldn't!" Fleischer thundered, wheeling around in a drunken motion. "You never should have sent your people in. Now he thinks we set a trap for him. You told me the plan was *No Interference.* We were going to make the payoff just like he wanted it and get Donnie back. All your men were supposed to do was write down license numbers, not go charging in like a herd of wild buffalo."

"We moved as quickly and quietly as possible under the conditions we were confronted with. If we hadn't moved when we did, those people could have gotten away, and then we wouldn't have had either Donnie or the money—"

"Don't you *understand?*" Fleischer interrupted, waving his arms wildly. "I don't *care* about the goddamn money. I've *got* more money. I've only got one son. Besides, how do you know those people in the dune buggies weren't in on it?"

Norton shook his head. "We've checked them out. They were just three families out for a night run in the desert. They do it all the time. They just happened to be at the wrong place at the wrong time."

Fleischer's eyes narrowed. "Yeah? Well, you lucked out. You couldn't have known that at the time."

"The probabilities were with us—"

"You don't play probabilities with my son's life."

"All I can tell you, Mr. Fleischer, is that these things happen. It's nobody's fault, and it can't be changed now. $400,000 is a lot of money to walk away from, and I don't think this joker is going to. Our main concern now is not to fix blame on who screwed up, but how we're going to convince him when he calls back that it was not our fault and that everything is still go. We're going to have to assure him that we'll cooperate with him one hundred percent."

Fleischer's eyes narrowed, distilling their fire. "*We* won't have to do anything. I'm going to call up the director if I have to, but I want somebody else in charge of this case."

Norton stared at him. "Look, Mr. Fleischer—"

"No, *you* look," Fleischer said, standing up and stabbing a finger at him. "You handled this job like a rank amateur, and I'm holding you personally responsible. You can't offer me any excuse for what happened. None."

Norton started to say something but clamped his jaw down on it. A silent tension stretched between them. To break it, I stood up and said: "Everybody's nerves are on edge right now. It's not the time to be making rash decisions."

Fleischer glowered at me and turned away. Norton said nothing.

"In the meantime," I continued, "I'm going to get cleaned up and try to grab a couple of hours' sleep. I suggest everybody else do the same. If anything happens, it probably won't be until tonight." To Norton, I said: "You want to drop me at my car?"

I told Fleischer I would be back before noon and went out to the garage with Norton. When we got into the car, I said: "I wouldn't take too much notice of what he said in there. He was just worked up."

He stared thoughtfully out the window. "Maybe he's right. Maybe I did screw it up."

"I was there," I said. "There wasn't anything anybody could have done. Fleischer was striking out, that's all. He's being eaten away by guilt. He never paid any attention to his kid, and now, suddenly, it's 'my baby, my baby.' Only it's too little, too late, and he knows it."

"You're a fine one to be distributing painkillers. You're the one who got into this because he felt responsible, remember?"

"And I still do," I said. "That kid is still out there, and one thing he doesn't need is for us to be sitting around whining in self-pity." To take his mind off it, I said: "Did you check out the Cleveland kidnapping story?"

He nodded. "That's all it was, a story. The Mafia stuff seems to be all bunk, too. The kid made it up." That seemed to snap him out of it. He looked at me. "You sure you can't ID that voice?"

I shook my head. "The voice on that tape could be McMurtry's, but I just can't tell for sure. It sounds like he had a handkerchief stuffed in his mouth. What I find strange is that your agents didn't spot McMurtry's car around the drop area."

"He walked up the wash," he said. "He must have parked way below somewhere."

"I suppose," I said. "So now it starts all over again?"

"Let's hope so. For that kid's sake, let's hope to God that's exactly what happens."

He started the car and was backing out when Garth came through the door of the house and called: "Inspector!"

We stopped, and Garth trotted to the car. "He's letting Donnie go," he said excitedly. "He just called."

Fleischer and Lainie were hugging each other tearfully when we came in, and Zach stood by watching them with a wide grin.

"The call came from a Denny's in Indio on Highway eighty-six," Haber said as he hung up the red phone. "We've got units on the way."

"Thank God, thank God," Fleischer kept saying. Tears rolled down his cheeks and splashed onto his collar.

Norton pointed at the recorder. "Let's hear it."

Garth stepped over to the machine and turned it on. There was a silent pause, and then Fleischer's voice said: "Hello?"

"Fleischer?" It was the same voice as on the other tape, and it still sounded as if he had a handkerchief in his mouth. "You called the cops. You shouldn't have done that."

"No, I swear—"

"Don't bother to lie about it. I *know.*"

"I have the money," Fleischer said rapidly. "I still have it. It wasn't our fault things went wrong. Some people—"

"Save it. It doesn't matter now anyway. Take this down: Jackson and Sixty-first Avenue. That's in Coachella."

"You want me to bring the money there?"

"No. That's where you'll find Donnie."

A pause. "I—I'm not sure I understand—"

"Your kid is there, Fleischer. I'm letting you have him."

"He's all right?" Fleischer asked anxiously.

"He's fine."

"You didn't hurt him?"

"No. He's not hurt. He's fine. Jackson and Sixty-first."

There was a double click and then a dial tone. Garth switched off the machine. "Okay," Norton said. "Let's roll."

Fleischer stepped in front of him. "I'm going, too."

"I don't think that would be such a good idea, Mr. Fleischer, until we find out what's there."

"He told me what's there. My son is there. And I'm going to be there with him." His voice was quietly determined. "I may have made some mistakes with Donnie, but I'm not going to make this one. I'm going to show him I'm there when he needs me."

"I'm going, too," Lainie said.

"All right, all right," Norton said, throwing up his arms in surrender. "Garth, you drive them."

Garth, Lainie, Fleischer, and Zach hustled out, and I stayed back with Norton while he issued some instructions to Haber. As we were about to leave, the red phone rang, and Norton picked it up. He listened, and dark lines of worry crossed his face. "That was all? Yeah, okay, thanks."

He hung up and stood grimly staring at the instrument.

"What was that all about?" I asked.

"That was the command post. McMurtry just called home."

"What'd he say?"

" 'I'm sorry.' That was it. Just 'I'm sorry.' I guess he said it a few times."

"How do you know it was McMurtry?"

"I don't have to. Mona Talbott knew. She said, 'Gerry, Gerry, where are you?' But he'd already hung up."

I didn't like the sound of it. "What do you think it means?"

"I wish to hell I knew," he said.

Garth had the Lincoln out in the street waiting for us when we pulled out, and he let us go in front. The sky had lightened into a washed-out yellow. We were driving east, into the sunrise. That was supposed to be a symbol of hope. At least it had been in every bad B movie I had ever seen.

We turned onto the highway and drove past a strip of elaborate restaurants built to look like Japanese pagodas and Spanish haciendas and railroad stations, past the mansions of Thunderbird Estates that sat on the hill behind guarded gates like temples devoted to the worship of money, through the commercial section of Rancho Mirage. We sailed through Palm Desert at seventy, and then the buildings turned into sagebrush and sand, offering a brief glimpse of what had been here ten years ago and wouldn't be in another one.

Just outside Indio a sign said JACKSON STREET, and Norton slowed down and signaled. About a mile after the turn he pulled off onto the shoulder and parked in front of a clump of paloverde. Garth pulled up behind us, and Norton got out of the car and went back to talk to him. When he came back, he said: "I told him to stay here until I give him the word to go."

The road ran straight through a wide, flat agricultural valley rimmed by mountains. Plowed fields alternated with groves of citrus and shaggy stands of date palms, and the air turned humid and thickened with the smells of alfalfa and manure. The fields were already filled with workers getting a head start on the heat of the day.

A couple of miles up, a clump of cars stood at the edge of a date grove. Norton slowed down and stopped behind it. A dozen men in street clothes, some with beards and long hair, stood by the cars, waiting for instructions. Part of the *new* FBI, I guessed.

One who looked more the part, a crew-cut young man who had to be older than his smooth, baby-faced good looks, came over to us as we got out of the car. "Hello, Inspector."

"Hello, Tighe. Tighe, Jacob Asch." We shook hands, and Norton looked past the young agent at the others. "What's the situation?"

Tighe pointed at the date grove. "Not sure. There's a shack in there. I've got it staked out, but I didn't want to move until you got here."

"How many men do we have?"

"Counting you two, thirteen."

"You got an extra gun?"

Tighe went to his car and brought back a Colt Python. He handed it to Norton, who gave it to me. "You do want to go with us?"

"I wouldn't miss it for the world," I told him.

He smiled and turned to Tighe. "I want every window and door covered. I'll take the front door. When I give the word, everyone moves at once."

"Right." Tighe moved off and issued instructions to the others, and they entered the date grove and fanned out in different directions.

Norton got out his pocket transmitter and his Colt, and we lifted a strand of barbed wire on the fence that surrounded the grove for me to step through.

Tangerine trees had been planted between the towering

palms, and the underbrush was almost waist-high with weeds. Clouds of gnats swirled in front of my eyes and sang in my ears. I waved them off, but they just danced away a foot or so and came back at me.

Twenty yards from the shack Norton put his hand on my chest, and we crouched down.

The shack was a small one-room adobe structure. Part of the wooden roof was caved in, and all its windows were smashed. It looked empty.

Norton picked up his transmitter. "How's it going, Tighe?"

"Everyone is in position, Inspector."

"Can you see anything?"

"Nothing."

"Okay," Norton said. "Everybody move in."

We left our cover and made a dash for the house, crouched down. The Magnum felt heavy but nice in my hand. I slammed against the wall by the hinge side of the door and spread out against it, breathing hard. My pulse was pounding, and I was perspiring freely. It was not all from the twenty-yard dash. My stomach quivered nervously.

Norton was on the other side of the door. There was a window behind each of us, and an agent had come up to cover them. The agents kept their eyes on Norton, waiting for the high sign. The inspector carefully set his transmitter on the ground, looked at all of us, then stepped back and kicked the door.

He went in fast, and I was right behind him. Three feet inside, he stopped abruptly and dropped into a crouch, and I nearly fell over his back. I sidestepped and kept my balance, and then the room was filled by the sound of shattering glass as the agents smashed in what was left of the windows. Then, just as suddenly, there was no sound at all. Norton's eyes swept the room from his crouch, and he stood up slowly.

My heart was still pounding; the gun grip felt soapy from the sweat in my palm. The silence was heavy, terrible, but then the sounds began to come back, slowly and one at a time. The buzzing of flies, the rumble of a jet passing overhead, the sounds of the birds outside as they chattered to one another in their own language, like computer language.

Sunlight streamed in through a huge hole in the roof, throwing long shadows across the room. The place was a shambles, filled with pieces of rotten lumber, old crumpled papers, and dirty rags. Some broken pieces of what had once been furniture lay about: table legs, a gutted box spring. In the corner, a sink, blackened with age, stood half torn from the wall. But no Donnie.

Tighe entered the front door with two other agents. Norton probed a plank of old lumber with his foot and said: "I want this place searched. Every inch of it. I want to know if that kid was here."

"Right, Inspector," Tighe said, nodding.

Norton slipped his revolver back into his shoulder holster. His eyes were rimmed with red, and his face was seamed with fatigue. We went out into the daylight, and he looked around at the date grove as if it had betrayed him.

"What do you think?" I asked, tucking the Magnum into my belt.

He shook his head. "I don't know."

"Maybe McMurtry intends to deliver the kid and turn himself in. Maybe he picked this as the meeting spot."

"Maybe," he said as if he did not really believe it. "Let's go back to the car and call Garth. I have to break the news to Fleischer. Let's go out this way. It's closer to the road."

We waded through the grass, and someone called out: "Inspector!"

One of the agents from the house was walking toward us. He didn't seem to be in any hurry about it, so I kept on walking toward the road. Probably wanted advice on a little piece of police procedure.

I ducked through the wire fence and straightened up. A gentle breeze brushed my face, rooting me to the ground. The scent was there, faint but unmistakable. I had smelled that smell many times before. It was a smell you never got used to and one you could never forget.

The foul breeze blew against my cheek again, and for a second I imagined I heard someone giggling. Probably my own thoughts, sneaking up to tap me on the shoulder with long, spidery fingers before scampering back into their dark corners to hide. Sweat stood out all over my forehead. I licked my finger and tested the breeze. It was coming from the north.

A cylindrical concrete irrigation standpipe stood at the northeast corner of the date grove, maybe nine feet tall. With every step toward it the smell grew stronger.

"Over here!" I shouted.

Norton and the other agent came trotting over to the fence. "What is it?"

"Take a whiff," I said.

They smelled the air and looked at each other, then picked their way gingerly through the fence. We all went over to the base of the standpipe. Norton pointed to the iron rungs that ran up its side and told the young agent to go up and take a look.

The man grabbed the bottom rung and went up slowly, hand over hand. He reached the top and looked down inside, and his body shuddered violently. Then he leaned over the side and puked.

"Goddammit," Norton said.

There were tears in his eyes.

SIXTEEN

The face was a creation for a horror movie, a blue-green Halloween mask. The cheeks were bloated and lumpy, the lips black and so swollen they looked like two slabs of liver. The belly had ballooned up from gases, and the maggots had already started their work. You could hear them.

I dropped the blanket back over the face and walked away, fighting the urge to retch. The other agents stood by their cars, as far away from the thing as they could. A lot of them smoked cigarettes, and some had lit pipes in an effort to kill the stench.

Norton approached me. "Well?"

"I can't tell."

"Christ," he said. "Fleischer will go to pieces, he sees the kid like that."

"I can't help it. I only saw him once and then just for a few seconds."

He nodded and looked at the sheriff's black-and-whites that were pulling into position to seal off the road. "I'm no coroner, but there's no rigor. That means he's been dead at least forty-eight hours. Disfigurement like that doesn't start until at least that long, even as hot as it's been. I'll bet the kid was dead an hour after he left Sambo's."

"How do you think he was killed?"

"There's a bullet hole in his head, but we'll have to wait for an autopsy." He looked at his watch, and his expression grew petulant. "Speaking of autopsies, I wonder where the hell the coroner's man is? They said they'd have somebody out here ten minutes ago."

His attention shifted to a spot down the road. I had turned to see what he was looking at when suddenly he broke away from me and started for the sheriff's car blocking the road. "The stupid son of a bitch," he muttered. "I told him to keep them away from here."

Fleischer's Mark V pulled up to the sheriff's unit, and Simon Fleischer stepped out. He spied Norton and started for him, but the young uniformed deputy stepped in front of him, cutting off his progress. "Let me by," Fleischer commanded.

"I'm sorry, sir—"

"I'm the boy's father!" Fleischer screamed, his face red with rage.

"I'm sorry, sir," the deputy said, this time more firmly. "Nobody goes beyond this point."

Lainie and Zach got out of the car, and the deputy, his attention diverted by the movement, turned his head. Fleischer took the opportunity to rush around him. Realizing he had been had, the deputy spun around. "Hey! Hold it!"

Norton had reached Fleischer, his arms outstretched and his palms outward, as if trying to hold up a collapsing wall. "It's all right, Officer!" Norton yelled.

The deputy relaxed and turned back to try to deal with Lainie and Zach.

"Where's Donnie? Where's my son?" Fleischer asked. His voice fluttered with apprehension.

"What happened to Garth?" Norton asked.

"Never mind about Garth. Where's my son?"

Fleischer's head was bobbing over Norton's shoulders as if it were on a string, and his face was pale and wooden, like a painted puppet's. He spied the blanket on the ground by me and pushed Norton out of the way to start toward it. The FBI man grabbed his arm to restrain him, but Fleischer shook off his grip as if possessed by some supernatural strength and rushed over. I would have tried to stop him, but I did not know what I could have done, aside from knocking him down.

Fleischer bent down and lifted one end of the blanket. He gasped and dropped it and staggered back a step. "Donnie. . . . "

His voice was a croaking whisper. I watched as a chalky white ring appeared around his mouth and his face turned ashen gray. "Jesus Christ!" I yelled, and lurched forward, catching him as he fell. "Somebody help me with him! Somebody help me!"

I struggled to hold him up, but I was off-balance; his dead weight was carrying me forward toward the thing under the blanket. I screamed again for help, and someone yanked on Fleischer's other arm, pulling us both backward. I looked up and saw Norton. "Put him down on the ground," I said. "On his back."

We pulled him away from his son's body and set him down easily on the ground. I bent down and put an ear to the man's chest. Nothing. I felt his throat for a pulse. Nothing.

"What is it?" Norton asked, his face white. "His heart?"

"Yeah," I said. "Go call an ambulance. And get Lainie over here."

"Right." He jumped up and ran to his car, and I turned my attention back to Fleischer.

His face was grayer now, almost a pale blue. I ripped open his shirt and dug two fingers in just below his sternum and began pressing upward with the heel of my hand as hard as I could. I tried to time each push to coincide with his breathing, or how he would have been breathing if he were breathing at all. I did that for what seemed like twenty minutes but was probably only two and then felt again for a pulse. Still nothing.

Lainie was standing over me now, crying fitfully and wringing her hands. That made me angry somehow.

"Listen," I said forcefully. "We have to give him mouth-to-mouth. You know how to do that?"

Her eyes darted around uncertainly, but she nodded and bent down. She pinched off his nose and put her mouth over his and began to breathe into it.

"Not so fast," I said. "Take good breaths, and breathe evenly."

She adjusted her breathing, and I kept pushing on his chest, timing each push so that it alternated with her breathing. I pushed down harder, and one of his ribs gave with a loud crack. She looked up at me, startled, but I said: "Just keep breathing, goddammit! Don't stop."

After another minute or so I touched his throat. His pulse was back, irregular, but there beneath my fingers.

Norton ran over. "How is he?"

I looked up and noticed for the first time that a crowd had gathered around us. All the faces appeared featureless, like a characterless crowd of gawkers at an accident, and as I looked around I felt strangely numb, as if coming out of a dream. "He's breathing." My voice sounded tired, far away. "What about the ambulance?"

"It's on its way."

I nodded and kept my fingers on Fleischer's carotid artery. The pulse seemed to be more regular now, and his color had come back a little. I was exhausted and wringing wet. "You wanted to know what else could go wrong?"

Lainie picked that up and looked at me fearfully. Her eyes

160

were full of tears, and her mouth was trembling visibly. "He'll be all right, won't he? He *will* be all right?"

"He'll be fine," I said.

It seemed to me I had used that line on someone, somewhere, recently, but I could not remember when or where. I dropped my gaze down to Fleischer to avoid looking into her searching eyes.

SEVENTEEN

The carpeted waiting room outside the hospital Emergency Room was well stocked with magazines—*Sports Illustrated, U.S. News, Golf Digest*—and a nice hardback assortment of *Bible Stories,* but nobody seemed to feel much like reading, and the magazines only managed to look ridiculously out of place.

Zach Fleischer sat slumped forward in his chair, his elbows on his knees and his eyes glued to the carpet. He had been sitting that way for the past half hour, saying nothing. Lainie in the meantime alternately paced and sat, occasionally breaking into racking sobs, which she tried to stifle with a handkerchief Zach had given her.

Her strength had deserted her hours ago. Her eyes now were quick, frightened animal eyes. At the sound of footsteps they would snap immediately toward the door in fearful anticipation, but then a green-frocked doctor would walk by, looking in no particular hurry, or a nurse would pass, her uniform making crisp rustling sounds as she walked, and Lainie would resume her pacing and sobbing.

She was pacing when a short, balding doctor came into the room. She rushed toward him and said: "How is he, Phil?"

The doctor smiled assuringly and patted her on the arms. "He'll be all right. He's still serious, but his condition has stabilized."

Zach Fleischer slumped back in his chair. "Thank God."

"Can I see him?" Lainie asked.

"I think that might be all right," he said. "But only for a minute. He was asking for you, but I don't want him to get worked up."

Lainie started out with the doctor, then stopped and said to me: "I want to thank you for what you did. Simon would be dead now if it hadn't been for you." She said it reluctantly, almost resentfully, like a six-year-old whose parents had made her apologize to her brother. Then she was gone.

I stood up. "I need a cup of coffee. I'm going to see if I can't find a cafeteria in this joint."

"I'll join you," Zach said.

The corridor was brightly lit and smelled of disinfectant. I stuck my head in the cubbyhole of a nurse's station across from the doors of the Emergency Room and asked where the cafeteria was. One of the nurses said down the hall and to the right.

We were almost to the end of the corridor when Norton came around the corner. There were dark circles under his eyes, and his face was pale and drawn. I didn't know how he was still on his feet. "Asch," he said, and made a quick movement with his head. He said to Zach: "If you'll excuse us for a minute."

We went down the hall out of Zach's hearing, and he said: "I've got one you can ID."

"What do you mean?"

"McMurtry. It looks like they've found him. At least we think it's McMurtry. The sheriff just called me."

"Where?"

"About four miles from the kid."

The smell of disinfectant in the hallway was overwhelming. I felt as if I were being pursued by sickness and death. "Okay."

I went back to tell Zach he would have to have coffee alone, then left with Norton.

Norton had parked in one of the doctors' slots outside the Emergency Room entrance.

The morning heat had collected in the car, creating a furnace. Norton turned on the air conditioning and pulled out of the lot, heading in the opposite direction from where we had found Donnie.

I suddenly remembered Garth, I don't know why. "Whatever happened to Garth? I forgot to ask."

"Fleischer left him. When the sheriff's units started coming, Garth got out of the car and flagged one down to find out what was happening. Fleischer took off and left him. He's going to meet us."

We passed through an especially seedy section of Indio, filled with dirty brick flophouses and discount clothing stores. Half the signs on the stores were in Spanish. We turned onto a four-lane divided highway that paralleled a set of railroad tracks. At Jackson, Norton hung a right, and we bumped over the tracks and drove another half mile or so before turning onto a dirt road. The road was badly cross-washed and ran along the edge of a grove of tangerine trees. After a while we passed a tin-roofed packing shed set back in the orchards and turned left onto another dusty dirt road.

That road was less bumpy and ended in a dirt embankment. A sheriff's black-and-white was parked on the embankment, and two uniformed deputies stood beside it. Norton flashed his ID out the window, and one of the deputies nodded. "The road is only wide enough for one car, and it's getting kind of congested down there, Inspector. I suggest you park it here and walk down."

Norton said fine and swung off to the right and parked. The embankment we were on ran along the edge of a steep-sided concrete canal maybe fifteen feet wide, filled with swift-moving, murky green water. On the far side of the canals stubs of grapevines ran in neat rows toward some low mountains. Above the mountains the sun burned the sky white.

"The Coachella Canal," he said. "It runs off the All-American Canal. The system runs through the whole Imperial and Coachella valleys. It's what has turned this desert into some of the richest farmland in the country."

His voice was flat, and the monologue struck me as curiously incongruous. I felt like a sightseer being conducted on a tour to dusty death.

A group of people were gathered around the cars, some uniformed, some not. Garth was there. When he spotted us, he broke away and came out to meet us.

Garth nodded to me and went right into his spiel. "He was found about half an hour ago by those people." He indicated a chubby Mexican man dressed in farm clothes and a straw hat, standing off to one side with two small brown-faced boys. The man was talking in Spanish to a sheriff's deputy, who stood stone-faced, taking notes. The children seemed totally undisturbed by anything that was going on. They played hide-and-seek behind their father's rotund body and giggled while the man kept swatting at them and telling them to shut up.

"Name's Chacon," Garth went on. "He and his kids came out here to fish. He says they come out here all the time to fish for cats. One of the kids saw McMurtry's car sitting out there and got curious."

"Anybody touch anything?"

"Only the coroner's investigator," Garth said. "He's over there now."

He led us past the line of black-and-whites and unmarked county cars to where McMurtry's black Cutlass stood by itself, both of its doors flung open. A photographer moved around the car, taking pictures of it from all angles. A short, squat man stood nearby, dispassionately taking notes. Garth called him over and introduced him as Sid Cutter, from the coroner's office.

"What does it look like?" Norton asked him.

"Gunshot wound in the head. Probably a twenty-two. There's no exit wound, which means that the bullet probably got busted up by bone. That happens in a lot of these cases because of the angle of the bullet."

"Suicide?"

The coroner's man shrugged. "That would be my guess, but we'll have to wait and see. There's a note there. It might be a suicide note."

"How long's he been dead?" Norton asked.

"Three hours, maybe four."

I went over to the car. The body was slumped over the wheel, and the left hand dangled loosely beside the seat. The face was turned away from me. I went around to the other side to get a better look.

It was McMurtry. He was filthy. His clothes were rumpled and dirty, and his face and hands were streaked with grime. There was a tiny red-black hole in his temple, just in front of the right ear. There was not much blood at all. His right hand lay limply on the seat next to him, and gripped loosely in it was a .22-caliber Iver Johnson revolver, of the Saturday Night Special variety. Next to it were a crumpled piece of paper with some writing on it and a box of Mini-Mag .22-caliber long rifle shells. The box was open, and a few of the shells had spilled out onto the seat.

The car was filled with flies. They kept landing on the wound and on the closed eyes, trying to lay their eggs on the lids, and I shooed them away angrily. I did not know why that seemed important to me. McMurtry's Vision would never be in his eyes anymore. Whatever was left of that had already been committed to canvas.

166

I straightened up and turned to Norton. "It's McMurtry," I said to Cutter. "His grip on the gun is pretty loose. Isn't there usually a death spasm when a person shoots himself in the head?"

"Not necessarily. It happens sometimes; sometimes it doesn't. Nobody knows why."

"Be sure and bag his hands," Norton said. "I want dermal nitrate tests run on them."

"I intended to do that," Cutter said sullenly, as if his intelligence had been insulted. A sensitive coroner.

The man's tone did not seem to affect Norton. He asked blankly: "Pictures already been taken of this?"

"Yeah."

He slipped a pair of tweezers from his coat pocket and used them to pick up the piece of paper from the seat. The handwriting was sloppy, almost an illegible scrawl. There were a few drops of blood on it.

No way out. No matter.
We're even now, Lainie.

Garth handed him a cellophane envelope, and he slipped the note into it. "We'll have to get a sample of McMurtry's handwriting."

Garth took the piece of evidence carefully. "Right."

Norton bent down and peered inside the car. "Asch," he said, "look at this."

On the floor on the passenger's side of the car was a map of the Palm Springs–Indio areas, partially unfolded. Norton used the tweezers to indicate a circle that had been penciled in on it. The drop site.

He gave me a significant, somber look, then told Garth to get some more cellophane envelopes. Garth went to get them, and Norton went back to poking around inside the car with his tweezers.

I suddenly felt nauseated. I stood up and walked away from the car, along the canal. A few steps away the dirt embankment sloped down into a dry cement channel that ran off at right angles from the main canal in both directions. There was a painted iron railing there enclosing some heavy machinery, and I went over and leaned on it.

I found myself looking through a rectangular grate, forty feet straight down. Above the grate was a thick axle wrapped with steel cable. A sign there said:

DANGER   AUTOMATIC EQUIPMENT
SUBJECT TO OPERATION AT ANY TIME

A huge steel door, thick with rust, ran all the way to the bottom of the dry channel bed. Invisible rivulets of water made lonely trickling sounds far below.

I stood there for a while, listening to the water, and then Norton came over. He had a cellophane envelope in his hand, inside which was another piece of paper, smaller than the other. He showed it to me.

The writing was in the same hurried scrawl as the other note:

Mexicana Airlines   Flt. 901   May 17   9 pm

"That was in the glove compartment," he said.

"May seventeenth is tomorrow."

"I don't think he's going to make his flight," he said. "There's a blanket in the trunk with some stains on it that could be blood."

They would be blood. They would be whatever type blood Donnie Fleischer's had been. And the ballistics on the gun in McMurtry's hand would match the bullet that had been put into Donnie's brain. I knew all that. It all fitted together. But it still did not make any sense.

But then nothing made much sense anymore. I had come to

that conclusion the day I was driving down the freeway and realized I was looking up at every overpass to make sure there was not some twelve-year-old sociopath up there grinning down at me with a rock in his hand.

I said to Norton almost testily: "Look, how long do you think you're going to be here?"

He caught my tone. "You don't have to stick around."

"I just don't feel too hot."

"I'll have somebody drive you back to your car."

"Thanks."

Before he turned to go, he said: "By the way, I'm still keeping the lid on this, at least until we find out exactly what we have here."

"What about Mona Talbott?" I asked. "She deserves to know that he's dead, at least. She must be going crazy by this time, after that phone call."

"Don't worry. She'll find out soon enough."

"I know. And I'd rather she heard it from me than somebody else. I owe her that much. After all, she still is my client, at least technically—"

He balked, then said: "By the time you get back to your motel she'll already know. We've had search warrants ready for McMurtry's house and studio ever since we lifted that first print from the note. We didn't move on them only because of the kid. Agents are on the way there right now."

He turned away and strode off with his cellophane envelope. I went back to waiting for the rain of blood, the vermin, the boils. I knew we were the butt of some cosmic joke, that any minute a booming voice would rupture the sky and announce: "This was only a test. If it had been real, you would have been instructed to turn to ten-forty on your radio dial and wait for further instructions. This was only a test."

I waited, but there was nothing. Only the sound of trickling water, far below me.

EIGHTEEN

There was a message in my key slot at the desk when I got back to the motel. Detective McDonald of the Palm Springs Police Department had called at 12:10 P.M. and wanted me to get in touch with him as soon as I returned. It was important, the message said. I used the pay phone outside to call the number on the message. McDonald answered right away.

He sounded glad I called. He told me he had something that he thought might interest me and asked if we could meet somewhere for coffee. The suggestion of coffee made me realize that I had not eaten in about fifteen hours, so I told him I would meet him in an hour at Lindy Lou's, a coffee shop just down the street from the Royal Western.

I hung up and stood there, thinking about making the call. I thought about it for a long time, then finally picked up the phone again and got the long-distance operator.

Mona's voice was a hysterical song in my ears. "Jake, where are you? I've been trying to find out where you are for days. What's this all about? The FBI has been here. They said . . . it couldn't be true. . . ."

Her voice trailed off momentarily, and I tried to jump in, but she did not seem to hear me. "It . . . they said . . . Gerry couldn't have done what they said. He couldn't, he couldn't be dead. Not Gerry. It has to be somebody else—"

"It's not somebody else."

"But—"

"Mona, now *listen to me.* You're going to have to get a grip on yourself—"

"They were here looking through everything. They took some things away. Some papers and things. But it couldn't be true what they said. Gerry never could have killed anyone. Not a child. A *child,* Jake. He never could have done that—"

"Mona. *MONA!*"

Then her voice broke, and there was only the sound of her tears on the other end. I waited until her crying had quieted down to sniffles and nose blowing. That took a few minutes. "You're going to have to come down here as soon as you can. You've got to claim the body. Do you understand me?"

There was a pause. "Yes."

"Okay. I'm going to call Howard Winter. He can drive you down. If he can't, I'll come and get you."

I told her to get a pencil and paper, and she sniffled and said to wait a minute and put the phone down. When she got back on the line, I told her where I was staying, then hesitated.

I did not want to get her started again, but I wanted the answer to the question, and I wanted it now. "One more question, Mona. Did Gerry own a gun?"

"No. Of course not. He hated guns."

"Okay. Now, just take it easy and try to get a grip on yourself. Try not to think about any of it. You have any friends you can call?"

"No." There were no more sobs or sniffling. Her voice was soft and steady. "I'll be fine, don't worry."

I hung up and got the number of Winter's gallery from long-distance information and called it. Susan Lamb answered. She said Winter had not been in all morning, but she expected him soon. I gave her my number at the hotel and told her that it was absolutely urgent that I get in touch with him as soon as possible. I told her that if he checked in, she should relay a number to me where he would be. She promised to do that.

The swimming pool was packed with people lying on chaise lounges or floating on rafts, soaking up the rays; and passing by all those greased, healthy-looking bodies, all dark-skinned and white-toothed, I felt contaminated, leprous.

Up in my room I flung off my clothes and sat naked on the edge of the bed, staring at the phone. My stomach was queasy; my hands were shaking. The last few days had gotten to me more than I cared to admit to myself. I was shell-shocked, battle-weary, overwhelmed by feelings of emptiness and futility. The barren walls of the motel room merely amplified my feeling of being totally alone. I needed to feel the touch of healing hands, to hear the sound of a sympathetic voice.

I thought of calling Erica but realized immediately that would be like a man caught in a riptide calling a shark for help. I tried to think of someone else to call, someone whose voice I wanted to hear, but could not come up with a name.

I went into the bathroom and turned on the shower as hot as I could stand it and stood under the spray for a long time, trying to lather away the taint of death that seemed to have seeped into my pores. I shaved and doused myself with cologne, but the smell kept coming back to me. Hoping nobody else could smell it, I slipped into a clean pair of jeans and a sports shirt and left the room.

The waitress at the coffee shop had already refilled my cup twice when I looked up and saw McDonald standing in the doorway. I didn't recognize him at first. He wore a double-breasted beige suit over a pale yellow dress shirt and a dark brown tie. His shoes were two-tone patent leather, chocolate brown and tan.

He came over and put the manila envelope he was carrying on the table and pulled up a chair.

"What's the occasion?" I asked, indicating his attire.

He plucked at his lapels. "This? I had to go to court this morning. An asshole I pinched for burglary is on trial, and I had to testify."

He put his elbows on the table, causing the sleeves of his coat to slide past his french cuffs. His cuff links were two tiny silver derringers. I pointed to them and said: "That's a cute touch."

He smiled at me and winked. "The troops dig it."

Our waitress was a plain-looking young girl whose only outstanding attribute was her hair. It looked as if it had taken a couple of carpenters three days to put up. She filled our cups, and I ordered sausage and eggs, and McDonald told her just coffee. She nodded as if she had known all the time that was what he was going to have and left.

"How was your Swinging Singles convention?" I asked.

"About normal. Right after we got there, some guy and a chick did a sixty-nine on the high dive. He fell off and missed the water. Broke his collarbone."

"What about the rape?"

"Pretty much how I figured it," he said, shrugging. "The broad dropped a few too many Quaaludes and decided to pull a train. After the fourth guy she got tired; only things were rolling by then. She got pissed off when she found out it was a runaway."

"What happened?"

"I convinced her she wouldn't come out looking too good in court if she pressed charges."

I nodded and looked at the front doors. A sunken-cheeked old man had come in and was trying to make it to one of the tables with the aid of a metal walker and a nurse. He looked as if he were having a time of it. His mouth was open slightly, and his eyes stared straight ahead, unblinking and vacant.

The ones that didn't come here for the sex and the dope and the fast life came here to die, I thought. They worked all their lives and scrimped and saved so they could come to Palm

Springs and spend their last few years like that, shuffling along with spittle dripping from their lips. Half of them probably hadn't seen the insides of their bathrooms in years. There was no need. They just walked outside and threw away the bags, all neat, clean, prepackaged. They had great lawns, though. The grass grew real good in Bypass City.

I sipped my coffee, feeling as if I had had a life bypass.

"I heard about the Fleischer kid," McDonald said. "Too bad."

"Yeah."

"Do they think it's McMurtry?"

I shrugged. "The way it looks is McMurtry flipped out and killed the kid, then decided he wanted to live after all and tried to arrange a payoff so he could get away. When the payoff got botched, he couldn't see any way out. He must have known by that time that the cops had him figured for it. So he called his girl friend to say his farewells, then called the Fleischers to tell them where they could find the kid."

He nodded as if it all made sense to him. "How's the old man doing?"

"His doctor seems to think he'll be all right after he recuperates for a while."

"How about the wife? Lainie? How's she taking it?"

There was something in his tone that made me think there was more in the question than the question itself. "Not too good. Why?"

He sipped his coffee. "Anybody figure out yet what set McMurtry off?"

"No."

The corners of his mouth turned up in a self-satisfied smirk, and he slid the manila envelope across the table to me. "Take a look at that, but not here. And you didn't get it from me."

"What is it?"

"A copy of an arrest report from 1972. Section 273a of the

174

California Penal Code. Felony child abuse. Guess who?"

"Lainie?"

"Bingo."

He draped one arm casually over the back of his chair and said: "You know, the first time I saw that broad up at the Fleischer house, when she was raising all that shit about McMurtry, something about her bothered me. I knew I'd seen her before, but I couldn't pin it down. Then yesterday it clicked. It was the name that threw me. The name on the report was Ellison, and I didn't put it together. I didn't know McMurtry had changed his name, and I only knew her maiden name was Bowen."

"What happened?"

"A woman who lived in the apartment below her heard the kid screaming one day. At first she didn't do anything about it because she'd heard the kid scream before. This time the kid kept it up, so she went upstairs and knocked, but nobody answered. So she went and got the manager of the building, and they went inside and found the three-year-old kid locked in the closet. He told them his mother had gone off to work and locked him in. Anyway, when they got the kid quieted down, he told them that his mother cuffed him around pretty regular and that one time she burned his arm with a steam iron. That was to teach him a lesson not to touch hot things. That was all they had to hear. They called the PD, and they had a couple of guys waiting for her when she got home."

The iron would be the triangular burn scar in the autopsy report. The broken wrist could have been a result of the beatings, too.

The waitress brought my order, and McDonald watched her with a lecherous glint in his eye.

"What happened?" I asked as she left.

"Huh?" he asked, distracted by her rear end doing its happy wiggle toward the kitchen. "Oh. The same thing that happens in most battered children cases. Lainie claimed it'd been an accident. She said the kid must have been playing in the closet, and she must have locked him in there without knowing it when she went to work. She denied ever hitting him. The iron she said had been an accident, too. She said she'd set the thing down on the ironing board and the kid had been crawling around on the floor and bumped into it and the iron had fallen.

"It was all shit, of course, but there wasn't much we could do about it, especially after the kid started crying that he wanted his mommy and he wanted to go home. He said he'd lied, that he'd made it all up about the beatings. That's the funny part. It happens a lot. You get three kids in a family, and the old man picks one of them to kick the holy shit out of, and a lot of times that's the kid that really loves his father. He loves him right up to the time he bleeds to death from internal injuries or dies of starvation from being chained up in a packing crate without food or water. It's sick. It's like a dog licking the hand of the master who whips it."

"So the case never got to trial?"

"There was nothing to go to trial with. The kid wouldn't testify; there was no eyewitness testimony, just the word of the woman downstairs, and she really hadn't seen anything. The DA wouldn't touch it."

I tapped the envelope with a forefinger. "How could McMurtry have found out about this?"

"Your guess is as good as mine. I don't even know that he did. I just thought you'd like to know about it, that's all."

"Thanks," I said. "I really appreciate it."

The waitress came back and asked if there would be anything else. McDonald looked up. "Yes. I'd like to see some ID, miss."

She put the check down on the table and stuck her jaw out insolently. "What for?"

"I'm a police officer," he said. "And you were speeding."

He broke into a boyish grin, and her expression softened. "You a cop for real?"

He flashed his badge and said: "Detective McDonald, Palm Springs Police Department." He slid a paper napkin over to her and said: "You can write down all the pertinent information on here. Name, address, phone number. I'll let you off with a reprimand this time, but I'm warning you, three of these violations and we take away your shoes."

"You're funny," she said, giggling, and moved away from the table.

The napkin was still there, blank.

McDonald shrugged. "Beats the shit out of Godzilla."

I took the report back up to my room and went through it slowly. It was just about as McDonald had said.

Lainie had been arrested on August 14, 1972, by Officers Monroe and Houts of the PSPD, who had been summoned to the apartment building on Ramon Road by a neighbor, Mrs. Jergens. The officers had found both the child and Mrs. Ellison's apartment in an "unsanitary, unhealthful condition," and after talking to the child, Brian, age three, they determined they had grounds for arrest of the mother under Section 273a of the Penal Code. Lainie was arrested later that day upon coming home from work and was held for thirty-six hours before being released. She was never formally arraigned. She had been picked up by a Mr. Darrell Dennard, of 4432 Sunrise Way, Palm Springs, who had signed the necessary release papers.

A young girl's musical laugh drifted up from the pool. I put the report back down on the bed and went to the door and opened it. Something was moving around in the back of my mind, something about that name. Darrell Dennard. Darrell Dennard. I had seen that name somewhere, and recently.

I went out onto the balcony. The laughter was coming from

a tanned, sun-bleached blonde in a red bikini who was sitting on the stairs of the pool, talking with a young man. They seemed totally engrossed in each other. I watched them for a while, and then they faded out. Everything faded out as it came to me.

Darrell Dennard. I had seen that name recently. On a list of license plates compiled by the FBI. Son of a bitch.

I went back inside and called the Sands. Norton was not back yet. I left word for him to call me whenever he got in and tried McDonald's number. He was not in either.

Almost as soon as I hung up the phone, it rang.

"Hello, old boy," Winter said. "You called?"

"Yes, I called. Listen to me now, Howard. This is important. McMurtry is dead."

"Dead? Good God. How?"

"Murdered, suicide, nobody's sure right now. You and Mona have to get down here as soon as you can. She's got to claim the body, and she's in no shape to drive. You're going to have to take charge."

"Yes, yes, of course, but. . . ." His voice faded into shocked silence. "Jesus Christ, this is hard to believe."

"Believe it, it's true." I gave him the name of my motel, and he said he would try to make it down by tonight. I was not counting on its being early tonight, though. Knowing Winter, I realized that before he would take charge of Mona he would probably first try to take charge of every existing McMurtry of which he knew the location. Now that McMurtry was dead, the basic law of supply and demand would dictate that the prices of his existing paintings would skyrocket.

I sat around for a while, waiting for Norton or McDonald to call back, then said to hell with it. I would get in touch with them later. After all, I was not a man completely without sources. It was just going to be a matter of whether my sources wanted to talk without having their fingernails pulled out with a pair of pliers.

NINETEEN

The house was a small, low-slung boxy tract home much too cheap for the assortment of Eldorados and Porsches and Mercedes parked out front. As I cruised by, I could hear the throbbing electric beat of rock and roll playing inside. Two doors down where I parked, I could still hear it.

I cut across the gravel front yard and through the carport to the backyard. I could have rung the front doorbell, but that would not have been any fun. It would have ruined my little surprise.

The backyard was deserted. It was gravel, too, surrounded by a high wooden fence. A small swimming pool sat in the middle, and around its perimeter were scattered some broken-down deck chairs and chaise lounges. A wooden awning was built out from the roof of the house to shade the concrete slab that served as a patio, and there was a sliding glass door there, but the curtains were drawn across it, and I could not see in.

I went to the door and pulled gently. It gave. They were careless. Stoners usually are. I pulled open the door and was immediately assaulted by the savage volume of the music and the thick, sweet smell of marijuana.

The small living room could have been a scene from a teenage disaster movie. Beer bottles, cans of soda pop, paper napkins, and bags of potato chips littered every tabletop in the place. Bodies were draped over couches and chairs, strewn across the floor as if flung there by some cataclysm of nature, and their eyes all had the heavy-lidded, glazed stare of fresh corpses.

I counted nine, three of them female, and I recognized some of the faces from Pam's yearbook. One of them was standing by the kitchen counter as I came in, a tall wired kid with red hair and a red face and red eyes to match. One of the Donovan twins. He was shirtless, and freckles dotted his chest and shoulders.

"Who are you?" He stepped away from the counter, blocking my way. There was a hostile edge in his slurred voice, and I did not like the knots of tensed muscle around his neck. I always felt uneasy around red freaks. Of all drug users, they are the most violent and the most unpredictable.

"Name's Jake," I said, smiling. "Tommy around?"

"Somewhere," he said belligerently. "You still didn't say who you are, man."

"A friend of Tommy's from L.A. I just got in." I cocked a thumb back at the door and said: "You dudes should keep that door locked. The Man comes walking in here, Tommy's gonna be in some deep shit. Everybody else, too. You get loose, and you get ripped off."

He looked at me, then the door. His eyes did not seem to focus very well on either. The bunches of muscle around his neck seemed to relax, and his hostility turned like a roaming searchlight on the rest of the room. "Hey, who's the asshole who left the door open? Who went out last?"

Nobody answered, but that did not seem to bother him. He was probably used to it. He went back to holding up the end of the counter, and I stepped around him, careful of the tangle of arms and legs on the floor.

180

The deafening din of electric guitars died in the four huge speaker cabinets that anchored down the corners of the room; then Jackson Browne came on, lamenting that he was "running on empty." Some heads nodded solemnly, as if they knew just where he was coming from. They had been running on empty for years.

As I stepped over one black-haired boy who was lying against the couch with his head propped up on a pillow, he looked at the girl sitting above him and said: "Hey, Lisa, pass me the 'ludes."

Lisa obligingly picked up a candy dish filled with white pills from the coffee table and handed it down to him. Another candy dish next to it was filled with reds. At least they had a good selection of colors.

The boy picked one of the Quaaludes from the dish and popped it into his mouth and washed it down with some 7 UP in a can.

"Go for it," a mousy-haired girl said from a chair nearby, and chuckled. "I'll take one of those."

As the bowl made its rounds, I went down a white hallway by the kitchen. The first doorway was open, and I stuck my head in.

It was a small sparsely furnished bedroom with dirty white walls. Sitting on the edge of the bed were the horse-faced Spanish teacher from Piedmont and a thin dark-haired boy of about seventeen I didn't recognize. She had on a suede poncho, and the boy's two hands were underneath it while she held a joint to his lips.

She took a hit from the joint herself, then looked up and smiled with too many teeth. "Hi," she said through held breath.

"Hi," I said.

"I'm Margot. Who are you?"

She disentangled the kid's hands from underneath her poncho and stood up. The boy looked disappointed. I had interrupted his day's instruction.

"Name's Jake. I'm a friend of Tommy's. Seen him around?"

"I think he's in the other bedroom," she said. When she got close, I could see that she was over thirty. How far over, I was not willing to guess. She held out the joint to me. "Want a hit?"

"No, thanks, not right now."

"It's Colombian."

"Maybe later. I have to see Tommy first."

"Come back after you do," she said, giving me what I guessed was supposed to be a significant look. To her maybe it was. To me it was just a look.

"Sure."

I backed out of the room and went down the hall to the next door, which was shut. I tried the knob gently. It turned. I put my ear to the door. Someone groaned behind it. I removed the Instamatic from my shirt and opened the door quietly and stepped into the room.

They both were naked on the bed and so engrossed in what they were doing they did not notice anybody had come in. Either that or they were used to it. I closed the door behind me softly, took aim with the camera, and popped off a flash.

That got their attention. The one on the bottom bolted upright, kneeing the kid hovering over him in the nose. His nose was bleeding, and his eyes were watery, and he blinked through tear-blinded eyes right into the camera as the second flash went off.

"Shit!" he screamed, and dove under the sheets. But not quick enough for me not to recognize him.

The other one jumped out of the bed and snatched a pair of jeans from the back of a nearby chair. He had some trouble zipping them up, and I popped two more flashes in his face before he finally managed that.

He was short and skinny, and his bulgy eyes, combined with an overbite and buckteeth, gave him the appearance of a gopher that had gone through a rough winter. "What the fuck is this, some kind of a joke?" he asked, stepping toward me.

"No joke, Tommy. You are Tommy Walsh, aren't you?"

"What about it? Who the hell are you? What are you doing in my house?"

"I'm a research analyst," I said, smiling politely. "See, I've been hired to conduct a survey on how students in private schools spend their leisure hours as compared to those who attend public schools. Parents like to know such things, you know."

A low groan came from underneath the sheets.

"Parents like Mr. and Mrs. Bowles."

The groan turned into a plaintive wail. I looked over there. On the nightstand beside the bed was a solid rock of cocaine that must have weighed well over an ounce. Some of it had been shaved off with a razor blade and chopped into three neat parallel lines on a small hand mirror.

The coke distracted me, and Walsh took the opportunity to come at me. His fists were clenched into small, hard balls, and rage burned in his eyes. Some of the burning was being done with a hundred-watt cocaine filament.

He grabbed for the camera, and I pulled it back and backhanded him with my other hand. The blow was not that hard, but it sent him reeling backward onto the bed. He landed on the lump under the covers, and the kid came flying out of the bed.

"You're not going to tell my parents," he whined. "Jesus. Shit. Please don't tell my parents. I'll do anything you say—"

"Get your clothes on, and wait outside the door. And when I say *wait,* I mean *wait.* You read me?"

There was a smear of blood at the corner of Walsh's mouth. He stood up and daubed at it with the back of his hand. "You can't—"

I pointed a finger at him. "*You* just shut the fuck up and stand there." I turned to the kid. "*You, move!*"

The Bowles kid got out of bed and tried to get dressed. That took him awhile. He was trembling like a dog trying to pass peach pits, and he kept stumbling as he tried to get into his pants. When he had finally managed to get everything on, he slunk past me and out the door.

Walsh was watching me, the rage still burning in his eyes. "Who are you?"

"A private detective," I said.

"Who are you working for?" he said out of the corner of his mouth, no mean feat through those teeth. The voice was thickened by a distinct southern drawl.

"That doesn't really matter, does it?" I asked. "What matters is that we have here, what they call a, uh, situation. Now, why don't you sit down there and we can discuss it like gentlemen?"

"Fuck you," he said, and took another step forward.

The cocaine was perhaps making him overconfident. I was going to have to make compensations for that. I kicked him hard in the shins, and he yelped in pain and staggered back, hopping up and down on one leg. "Now, Tommy boy, sit down. Please."

He sat back on the edge of the bed and rubbed his shin. He made airy, sucking noises through his teeth. I put the camera in my belt and stepped toward him. I tried to look menacing. I must have succeeded because he drew back on the bed, his eyes clouded by fear and pain.

"Now," I said. "Let's talk."

"What do you want?"

"Information."

"What kind of information?"

I pointed at the coke on the table. "Where'd you get the rock?"

He stared at me hatefully.

"Okay. Let's try another approach. Who does Donnie Fleischer buy his dope from locally?"

He still said nothing. I stepped forward and kicked him hard again on the same shin, and he screamed and fell onto the floor, writing in agony. I was not worried about anybody hearing him. The music in the other room would drown out any sound he would make.

"Jesus Christ! Shit! What did you do that for?"

I bent over him. "Just to get your undivided attention, Tommy baby. You don't seem to be listening to my questions. You don't seem to have gotten it through your gopher brain what kind of position you are in here." I pointed at the bedroom door. "You know who the parents of those lovely fair-haired stone freaks are out there? Between all of them, they could probably come up with a hundred million bucks or so. You know what a hundred million can buy, Tommy? A lot of juice. You know what that juice would buy if they found out what you were doing with their kids, Tommy? You know what they'd do if they found out you are filling their kids full of dope so you can bring them in here and pack their little poopers, Tommy? They'd have you skinned alive. You couldn't run far enough to get away from a hundred million bucks, Tommy."

He threw up his hands. "What do you want from me?"

"I already told you." I spoke slowly and clearly, letting him watch my lips move, as if I were talking to a retarded child. "Once more. Who does Donnie Fleischer buy his dope from?"

He didn't say anything. His mouth turned surly around the edges.

"Of course, I don't have to turn these pictures over to these kids' parents. I can always give them to the cops. That wouldn't be bad either. Sodomy, contributing, statutory rape, child molesting. You could go up for a long time."

He didn't say anything.

"Then there's always murder."

That got his attention. "What are you talking about? What murder?"

"You seen Donnie Fleischer around lately?"

"He's back east."

"Who told you that?"

"His stepmother. I called the house yesterday."

"That was just the story they were giving out."

"What are you talking about, man?"

"Donnie's dead, Tommy. They found him this morning. He was murdered."

"Murdered?" His eyes were two white saucers.

"That's right, Tommy baby. Murdered."

"But . . . you can't think I . . . hey, man, I don't know nothing about no murder—"

He started to stand up, but I put a hand on his bony chest and pushed him back down. I hovered over him and growled: "You were messing around with him, weren't you?"

"No, I swear. . . ." His head wagged violently back and forth, like a rag doll being shaken by some invisible hand.

"Maybe he decided to lean on you a little, huh? Maybe he threatened to tell some of these kids' parents what was going on here at your parties and tried to hit you up for some bread, and you decided to get rid of him. From what I hear about him, he was always lacking for spending money—"

His head still shook back and forth. "No, no, hey, look, man, you've got it all wrong. Donnie came around here, sure, but he never, we never got it on or anything like that."

I put my foot up on the bed and shrugged. "I might believe you. If I get the right answers to some questions."

"What questions?"

"On Friday night Donnie was supposed to meet a man to score a lid. Who?"

"I haven't seen Donnie in a week," he said in an agonized tone. "How would I know?"

"Take a guess."

"I don't know."

"The most likely candidate."

His eyes darted around the room. The search they were making, though, was going on inside his head. He licked his lips. "I—I don't know. Honest, man."

"Don't give me any of that shit—"

He held up his hands. "No, really, man, I—"

"How about Darrell Dennard? Does that name mean anything to you?"

His eyes locked onto mine. Something moved behind them. Something like fear. "No. I don't know the cat, man."

I kicked him again as hard as I could, aiming at the same place to compound the pain, and he shrieked, a girl's shriek, and grabbed his leg and fell on the floor. I cocked my foot back, and he said quickly: "All right, all right, yeah, I know him, I know him."

"Does he deal?"

"Yeah, yeah, he deals."

"Would that have been who Donnie went to meet?"

"Honest to God," he whined. "I don't know. Look, is that for real about Donnie being dead?"

"As real as you can get," I said. "Did Donnie know Dennard?"

He grimaced in pain and kept rocking back and forth with his eyes closed, holding his leg. "Yeah. Donnie was in the car one night when I bought some coke from Darrell. I guess they knew each other because when Donnie saw Darrell, he freaked out. He asked Darrell not to tell his stepmother he had seen him."

The cocaine high was backfiring on him now. His nerves were strung out, and he was starting to tremble.

"How did Dennard know Donnie's stepmother?"

"I—I'm not sure. Darrell is a bartender at a disco joint downtown called the Silver Cockatoo. I think Donnie and his stepmother eat in there every once in a while."

"What does he look like?"

"Dennard? Tall, blond hair. Thirty or so. He used to be an actor. He looks a lot like David Soul."

I got a rush. "You mean the one who plays on 'Starsky and Hutch'?"

"Yeah, that's him."

"What's he like?"

He shrugged. "A nice guy. A gentleman. And a sport. He spends a lot of bread. He's cold, though. Darrell is one cold dude."

"How cold?"

He sucked in a breath. "Well, one night Darrell came over here to deal me some coke, and he brought his dog with him. It was a gold Afghan. A real nice dog. He'd had it since it was just a pup. Anyway, the dog got kind of excited and jumped up on Darrell and made him drop about five hundred bucks' worth of coke. He didn't say nothing about it then, but I saw him a couple of days later and asked him how his dog was, and he said it'd died. The door of the car had opened on the freeway, he said, and the dog had fallen out. But it was the way he said it that got me. It was like he was talking about one of his hubcaps falling off or something." He gave me a worried look. "Is that what you think, that Darrell killed Donnie?"

"I don't think anything. All I know is that somebody killed him, and I'm going to find out who." I straightened up. "I wouldn't want Mr. Dennard to get the word that I've been asking questions about him."

"Don't worry about that, man. If Darrell found out I'd snitched him off—" He didn't finish the sentence.

"It might be a dog's life," I said, finishing it for him. "If anything happens that makes me think you made any phone calls, I'll make sure these pictures get to the right people, Tommy. But I know you won't do that. The word of a southern gentleman is always good."

Speaking of dogs, Andy Bowles was waiting like an obedient one when I came out the door. He would not look me directly in the eyes. "Let's talk outside," I said.

We went down the hall into the living room. A new group had replaced Jackson Browne, one with thirty more singers and fifty more electric guitars. Nobody asked us where we were going as we went out the front door.

The air outside was fresh and clean after that stale marijuana smell in the house.

"What are you going to do with those pictures?" he asked, his head bowed.

"That will depend."

"On what?"

"The answers you give me to a couple of questions," I said. "Where do your friends buy their dope?"

He looked up at me sharply. His pupils were constricted pinpoints. His mouth dropped open. "Are you a cop?"

"No."

"What do you want to know about that for?"

"That doesn't matter, kid," I said in a purposely nasty tone. I patted the spot where the camera was tucked into my belt. "The only thing that matters is what's on this roll of film. If you don't want your parents to see it, you'd better start coming up with some answers. Fast."

"I—there are some kids at school, at the high school, I mean, who deal—"

"Where does Donnie Fleischer buy his dope from? Those kids?"

"No." He dropped his eyes. "I mean, I don't know."

I sighed. "Okay." I started away from him. "I guess I'll have to get these developed and mailed out—"

He chased after me. His voice cracked in panic. "Wait. Mister, honest, I don't know the guy's name. I saw him only once. I swear to God."

"Where?"

"On Palm Canyon. I was downtown one day with Donnie, and he pointed this guy out to me as he drove by and said,

'That's my dealer.' That's all I know. I don't know the guy's name or anything. I don't even know if it was true. With Donnie you never know. He likes to play the big shot and talk like that, like he's got all kinds of connections with hoods and stuff."

"What kind of car was the guy driving?"

"I don't remember. It was new, I think. And it was red, I remember that."

"What did he look like?"

"I saw him for only a second. He was young. Blond hair. That's all I remember. I didn't pay much attention."

I nodded. "Okay, kid. Go on home."

He reached for my sleeve, but his hand recoiled before he touched it. He chewed worriedly at the corner of his mouth. "What . . . what are you going to do with those pictures?"

"Nothing, kid. Absolutely nothing. Unless I hear you've told anybody about this."

He shook his head in vehement protest. "I won't. I swear to God. Just please, mister, don't tell my parents."

He disgusted me, as any cringing, whimpering animal disgusted me, but in a way I could not help feeling sorry for him. He was too pathetic not to. He and all the others inside who stayed fried out of their skulls to forget about the pain and about the people who didn't care. They were like plants. They grew up bent because that was the way the light was coming in.

I walked away from the kid without saying anything more, wondering how many of them would make their thirtieth birthdays and how many would wind up like casualties, like Donnie Fleischer.

I stopped wondering before I got to the car. On purpose. I already had enough victims to think about. Somebody else was going to have to think about the rest of them.

I checked at the motel desk on the way in. Nobody had called. I reserved two rooms for Mona and Winter; then I left a wake-up call for 11:00.

I must have fallen asleep before I had gotten out of my clothes because I still had half of them on when the jangling of the phone woke me. The room was pitch-black, and it took me a few seconds to remember where I was. The phone rang again, and I picked it up, mumbled a "Thanks" into it and hung up. I fumbled around until I found the light switch and turned it on, then reached for my watch on the nightstand: 9:30. That stupid son of a bitch.

The phone rang again.

An angry voice on the other end said: "Asch, why the hell did you just hang up on me?" It was Norton.

"I'm sorry, Inspector. I thought you were the desk clerk."

"Well, I'm not the desk clerk."

"Yeah, I realize that. Look, you want me to see what I can do? I have a lot of pull here. A word from me, they might put you on."

He sighed tiredly. "What did you call me for?"

"You find anything else out?"

"McMurtry did have a reservation on Mexicana Airlines for tomorrow night. To Mexico City."

"Did he pay for it?"

"No."

"Anybody could have made a reservation under his name. What else?"

"The handwriting on the note checks out. Our experts have definitely identified it as McMurtry's."

"What about the gun?"

"It was originally registered to a Samuel Whiddington of San Pedro. He reported it stolen in a burglary in 1976. It could have changed hands four or five times since then and probably did."

"Where would McMurtry have gotten it?"

"Who the hell knows? He could have bought it in one of the bars he used to frequent."

"How about the autopsies?"

"The kid will be done in the morning, McMurtry tomorrow afternoon. But I don't expect them to change anything. It's going to come out McMurtry, by himself."

"That seems like kind of a premature conclusion, don't you think?"

"Yeah, well, I'm one of the few that think Oswald was alone when he blew up Kennedy. So what the hell do I know?"

"Don't you think it's a little strange that McMurtry's car wasn't spotted in the vicinity of the drop?"

"Not particularly," he said defensively. "Our guys must have missed him. So what?"

"Do me a favor," I said. "Run a Darrell Dennard through your crime teletype and see what comes out. His car was on the list for the drop." I spelled the name for him.

"What's with him?"

I told him. I didn't tell him about Lainie, though. Until I

found out a few things, there was no sense loading her with any more trouble than she already had to deal with. In the end it all might amount to nothing, and I was already responsible for enough grief.

When I was done, he said: "Interesting."

"Yeah, I thought so. You might also try running his name through C Two."

"If he's on C Two, we've got him on our teletype."

"I've heard of things getting lost on your teletype."

"I'll call you back."

I hung up. Five minutes later the phone rang.

"The computer kicked him out. No priors, no arrests. The guy's clean."

"I'll bet he is," I said. "As clean as a ring in a dirty bathtub."

"What are you going to do?"

"I thought I'd do a little more checking up on Mr. Dennard."

"Yeah, well, if you come up with anything, let me know."

"But you don't think I will."

"I didn't say that."

"You didn't have to," I said. "I know you don't believe in conspiracy theories. Oswald killed Kennedy. Right?"

"Right."

"Yeah, well, there's a bit of information I've come across lately that isn't public knowledge. Did you know, Inspector, that Marilyn Monroe's doctor and her psychiatrist were both very good friends of the Kennedys and they were both in Dallas the day Kennedy was shot?"

"No, I didn't."

"I didn't either, but it sounds good, doesn't it?"

"Don't worry. Somebody will come up with that. Then we'll have three more Senate committees spend another ten million of the taxpayers' money investigating it, and Oswald will still come out holding the gun."

"I'm going to be doing this for free," I said. "I guarantee not one dime of the taxpayers' money will be spent on my investigation of Mr. Dennard."

"And McMurtry will still come out holding the gun."

"We'll see, Inspector. Talk to you."

I called downstairs to find out if Mona and Winter had arrived yet. They hadn't. I assured the clerk they would arrive later and told him to hold the rooms, then tried Mona at her home. No answer. They were probably on their way.

TWENTY-ONE

From the outside the Silver Cockatoo looked like a huge, ugly wooden warehouse. Inside, however, things were considerably more chic.

The bottom floor was strictly dining. It was all diagonal wood and hanging plants, and the chairs at the tables were canvas, the type directors sit in while shooting movies. The young waiters all wore shorts and waist aprons and tennies and looked as if they had all driven in from Rincón, where they had just gotten through shooting the curl. The waitresses wore T-shirts and jeans and looked like refugees from the Manson Family, and all of them would be sure to tell you their name was "Sarah" or "Bill" before taking your order, as if anybody gave a good goddamn what their names were. It was all very "in."

To the right of the reservations desk a stairway ran up through a zebra-skin tunnel. Music tumbled down the stairs like water. A burly black man with a shaved head stood at the entrance to the tunnel, rocking back and forth on his feet as if he were expecting trouble. I wasn't about to give him any. I said hello and went past his scowl, up to disco land.

The room upstairs was large, and it looked even larger because it was half empty. An amorphous-shaped dance floor rimmed by flashing lights ran through the middle of the room, and on it a few couples whirled and twirled, showing off the latest disco steps they had learned through hours of laborious practice. Their bodies were silhouetted by lights that strobed in synchronization with the music through a fabric-covered canopy above the dance floor.

Clumps of men stood at upright cocktail tables, sipping drinks and watching the room with predatory eyes. Single girls walked by them, trying to look available, and couples lounged on couches beneath the convex fish tanks that were set into the chocolate-colored walls or sat at tables, yelling at one another to make themselves heard over the music.

A sunken bar ran along the back of the room, overhung by Lucite light fixtures. My eyes scanned it slowly until they landed on him.

He did look like David Soul, except he was thicker through the back and shoulders and he had more hair. It was thick and so blond it was almost white. His eyebrows and eyelashes were white, too, and they provided a striking contrast with his dark tan.

I took a stool in front of him, and he put a cocktail napkin down on the bar. "What'll it be?"

He flashed me a white-toothed smile, but only with the bottom of his face. The eyes didn't smile.

"Vodka-water."

"Vodka-water it is," he said and went to the well to make the drink.

I watched him as he walked away. Six-one or -two, I imagined, and probably two hundred, two-oh-five, and not much of it fat. He had a springy athlete's walk, up on the balls of his feet, and he moved with a graceful, fluid roll to his upper body. A jogger, probably, and maybe some weights when he really got ambitious.

He came back with the drink. "Two dollars."

While he waited for the money, he stood holding his right hand turned palm up and tapped his index and middle fingers against his thumb in rapid succession. He didn't seem to realize he was doing it. After a long period of time heavy coke users developed a lot of unconscious nervous mannerisms.

I put three ones on the bar and asked: "You're new here, aren't you?"

He shook his head. "I've been here a year."

"I've been in the past four nights, and I haven't seen you."

"I've been down with the flu."

So far so good. "It's going around."

He went to the cash register and put the two dollars away, and then a cocktail waitress came over to the service station and he walked over to fill her order. After he came back, I said: "There was more action in here last night."

He nodded. "It'll pick up. It's only eleven. Things will start happening in another half hour."

"Seems like this is the place to be," I said. "I've been all over town the past week, and this place seems to have the best-looking broads."

As if that were a cue, a dark-haired girl slid onto the stool next to me. She had the pretty, painted face of someone who had not really experienced life but skated along its surface. Dennard put down a napkin and offered her the same dazzling, even-toothed smile.

There was something wrong with that smile, with the face, something that made me uncomfortable, and I studied him trying to determine what it was without looking too obvious about it. Before I had a chance to do that, the girl ordered a scotch-mist, and he went away to make it.

The girl next to me took a cigarette out of her purse and began rummaging around in her purse, looking for something to light it with. I picked the book of matches off the bar and did the honors. She cupped her hand over mine while I lit the cigarette, then exhaled and smiled. "Thanks."

"Sure."

"Isn't this weather just out of sight?" she asked, lowering her false eyelashes.

"Out of sight," I agreed.

"You from around here?"

"L.A.," I said. "How about you?"

"Mission Viejo." She took another drag on her cigarette and glanced down the bar. "What do you do?"

"Right now, I'm unemployed," I said. "Things are a little slow in my regular line of work."

She nodded as if she understood. "What do you do normally?"

"I'm a squire."

Her eyebrows knitted.

"Things have been kind of tough since my knight died," I explained.

She was still trying to figure that one out when Dennard came back with her drink. He was doing that thing with his fingers again.

While he collected her money, I watched him, trying to figure out what was wrong with his face, and then it came to me. It was the eyes. They were gray blue, and there was no expression in them, nothing, and there never would be, no matter how much he smiled. They were eyes that would never change, and looking into them was like looking through two windows at a bedrock of slate.

He caught me staring at him and frowned. "Something wrong?"

"No, it's just . . . Jesus, you look familiar. Did you ever do any TV or movies?"

He shrugged. "I did a few bit parts. But that was years ago."

"What kind of parts?"

"Some soaps. Daytime TV mostly."

"I think I've seen you."

"I doubt it."

"No, really," I said.

I got out my wallet and took out a card that said I was Gilbert Evans of Triforium Productions, Inc., Universal City. I hoped Dennard had been out of the business a whole lot of years and that while he had been in it, he had never auditioned for Gilbert Evans. I would have had to have grown five inches and lost a headful of hair, and even then, I would have looked as much like Gilbert Evans as the "Sesame Street" Cookie Monster looks like Jimmy Carter. "Which soaps did you do? The reason I'm asking," I said, pushing the card across the bar toward him, "is that I produce television shows. Mostly movies for TV."

He looked at the card and then smiled. "I did quite a few episodes of 'Days of Our Lives' and 'General Hospital.' And a couple 'The Streets of San Francisco.'"

"Really?" I said, with mild interest. "Why'd you quit?"

"The reason everybody quits, I guess. I had to eat. And I got tired of the rat race, of the cattle calls and the ass kissing to get a chance to say four lines on some crummy show. That gets really old after a couple of years. It can really screw up your head, you know what I mean?"

"How's your head now?" I asked.

"Fine, why?"

"Ever think of doing anything again?"

"Naw," he said, but his expression was pleased. "I couldn't get back into that again."

"What's your name?"

"Dennard. Darrell Dennard."

"Well, Darrell, you keep that card," I said. "If you ever get up into the L.A. area, stop by. I'd like to talk more. I know what you mean about the business. There are a lot of idiots in positions of power. But I've got a few things cooking that might be just right for you."

He pocketed the card and said: "Sure, thanks."

"You got anything with your name on it? A number where I can get hold of you?"

His expression turned cautious, as if he were trying to figure out the angle. "No, I don't. I just moved into the apartment I'm living in, and I don't have a phone yet. Excuse me."

He moved down the bar and the dark-haired girl next to me said: "I heard you tell that guy you're a producer."

"That's right."

She scoped me out with radar eyes and leaned closer. "That must really be interesting work."

"Sometimes."

The cocktail waitress was back at the service bar, and Dennard went over to where her long fingernails were making impatient clicking sounds on the plastic cocktail tray.

"What have you produced?"

"Ever see 'The Return of Gunga Din'?"

"No."

" 'Return of the Native'?"

"No," she said. "Sounds like you're big on 'Returns.' "

I nodded authoritatively. "There are more returns in 'Returns' than in any other type of movie."

Her mouth shaped itself into a suggestive orifice. Her face had probably gone down on everything but the *Lusitania.* "How about 'Return to My Room'?" she asked.

I raised my eyebrows. "That sounds like it would be a good one."

Her eyes promised me things. "It would be. I guarantee it."

I smiled back and, just to be sociable, asked: "Can I buy you a drink?"

She looked at her glass of crushed ice. "Sure. Why not?"

Dennard came back, and I ordered the lady and myself a

drink, then went back to half listening to her idle stream of chatter. Her name was Lisa. She knew mine was Gilbert Evans. I told her to call me just Gil. Lisa, it turned out, was a hairdresser who had always been fascinated with acting. She had not done much lately, but she assured me she had been simply superb in several plays in high school, which she proceeded to describe for me. Through all that I nodded and tried to look interested. When she put her hand on my knee, I must have really looked interested because the intensity of her sales pitch picked up.

Several dozen males cruised continually by the bar, performing dances other than the ones being done on the floor. They preened; they strutted; they swaggered, performing various mating dances like grouse in the mating season. They all wore tight Levi's, and their shirts were unbuttoned to display their chest hair and gold chains, and the women all wore peasant blouses and tight jeans with the cuffs turned up and dagger heels because that was what the fashion designers had told them that the male grouse would be reacting to this season.

One of the men, a lean, swarthy young man with an extra helping of chains and chest hair, had already been by five times, trying to look casual with a drink in his hand while he checked out the merchandise. On the sixth trip he stopped in front of the girl beside me and asked her to dance. She looked at me questioningly, and I said: "Go ahead."

"Will you watch my purse?" she asked me.

"Sure."

She bit her lip seductively. "You won't go away?"

"And leave you? How could I?"

That seemed to satisfy her, and she went out on the dance floor.

To make it look good, I went into the bathroom. I took her purse with me, and a few guys washing their hands looked at me, wondering. When I came back out, the dance number had ended, and she was sitting back on her stool, demurely wiping the perspiration from her upper lip with an index finger.

She smiled when she saw me. "I thought you'd left—"

"No, but I'm going to have to, I'm afraid. I just talked to someone on the phone. An emergency has come up."

She looked crestfallen. I knew that would last about forty seconds, until I was out the door and Macho Man cruised by again.

"Listen," I said. "You got a number in Mission Viejo?"

She nodded and dug through her purse until she came up with a pen. She wrote her number and name down on the cocktail napkin. I pocketed it and signaled Dennard I was ready to leave.

"Going already?" he asked. "It's only twelve-fifteen."

"I know, but something has come up." I put enough down on the bar for the drinks and a three-dollar tip and stood up.

"Thanks a lot," he said, as if he meant it.

"Right. And if you get to L.A., I'm serious about that offer."

He smiled easily and waved. "Okay, Mr. Evans. I might take you up on it. I'll be in L.A. next week. I'll look you up."

I pointed the pistol I'd made out of my hand at him and let my thumb-hammer go down on the firing pin, smiling. Then I said my tearful farewell to Lisa, who looked as if she were standing on a dock watching her fiancé skip out to Singapore, and left.

I went out to the parking lot and reparked my car so that I could watch the front doors. Lisa came out forty minutes later with Macho Man, and I remarked to myself how fickle true love was.

People trickled out for the next hour as if the place had a slow leak—the ones who had matched up looking artificially happy, the ones who had not looking glum. At 2:00 the leak stopped. I waited, stifling a yawn.

At 2:24, Dennard stepped through the glass doors, casually lit a cigarette, and went down the wooden stairs to a red Firebird parked close to the building. I waited until he pulled out of the driveway before turning on my lights.

You could have bowled on Palm Canyon. We were the only cars on the street. That made him easy to follow. It also made me easy to spot, so I dropped way back.

At South Palm Canyon he veered off to the right. His tail-lights sailed past my motel, past a string of apartment buildings and unfinished construction projects, and then his left blinker was on, and he was turning into the driveway of a condo project whose amber-lit roofs made jagged, repetitive patterns against the sky.

I took my foot off the gas as I approached the place. The complex was small, divided in the middle by a parking area. As I passed the driveway, I could see Dennard's brake lights in a stall down at the far end.

I drove up the block and parked. I gave him a couple of minutes to get to his place, then got my Slim Jim out of my trunk and started back on foot.

Up in the mountains behind me a coyote yip-yipped and was joined by a chorus of his friends. They sounded happy, but at the same time lonely, like a group of Christmas carolers singing to nobody.

At the corner of the wall by the driveway I was stopped by the sound of voices. A man's and a woman's. I recognized both of them.

"I told you not to come here—"

"I had to see you," the woman said, her voice pleading. "Everything that's happened . . . I had to. Don't send me home, honey, not now. Please. I need you. I need to talk to you."

"You're sure nobody followed you here?"

"Yes, I'm absolutely sure. I was careful, I swear it."

"Shit," the man said. "All right, come on."

I bent down and peeked around the corner. Dennard had a grip on Lainie's elbow and was hustling her down a walkway at the far end of the parking lot. They disappeared behind a wall there, and I listened to their footsteps fade on the walk before I stepped into the light.

Dennard's Firebird was parked in the space allotted to unit number twelve. The white Mark was parked next to it. Both cars were locked.

I peeked around the corner carefully. The cement walkway was empty. It ran about ten feet between two areas of low bushes before dead-ending in another walkway that ran off in both directions. I waited, then tiptoed down the cement trail. I tried the left first.

The units were rough plaster two-story jobs, each of them split into two mirrorlike halves. The numbers on the first two doors were 19 and 20. I turned and went to the right.

The door to Dennard's condo was closed, and the lights were on inside. I went quickly back to the garage.

A Slim Jim is a thin metal bar with a hook on one end, and when inserted between the outside of the window and the door, it will unlock eight out of every ten cars on the street. Dennard's Firebird was one of the eight.

The glove compartment was unlocked, and I started with it. It was filled with papers: car maintenance bills; car registration; receipts for various items; an empty plea envelope from the American Cancer Society. There were four or five cassettes for his tape deck: War, Boz Skaggs, Steely Dan, Atlanta Rhythm Section. There was a map of the Palm Springs–Indio area like the one in McMurtry's car, but that was hardly an incriminating piece of evidence. I pawed through it, and then my eye was caught by a heading stamped on the top of a receipt.

TINY'S GUN SHOP
781 Indian Ave.
Palm Springs

The receipt was for one box of Mini-Mag .22-caliber long rifle bullets, which had been purchased on May 2, 1978.

I thought about taking the receipt but decided against it. It would mean nothing if removed from the car, not if Tiny or whoever had sold Dennard the bullets could not identify him from his picture.

I buried the receipt under the other papers in the glove box and was starting to look around the floor by the front seat when the sound of voices sent a shot of adrenaline surging through me. I stepped out of the car and pressed down the lock button and closed the door as quietly as I could. That took too much time. They were coming around the corner, and I had to scramble to duck down behind the body of the Mark.

". . . I'm telling you, don't worry," Dennard was saying. "Everything will be all right. I'm really sorry about Donnie."

"I'm going to need you more than ever now," Lainie told him.

"I know." His voice was sugary sweet. Total solicitude. "But we're just going to have to be careful."

I crept along the side of the Mark and around the front of the Thunderbird parked next to it. The grille of the car was too close to the garage wall, and I found myself wedged in, unable to move any further. They came around the back end of the Mark and stopped in front of her door. I scrunched as far down as I could, trying to make myself invisible. Luckily they were looking at each other and not in my direction. I was not sure they would see me even if they did, but I still felt naked and vulnerable, like a roach on a wall when the lights go on.

"We're going to have to tell him—" Lainie said.

"Not now," Dennard answered sharply. "It would kill him now. We can wait. We've waited this long."

He leaned forward and gave her a quick peck on the mouth and started to back away, but she grabbed him around the neck and held on. They stayed like that for quite a while. He patted her on the back sympathetically, but over her shoulder his face was a stony mask of impatience. They parted, and his smile became tender once more. He hustled her into the car and stepped away, and I could not see him anymore as she backed out.

The sound of her motor grew soft, and then I heard her take off out on the street, but he had not moved.

His footsteps moved away from the rear of the Thunderbird, and I saw him move over to his own car and take out his keys. He unlocked the door and started up the motor and backed out of his stall. He peeled rubber out of the garage, heading somewhere in one hell of a hurry.

I straightened up and exhaled a sigh of relief. My watch said 3:10. I wondered where he would be going in such a hurry at 3:10 in the morning. There was only one way to find out.

By the time I hit the street his taillights were tiny red dots down South Palm Canyon. I sprinted to my car, tossed my Slim Jim onto the seat, and started her up. His right blinker was on by the time I got my car turned around and heading in the right direction. I punched it.

He had made a right on Highway 111, heading toward Cathedral City. As I turned, I saw his taillights at least a mile ahead of me.

I managed to close the gap a little by the edge of Cathedral City, but not by too much. He was driving fast, much too fast, and I found my excitement rising. Maybe Lainie's visit had reminded him of something, something he had forgotten. I just hoped there were no CHPs lurking around.

We sailed through Cathedral City at twenty miles an hour over the speed limit, and he was up to seventy in the stretch between Rancho Mirage and Palm Desert. After Palm Desert he slowed down to sixty and stayed there. I closed the distance between us down to about three-quarters of a mile and kept it there.

Just before we entered the outskirts of Indio, he signaled and turned right. I slowed as I approached the intersection. My lights flashed on a sign before I switched them off. Jefferson Street. The area was very patriotic. All the streets were named after past presidents. Dead presidents.

I leaned forward, squinting through the windshield, keeping my eyes glued to the dotted white line. The moon was a pale halo behind the mountains, but enough of its light remained diffused across the sky for me to drive on. Without headlights, the stars were almost startling in their brilliance. Way above, they spread across the sky like a fine mist, then condensed into bigger droplets as they fell toward earth. Beneath their blue-white radiance, the plowed fields on each side of the road looked like the eroded gray surface of some dead planet.

Dennard's taillights were ahead of me, and then they were not anymore. Panic surged through me, and I stepped on the gas. I was on top of the intersection before I had a chance to stop, and I caught a glimpse of red on my left as I sailed through it. I hit the brakes and threw the car into reverse and backed up. The taillights were gone again.

The road was a two-lane rutted concrete ribbon that ran between groves of date and citrus trees. Every quarter of a mile or so another road crossed the one I was on, and I slowed and looked both ways. At the third one I saw two tiny pinpricks of red to the right, and I turned.

His brake lights were flashing up ahead, and he swung off the road, to the right. I slowed down.

The Firebird sat at the end of a dried-mud driveway, alongside an old packing shed that sat recessed back from the road. Dark stands of date groves stood on both sides of it. I drove on another quarter mile to the edge of the date grove and pulled off onto a section of hard dirt.

I got my flashlight out of the glove compartment, locked the car up, then got a tire iron out of the trunk. I wished I still had the .38. It would have felt good in my hand right now.

I trotted down the road to the packing shed. It had a high-peaked corrugated tin roof, and most of the windows across its second story were smashed out. A loading dock out front was stacked with empty wooden flats. The place looked as if it had not been used in years. It probably hadn't. Chavez and his boys had put a lot of these outfits out of business.

The front door was padlocked from the outside. I started around back when I heard the engine of the Firebird turn over. I ducked down behind a stack of flats as the sleek red body of the car backed out of the driveway and took off in the direction we had come.

I waited and then went around back where he had parked. A rusted hinge creaked. I froze. A breeze blew at my back, and the hinge creaked again. I went forward cautiously toward the creaking sound. There was a door there. I flattened myself out against the wall and pushed on the door with my tire iron. The door was ajar, and it creaked again, but that was all. I waited for something else to happen, I don't know what, and when nothing did, I pushed the door open and stepped inside.

The interior of the place was one huge dirty room. I swept it with my flash. It was empty except for more wooden pallets stacked around and an old conveyor belt system that ran waist-high along the length of the far wall. The only sound in the place was a steady drip, drip, drip of water, and my flash identified the source as some old rusted water pipes on the ceiling over the conveyor system. Dates, probably. The water would have been used to spray them as they came down the belt.

The floor was littered with crumpled papers and old wine bottles, but they were too old to be what I was looking for. Two thick wooden doors stood open at the other end of the room. I went to them.

The doors opened into two fair-sized windowless rooms that

must have been walk-in refrigerators when the place was operating. The evaporator fans were still mounted in the corners by the ceiling. The lock on the first door was rusted, but the latch on the other had recently been replaced and had a brand new padlock on it.

I stepped inside. The room reeked of excrement. My flashlight found the source of the smell in the corner. A roll of toilet paper stood on its end on the dirty cement floor. Some of it had been used and lay bunched there in crumpled wads. My flash roamed over the rest of the place.

On the opposite side of the room were crumpled pieces of waxed paper and several brown paper bags. I went over and bent down and poked at them. Of course, he would eat as far away as he could from where he shit. Crumpled cellophane wrappers that had once contained Hostess Twinkies and cherry turnovers. An apple core covered with night-crawling insects. In the paper bags, several empty cartons of milk and Coke bottles. Not exactly your basic Jack LaLanne high-protein diet, but enough to keep a body alive for several days.

I stood up and looked around. All in all, a good place to keep someone on ice for a few days. With the insulated walls and the door closed, a man could scream his lungs out and nobody would hear him. I wondered how long McMurtry had tried screaming.

A sound outside the door made my heart flutter. I snapped off my flash and stood perfectly still, listening. I tiptoed to the door and eased up behind it, my grip tight on the tire iron. My heart was pounding in my ears as I stepped into the big room.

There was nobody there. A wind brushed by outside, moving the back door on its squeaking hinge. Nothing but the wind. Saved by the wind.

My grip relaxed a bit on the tire iron, and I snicked my flash back on and went to the door. Daytime would be a better time to go over the place anyway, and the FBI lab boys would be better equipped to deal with any evidence here.

I pushed on the door and stepped outside, and the front of my head exploded in a shower of light and pain. It seemed to me I was falling then, somersaulting weightlessly, tumbling head over heel, until I reached the bottom of a place that was hard and dark.

TWENTY-TWO

Something cold and wet hit me in the face, and I was being shaken awake. Consciousness dribbled into my brain little by little, drop by drop, like water from a leaky faucet. I didn't want it. With the consciousness came the pain. I tried to go back to sleep, but somebody shook me again.

A voice groaned. The voice sounded familiar. It was my own. I opened my eyes, and a light blinded me, and I closed them again.

I was on my back, and there was a hard lump under my tailbone. I tried to move my hands. The lump moved. My hands were the lump. My Holmesian powers of deduction were still intact. No puzzle was too difficult for Jacob Asch, private eye.

Strong hands grabbed me under the armpits and lifted me so that I was sitting up. My back rested against something hard. A wall. I tried moving my hands again. I couldn't. They were tied. I opened my eyes. The light was there again, and I turned away from it, but a hand yanked on my hair, pulling my head back.

Through squinted lids I saw a foot. It was propped up on a wooden crate in front of me, and my flashlight rested beside it, the beam aimed at my face. From the darkness beyond the circle of light came a soft, fluttering sound like the beating of moth wings. The fingers. "Well, well, Mr. Evans," a voice said. "You're finally awake."

Dennard's face moved into the light. He was smiling, and his teeth glistened in the beam of the flash. The stink of shit and urine drifted to me from the darkness. We were back in the icebox.

My face was wet. I hoped it was just water. Even a little blood would be okay, as long as it was not mixed with gray matter. Some people might be able to get along without parts of their brains, but I needed all of mine, just to get by.

I counted to myself from one to ten and back again. I made it without a slip. I told myself I was all right. The front of my head felt as if someone had pumped it full of latex, then hammered a wedge into it, but I was all right. Sure I was.

"I thought I would take you up on your offer of a part," Dennard said. "That was what you followed me out here for, wasn't it? To offer me a role in your next film?"

I tried to gather my thoughts. They floated freely inside my head, and trying to latch on to one of them was like bobbing for apples.

I licked my lips and said in a dry, croaking voice: "How . . . how did you . . . know?"

His eyes were vacant, except for a mild curiosity. He looked at me as if I were some fairly interesting bacteria he thought worthy of study before staining and filing. "I didn't. I guessed. When Lainie told me about it tonight and mentioned a private detective, I was curious, naturally. Her description of Jacob Asch sounded a lot like Gilbert Evans, movie mogul. I put two and two together. I figured you followed me home, which meant you saw Lainie. I couldn't have that, so I baited the trap. You fell right into it."

"Smart," I said. Talking was an effort, a painful one. But I knew I had to do it. It was the only chance I had.

He straightened up and said in a businesslike tone: "There's no sense prolonging this any longer than we have to. Who else knows?"

"Knows what?"

"About me."

"Everybody."

"You're a liar."

"Okay, so I'm a liar. Why ask me?"

He bent down and picked up a short length of thick iron pipe from the floor and began slapping it in his palm. That was probably what he had hit me with. "Let's try again. Who else knows?"

"I told you. Everybody."

He banged me hard on the knee with the piece of pipe, and I screamed as searing pain shot up my leg.

"Nobody can hear you screaming," he said. "So you see, Asch, I could systematically bust you into pieces if I wanted to. I don't particularly enjoy inflicting pain, but it doesn't particularly bother me either. So you might as well tell me. You're going to anyway."

I clenched my teeth against the pain and said: "The world knows about you, Dennard. How the fuck do you think I knew about you? Your license number is on an FBI list of cars spotted in the vicinity of the ransom drop. Your name also happens to be on an arrest report from 1972. For felony child abuse. You remember that little incident, don't you, Dennard? You picked up Lainie at the jail."

The muscles around his mouth tightened, and for the first time the self-assurance was gone from his features. Lines of worry pulled faintly at his brow. "It doesn't matter," he said finally. "They'll never be able to prove anything. Not once you're dead."

"How are you going to handle that? It might not be so easy

to convince the FBI that the ghost of Gerry McMurtry came back from the grave and murdered me."

His eyes were once more dead, dark holes staring at me. "You're not going to be murdered. You're going to have an accident. A drowning accident. Being the supersleuth you are, you are going to go back to the spot where McMurtry was found, and while searching for clues you're going to slip and fall in the canal. Tragic. But actually, it happens quite often. They pull at least a body a month out of those canals. The undertow in them is quite brutal. Especially if you're unconscious when you go in."

"You're forgetting about the pipe marks on my head," I said. "A coroner might find those kind of interesting."

"On the contrary. By the time your body gets scraped along the bottom of the canal and goes through a set of locks it'll be so smashed up it'll be lucky if it has any skin on it at all. The coroner will be able to determine you died by drowning, but that will be all he will be able to determine."

I tried to make my mind work faster, but my thoughts crawled along on all fours. I had to buy myself some time, keep him talking. "I have to hand it to you, Dennard. You set it up pretty for such short notice."

"Oh, I've been thinking about it for a long time. Ever since Lainie came into the Cockatoo with the kid last year. I hadn't seen her for five years, and she looked exactly the same. Then, when she told me who she was married to, she looked completely different. I could see right away she still had a thing for me. That was what started me thinking about how I was going to get my hand on Fleischer's twenty million bucks."

He spoke carefully, slowly, as if rehearsing a scene for one of the daytime serials he used to be in. "Actually, it all sort of fell in my lap. I was selling a couple of grams of coke to a guy and who happened to be with him? The kid. After that I made sure I got close to him. I laid a lot of dope on him for nothing so he

214

could be a big shot with his friends, and all the time I was thinking, thinking. I knew the first thing I had to do was get rid of him—he was Fleischer's heir. I was still thinking about how to do that when McMurtry came along and solved it for me."

"So you got McMurtry down here with a phone call and put him on ice until you needed him to turn up dead."

"Correct."

The pain in my leg had subsided to a dull, throbbing ache.

"You made the phone calls to Fleischer. I know that. But Mona recognized McMurtry's voice. What did you use, a recording?"

He nodded. "I had McMurtry convinced Lainie was behind the whole thing, that she'd hired me to teach him a lesson. When I told him Lainie wanted a taped apology for the suffering he'd caused her, he believed me."

"And when you called Mona and played it for her, she thought McMurtry was calling to apologize for what he was going to do—commit suicide."

He smiled, pleased. "Beautiful, huh?"

"Lovely."

"McMurtry was a little claustrophobic. That made everything easier. After being locked up in this freezer a few days, he started to break down. I kept telling him I was going to let him out in a few days, but that I had to keep him here until Lainie said it was okay to let him go. By the time I had him make the recording and write the note he wasn't quite right in the head. He would've done anything I said. He was like a drowning man grasping at straws."

A drowning man grasping at straws. That was exactly what I was going to be unless I kept him talking. It had to be close to dawn. If I kept him talking until then, he would have to wait for night. "You had everybody suckered," I said admiringly. "McMurtry, the kid, Lainie. That was a nice touch, having Donnie tell his date he was going to meet a man named Gerry."

"Wasn't it? The kid was my buddy. He'd do anything I said, too." He paused reflectively, and his eyes focused on a point over my shoulder. "Actually, I felt a kind of kinship with the kid. My father had money, too. He was also a tightfisted son of a bitch like Fleischer. He spanked me one day for asking for a dollar. *A dollar.* The man didn't teach me much about love, but he sure taught me all about money. Money is everything. Without it, you're nothing. Only I always looked up to my old man, not like Donnie. My father to me was like the Old Testament God I heard about in Sunday school. I wanted to be just like him when I grew up."

"What did he do?"

"My father? He was a lawyer. The best. Shrewd and smart and ruthless. I used to love to watch him try a case. He'd let me do that sometimes. Watching him, I learned the only side that was right was the side that won. Since then I've always tried to be on the winning side."

His tone was reverent. I tried to keep him on that track. "Why didn't you become a lawyer?"

"I never had the patience. See, I never did like to work."

"So you became an actor?"

He nodded. "I owe that to my father, too. I learned from him how important appearances were. Appearances were very important to him. I was my parents' showpiece. He made sure I was trained in all the social graces, so that I didn't embarrass him in public. I learned to act at a very early age."

Keep him talking. "One thing I'm really curious about. Did you tell McMurtry his son wasn't killed in the accident?"

"You figured that one out, did you?"

"Lainie called you that night, didn't she?"

"She depended on me for everything. That was one reason I had to get away from her. She hung on me. McMurtry really fucked her up when he split on her. The rejection really blew her away. She was really insecure anyway, and when he dumped on her, she just converted all that insecurity into hate for him. She hated him so much she used to beat on her kid because he looked like his father and he reminded her of him."

"And one night she beat on him too hard."

"She panicked and called me up wanting to know what to do. She said the kid wasn't breathing."

"So you thoughtfully told her to put him in the car and drive into a power pole, thinking you could kill two birds with one stone."

"Hey, man," he said, as if insulted. "I told her to drive into a ditch. I never told the stupid cunt to drive into any pole. She did that because she felt guilty and tried to kill herself. She told me that later."

"Was she in on the kidnapping?"

He took his head back, surprised. "Lainie? She never would've allowed anything to happen to Donnie. Donnie was her new son. The same guilt that made her drive into that pole made her latch on to Donnie. No, she's sure it's all McMurtry's doing."

"Why did she visit you tonight?"

He laughed. It was a high, tinny laugh, like the sound of a man beating on the inside of an oil drum with a stick. "Because she's crazy about me. She can't stay away from me. She never could."

"When are you going to do Fleischer in?"

He shrugged. "I thought I might have gotten rid of him today. In a way, I'm glad it didn't happen. This way he'll have time to get his affairs in order and change his will around. There's plenty of time for him, don't worry."

"What if Lainie won't marry you after you do it?"

He smiled and shook his head pityingly. "She'll marry me; don't worry about that."

"If you're so sure, why did you bother with the ransom at all? Why didn't you just kill the kid and get on with the plan?"

"Insurance," he said. "The plan was long-term, and I figured I might as well have a little something to tide me over until things were finalized."

"A little something to tide you over?" I asked unbelievingly. "Four hundred grand?"

"I went through two hundred in two years after my father died," he said proudly. "I like to spend money. It's a weakness I have."

Talking about yourself is another one, I thought. "Why did you give up the plan so quickly?"

"The price of the insurance policy was getting too steep," he said, shrugging. "It was getting late, and I knew the FBI was in on it. They wouldn't be likely to publicize the fact if they'd found Donnie's body, and if they had, they would have had nothing to lose by grabbing me as soon as I tried to pick up the money. So I decided to cash in and go back to Plan A."

"It won't work, Dennard," I said. "When I turn up dead, the feds are going to look right in your direction. When they do that, even if they can't prove anything, Lainie will know about it, and your plan will be dead."

He laughed again. His fingers were making their soft pat-pat-pat sounds again, faster now. "You just don't understand, do you, Asch? I can tell Lainie anything and she'll believe me. She's like a puppet. I know just what strings to pull to make her respond. It's taken years, but I know which ones are attached to guilt, which ones to fear, which ones to her insecurities, which ones to lust. I can make her forget, and I can make her remember. I know her better than she knows herself."

"Too many bodies, Dennard. She'll have to work things out."

"By that time," he said, "hers will be among the count. Right now I've only got one body to take care of. Yours."

"Wait," I said.

He shook his head and smiled. "Don't you think I know what you've been doing, Asch? Trying to keep me talking until morning? You think I'm an idiot? The only reason I've talked to you at all is because I had to share this with somebody. You don't know how frustrating it's been being so downright brilliant and not having anybody to share it with." He looked at me fondly. "But now there's you."

"You don't want to do this, Dennard," I babbled. "You can't get away with it—"

He raised the pipe and said softly: "Good-bye, Mr. Evans. I'm sorry I can't star in your next picture, but I have a previous commitment I'm afraid I can't back out of."

I turned my head as the pipe came down, but not far enough. My neck took some of the blow, but most of it landed behind my right ear. The light exploded behind my eyes again, white-hot, and I was spinning once more, down, down, into darkness.

TWENTY-THREE

I was awake, and then I wasn't, and then I was again. Memories floated up to the surface of my mind like slow, rolling bubbles, then burst, turning into gaseous nothing. Things began to fade again, and then something physically jolted me and I jerked myself awake. I had to stay awake. I knew it was important, but I could not remember why. Maybe if I opened my eyes. . . .

Lights slid along the ceiling as if it were made of Teflon, left to right, left to right. They were not lights like in the Silver Cockatoo, not at all, but there was a rhythmic regularity to them.

I tried to move but couldn't. I was lying on my back, wedged between two seats. I was in a car, and the car was moving. With that a lot of the rest of it came back to me. Not all of it, but enough to flood my mind with fear. I tried to move my hands. They were tied behind me. I knew that because my arms were attached to them, but there was no feeling in them.

You're not going to go like this, I thought. You can't. Not like this—alone, with nobody knowing. I wrestled with the panic that threatened to engulf me. Norton would know. He would do something. Somebody would do something. Sure they would.

The car slowed and then turned right, and the road became bumpy. My mind raced the car, trying to get to the canal before it did. I had to think. *Think.* He couldn't dump me with my hands tied. Not if he intended to make it look like an accident, he couldn't. He had to untie me sometime before. That was my only chance. A slim one, but the only one I had. I just hoped my hands still worked. I was going to need them.

We were turning again, and then the car went up a little hill and stopped, and the motor died. I listened to him get out and closed my eyes. The door by my head opened, and a warm hand rested on my forehead, and a thumb lifted my right eyelid. I rolled both eyes as far back into my head as I could, trying to give him only white. He dropped the lid and grabbed me under the arms and pulled me out of the car.

I stayed limp as he dragged me backward, and I could hear his breath laboring behind me. Maybe he was not in as good shape as he looked. I hoped not. I hoped he had to drag me a long way and got nice and tired. My hopes were dampened when he stopped a short distance away and dropped me.

He rolled me over onto my face. The water was very close. It made quiet, rushing sounds a few feet away to my right. The sandy stink of the canal filled my nostrils.

He lifted my arms up behind me and cut the rope tying my hands together. I had to force myself not to scream as the blood rushed back into them. He moved over to my left side and got two hands under my shoulder and started to roll me over, and I knew it was now or never.

His face registered surprise as I opened my eyes and reached up and grabbed a handful of his shirt. I was already halfway over the edge of the canal, and he was bent over me. He tried to pull back, but with my weight attached to him, his center of gravity was somewhere in front of him, and his balance was gone. He tried desperately to thrash my hand loose, but by that time it was too late, and we were both falling.

I let him go as soon as I hit the water and was immediately sucked under. He was right; the undertow was brutal. I fought frantically for air, and broke the surface, coughing and gagging.

The water rolled me over, and my shoulder slammed into something hard, sending an electric pain shooting down my side. The concrete side of the canal passed by my face as if I were on some gigantic conveyor system. I reached out and tried to slow myself down, but all I managed to do was scrape all the skin off the palms of my hands.

I was sucked under again and gulped in a mouthful of foul water. I clawed my way back to the surface, my lungs panicking for air. Something came to me, something Dennard had said to me about locks. I was already exhausted, and I knew I would never make it through them. I dog-paddled in the current and looked around for Dennard, but I could not see his head bobbing anywhere above the dark water.

The current carried me into the side of the canal again, and as I put out my hand to cushion the impact, I touched something fuzzy. Clumps of sagebrush grew out of the cracks in the cement embankment like tufts of hair. As I passed another one, I grabbed for it, but it broke into pieces, and I came away with a handful of brittle bush.

The current seemed to be picking up now, and the rushing sound of the water was louder up ahead.

Another bush loomed out of the dark water, coming up fast. I concentrated on the spot I was going to grab it, down by the root where the bush came out of the cement, and as I passed it, I made a desperate grab. The grab was good, and the bush held.

I stayed there for a few minutes, trying to get my breath back, then looked up. The top of the bank was four feet above me, and between it and me, about halfway up, was another bush. I took a deep breath and reached for it.

I couldn't make it. Stretched out as far as I could reach, I was still a good foot short. The current pulled at my legs like a jealous lover. It wanted me back. I didn't want to go back.

The sky was starting to turn a dull gray. It would be day soon. I might be able to hold on here until somebody happened to come by to go catfishing, but I doubted it. My arms were already becoming cramped from holding on to the bush. And if Dennard had made it out, he would be looking for me.

I let the current carry my legs away from the bush, and when I was almost prone, I swung one leg out and tried to get a footing on the cement. The sides were steep, but if I used my body weight, I figured I might be able to use the foot as a pivot. I pushed down on the foot and made a lunging grab for the bush. Pain shot through my hand as needlelike pieces of the plant struck into my palm, but I held on.

I was out of the water now, and even though the muscles in my arms and back ached and I was totally exhausted, my body felt almost weightless. I used my knees to pull myself over the top of the bush and lay staring up at the sky, my breath rattling in my chest. Then I remembered. Dennard.

I stood up unsteadily, trying to get a visual grip on the horizon, then started down the edge of the canal.

The current had carried him farther down toward the locks. He was clinging like a wet monkey to a bush just above the waterline. He looked up and saw me, and his eyes were not dead anymore. Behind a heavy-lidded exhaustion they were alive with fear. "Help . . . Asch . . . please."

He made a dry, sucking noise as he gulped for some air.

"You've got to be kidding."

"Please. You can't let me drown. Turn me in, but for Christ's sake, don't let me drown."

"Why shouldn't I? Give me a reason, Dennard, and then I'll consider it."

"I—I don't want to die, Asch—"

The fear crackled in his voice.

"Please, you're touching my heart."

There was a rock by my foot, and I bent down and picked it up, testing the weight in my hand. Good. Heavy enough to hurt, but not enough for a KO. I took aim and tossed it down, and it hit him on the left shoulder. He emitted a high shriek of pain, more like a woman's scream, but held on to the bush.

"Good, Dennard. Just keep holding on."

The next one hit him on the back of the neck, and he screamed again. "Asch! For God's sake, what are you doing?"

His voice was turning blubbery and incoherent. I picked up another rock and was about to let it go when I stopped. I was enjoying this, I realized. His pathetic pleadings struck some deep, dark responsive chord somewhere, and I was enjoying it. I dropped the rock and stood there.

He seemed to pick up my vacillation, and the intensity of his pleadings picked up. I stood, wrestling with my conscience, and he yelled again. I told him to hold on and limped back to the car. My knee felt as if it were twice its normal size.

A coil of nylon rope sat on the front seat, next to the piece of pipe. I took them both. I may have been softhearted, but I was no fool.

I was on my way back when I heard it. I froze, listening.

It was up ahead of me, ahead of him. A loud click, a high-pitched motor whine—a big motor—then a metallic meshing of gears and the creaking of straining cables. I started to run, but I knew I could never make it. The water in the canal was already boiling, picking up momentum as it surged toward the great rusted door.

Dennard's eyes were wide in terror, and he was screaming, but I could not hear him over the roar of the water, and then the bush ripped loose from the side of the canal, and he was swept away. I ran alongside him as the water carried him down, and he managed to stay on top for a short while, but then his head was ripped under by the suction, and he was gone.

I ran to the other side to see if I could spot him going through, but there was nothing but the roaring, raging torrent as the white water raced down the channel bed, out across the valley. I stayed there for a while, watching the channel fill up; then the motors whined again, and the huge door shut, and the deafening waterfall was turned back into a faint trickle.

It was getting light. The features of the landscape were developing slowly, like a negative in a photographic solution. The mountains stretched darkly across the bottom half of the sky, jagged, as if drawn there by some palsied hand, and orange-pink wisps of cirrus cloud rose off their peaks, like steam.

I spent fifteen minutes searching the car for a set of keys.

The inconsiderate bastard, I thought, finally giving up. If he was going to take off like that, the least he could have done was leave me a set of keys.

It took me forty minutes to walk to a pay phone.

TWENTY-FOUR

"Some outfit that has five thousand acres south of Coachella called the Valley Water District yesterday and put in an order for water for five-thirty this morning," Norton said. "Everything in the canal system is controlled from a central station. The guy working the board there came in this morning and punched the buttons to fill the order, and that was it for Mr. Dennard. He might turn up in the Salton Sea in a month or two. If we ever find him."

I was only half listening to him. I was surrounded by whiteness, and the smell of the antiseptic was making me nauseated. Even lying down, I was still dizzy.

"You should make sure that outfit gets an extra parity payment from the government," I said. "They saved the taxpayers a lot of money."

"Huh?"

"The trial."

"Oh. Yeah."

The man on the other side of the curtain was wheezing louder now. Pneumonia, I guessed. He had been there when I had come in, but nobody seemed to be doing much for him. He had probably let his Blue Cross lapse.

I clenched my teeth together to keep whatever I had eaten yesterday from coming up, then swung my feet over the edge of the bed. "Excuse me."

I pushed through the curtains and found the bathroom and spent five minutes with my head in the toilet. After I had worked into the dry heaves, things finally settled down, and I washed my face and rinsed my mouth out with cold water and went back out into the ER.

Norton gave me a concerned look as I parted the curtains and lay back down on the bed. "You all right?"

"Peachy," I said. "Did Mona get here?"

"Yeah. She and Winter are at the motel."

"I want to talk to her."

"Don't worry about that right now. You're in no shape to talk to anybody."

The curtains parted, and the doctor, a pale, dark-haired man who looked too young to be a doctor, stepped in, holding a set of X-rays. "You don't have any fractures, Mr. Asch, in either your head or your knee, but you do have a concussion. I suggest you stay in the hospital for a day or so, just so we can keep an eye on you."

"I've seen how patients get watched in hospitals, Doc. There's a good case right next door." I jabbed a thumb at the curtain.

"That man has his *own* doctor," he said petulantly. "We're waiting for him to arrive."

I nodded. "Well, I'd just as soon skip it. All I'll be doing here is staying in bed and resting. I can do that at home a lot cheaper. So if you'll just finish bandaging up my hands, I'll get out of your way."

Displeasure turned down the corners of his mouth. "You realize you might be hemorrhaging. There's no way to tell. If you don't stay here—"

"I can't get a staph infection."

He started to argue with me, but I said: "Look, Doc, I don't have any money and I don't have Blue Cross or Blue Shield."

The displeasure on his face turned to alarm. "Who's going to pay for the X rays and Emergency Room fees?"

"I am," Norton answered.

"Oh." He seemed relieved. "All right then. But we can't be held responsible."

"I'm not asking you to be."

He went out in a huff, and I pointed to the dry clothes on the chair that Norton had had dropped off for me. "You want to hand me those?"

I slipped off the breakaway robe I was wearing and got dressed painfully. My head hurt like hell. My knee hurt like hell. Everything hurt like hell. Norton watched my face contort in. pain as I slipped into the pair of pants and said: "Maybe you should stay in the hospital for a day or two."

"At two hundred a day? Are you kidding? Besides, I can't stand hospitals. They make me sick."

"Don't be so damned stubborn. If there's a chance you could have a brain hemorrhage—"

I laughed. "It's not my time, Inspector. I couldn't have gone through everything I did last night and come out of it if it was. Walk out on the street now and drop dead of a brain hemorrhage? Don't be ridiculous."

He made a grunting noise and crossed his arms in irritated resignation.

The doctor came back in and hurriedly put antiseptic on my cut hands and wrapped them with bandages. He made me sign forms releasing the hospital of all liability should something happen to me, then let us go in a huff. Norton paid the bill, sixty-four dollars, and I told him I'd write him a check when we got back to the motel. My wallet had taken a trip to the Salton Sea, along with Dennard.

I was dizzy and weak as a cat, and I used Norton's arm several times to brace myself as we walked up the ramp to where his car was parked. The sunshine felt like hot salve on my skin. I got into the car, slowly.

There were rough edges on everything—the palm trees, the mountains, the sky. The world had psoriasis and was flaking off. We backed out of the space and I turned to see a white Mark V pull into the parking lot. "My life, it seems, is full of meaningful coincidences lately. It's enough to make me start reading Jung again. Pull over there."

Norton swung the car around and pulled behind the Mark. Norm was driving. Lainie opened the door and stepped out.

I got out of the car to meet her. That took a lot of effort. I had to brace myself against the body of the car to keep from falling.

She looked with alarm at the stitches on my forehead and my bandaged hands, but before she could say anything, I asked: "How's your husband?"

"Better this morning, thank you," she said. "What happened to you?"

"A goblin tried to give me a kiss," I told her. "I fought him off, though."

She looked at me strangely. "I'm glad to hear it."

I stared at her, and she fingered her purse nervously. "Well, if that's all you wanted to know—"

"He's dead, Lainie."

Her smile evaporated from her lips. "He? Who?"

"Dennard."

Her eyes went blank. "What, what are . . . you talking about?"

"He tried to kill me last night. He killed Donnie and McMurtry, and he was going to kill your husband. Divorce wasn't good enough for him. He didn't want half of Fleischer's money. He wanted all of it."

Her grip tightened on her purse, but she said nothing.

"He set it all up to look like McMurtry. He had to get rid of Donnie first. Donnie was the principal heir. He set *you* up, Lainie. You were going to be the last one on his list."

"It's not true. You're lying." Her face melted, and her features seemed to be trying to rearrange themselves. Then some internal catalyst hardened them in their original form. She was trying to regroup. Her knuckles whitened on her purse, and she shoved her face at me. "You're despicable. You're just saying these things because you have a sick and twisted mind."

I don't know why I bothered. It wouldn't change anything. I just couldn't stop myself. The words came out by themselves. "My mind may be sick and twisted, but the cops have enough physical evidence to make the case against Dennard, or at least they will within a few days. He was careful, but his type is never careful enough. They always leave something behind for the lab boys to work on. Of course, it doesn't matter much, not with Dennard dead. It's just a matter of clearing McMurtry's name."

She stepped forward unsteadily, and tears filled her eyes. "Then, it's ... true? Darrell is ... ?"

"Dead. Which is probably a good thing for you, since there is no statute of limitations on murder. Now he can't testify against you. You lucked out."

"*Me?*" she said shrilly. The gleam of hysteria blended with the tears and gave her blue eyes a special brilliance. "You have to be insane. You can't be saying *I* had anything to do with this?"

"The kidnapping? No. I was talking about Brian."

Her hand flew to her throat. "Brian?" The word was almost a squeak.

I leaned toward her and said softly: "I know, Lainie. I *know.* And Norton knows. And McDonald knows. Your husband doesn't know yet, but he'll probably find out. You know how hard it is to keep these things hushed up."

She staggered forward a little and reached out to grab my arm, but I stepped back. "Don't try to lean on me, lady. We'll both fall, and I don't think I could handle that right now."

Her hands and her mouth were working furiously, making all kinds of little, jerky movements. "I—I have to explain—"

"Not to me, you don't," I said. My legs were going to fail if I didn't sit down, so I got back into the car and shut the door. There were three of her outside the window. One had been enough.

I closed my eyes and rested my head against the seat and tried to get control of the nausea. I was going to have to heave, but I didn't want to do it here, not with her standing there, watching. "At least you killed Erica," I said softly. "That was one good deed you did."

She took a step toward the car, but I said, "Go," and Norton drove out of the parking lot.

When we turned onto the street, he said: "What were you saying back there? Who is this Erica?"

"Nobody," I said.

When he got up the road a ways, I told him to pull over.